BROWN GOLD

BY

STEVEN LUSK

Casper Books

First publication: Casper Books, Johnson City, Tennessee 37604 November, 2011

Cover art copyright by Steven Lusk November, 2011

ISBN 10: 0983989427
ISBN 13: 978-0983989424

The beginning of the saga

A Roar in the East
by Steven Lusk

Available through Amazon.com
And
as an Ebook on Amazon Kindle

PROLOGUE

Roaring out of the night like an avenging angel of death, its glossy black sides gleaming in the glare of the streetlights, the sparkles of its chrome flashing like stars, the car squealed as it turned from the street into the parking lot. A dark smear of rubber pointed like an arrow to the cars path. The gears clashed as the driver downshifted. Then clashed again. And once again. A muttered, "Blast it," could be heard above the engine roar.

With a "Squeeeech" the car came to a stop. Banging and clanking could be heard from the inside and an exasperated, "Finally!" The clanking and groaning stopped and the car shrieked into the night, the front tires billowed smoke as they sought to gain traction on the pitted and dark surface of the lot.

Suddenly the car leaped forward and then, with a roar of its engine and a squeal of tires, the black car stopped with its bumper inches from the guardrail that protected the parking lot. Fifteen feet below the guardrail, an alley ran parallel to the upper roadway, going right to a street and left to a dead end. Directly in front of the car, across the alley, the brick wall of a building rose into the night, its windows shining dully from the streetlights.

With another clash of gears, the car reversed and accelerated, moving backward up the lot. The tires screamed again as the car came to another stop. Again the gears crashed and the tires spun, smoking as they slid on the macadam. With a howl the car surged forward, aiming for the guardrail and the drop off.

At the last second before hitting the guardrail the driver stomped on the brake and spun the steering wheel to the right. The car rotated ninety degrees, slammed into the guardrail with the passenger side, tore the guardrail away and allowed the car to plummet to the alley below. As the car dropped it made one complete rotation from roof to tires and back again. The vehicle slammed down on its wheels, rocking the entire chassis. The driver banged his head on the roof and pressed hard on the gas pedal.

With more smoke coming from the spinning tires, and the sound of tortured metal from the dented right side panels, the vehicle bounded forward toward the right end of the alley. The driver again smacked the brakes and spun the wheel to the left. The car did a quarter circle rotation and roared out of sight down another street on the far side of the brick building.

Up in the parking lot a silver-gray SUV screeched to a halt inches from the broken guardrail. Inside the big gas guzzler the driver watched the black car disappear around the building. His gloved hand reached down and moved the stick shift as his foot depressed the clutch pedal. The foot lifted and his other foot pressed down on the gas. With a roar of its engine the silver car leaped backward and spun around. The gloved hand and the feet worked the clutch and gear shift again and the car squealed its tires leaving a black patch on the macadam as it accelerated toward the entrance to the parking lot. There, the car turned left and roared to the end of the street, spun to the left again and rocketed down a hill.

Seconds after the gray car was out of sight the black car raced back into the alley, squealing to a halt within inches of hitting the wall at the dead end. Pushing the stick shift into neutral the driver turned off the engine, grabbed the keys from the ignition and leaped out of the car, running toward a metal door that opened into the wall of the drop off under the parking lot above.

Behind him the car began to slowly roll backward, the uneven road surface causing the tires to turn to the left. Within seconds the rear end of the vehicle bumped into the brick wall causing the car to rock back and forth. Inside the car there was a "Whoosh" sound of an air bag inflating creating a large white balloon in the front seat.

The driver pulled the metal door open and raced down a dank passageway cluttered with old boxes and waste bins. In the dim light he hit the wall when the hall turned to the left. With a loud "Thud," he rebounded from the wall and landed on his back on the floor, striking his head on the concrete with a loud "Crack." For a moment he lay there, too stunned to move. Slowly his hand came up and felt the back of his head. With effort he stood up and leaned against the wall. He looked at his hand for signs of blood and found only a couple of black hairs and a mouse turd.

Shaking his head he staggered down the passageway a number of feet before he realized he was headed back toward the outside door. Turning around he moved more quickly back down the passage, turning left to follow the hallway before running into the wall again.

Getting up again he started running, his hand held in front of him in anticipation of another wall. Rapidly increasing his pace he ran down the hall another fifty feet until he entered the basement of a building. Frowning he slowed to look quickly around before spotting a set of stairs leading upward. With a grin he started running up them two at a time, using the handrail to spin through each of the landings he came to.

Ames Blond began to sweat as he hurried up the stairs, his coat flying behind him like a set of dark wings. The agent for DORK was in his element. The chase was his forte.

"Yeah, what you want?" muttered Ben Forte, the African American driver of the silver-gray car, as he slammed to a stop at the intersection at the bottom of the hill.

No Ben, we were not talking about you. You lost Ames.

"Then why'd you bring up my name?" asked Forte, looking left and right.

We didn't mention your name. We were talking about Blond's forte, you know, his abilities.

"Sure, talk about that suckers abilities while you leave me lost out here," complained Ben. "For that matter, you even told everybody where I am."

Don't get uptight. We told you where Blond is too.

"Yo, you did, didn't you!" exclaimed Forte as he took his foot from the brake and transferred it to the gas. With a rapid movement he spun the steering wheel, jerking the car to the right. He roared down the street to the alley and spun the wheel again, putting the car on two wheels as he went around the corner, barely missing the black car with its rear against the building. Slamming on the brake, he was pulling out the key even as the car came to a stop. Within seconds he was racing through the same door Ames had disappeared through.

In the building Ames had passed the fifth landing and slowed to taking the steps one at a time. He was sweating heavily and his breath came in a rasping pant as he forced himself to continue the upward charge. By the time he reached the eighth landing, his steps had turned into a heavy slog, forcing each foot from one riser to the next.

He was wheezing and huffing, using his arms to help pull him onward.

At the eleventh landing he fell to the floor gasping for breath. His mouth was opening and closing like a fish out of water, trying to draw in sufficient air to his lungs. With bleary eyes he looked at the floor marker, barely seeing the 11.

"Whoa," he gasped. "One floor too many."

With effort he dragged himself to his feet and trudged back down to the tenth floor.

In the basement, Forte came to the stairs, looked around, and saw the elevator. He punched the button to go up, then waited for the car to reach him while whistling under his breath and tapping his foot lightly to the tune. He reached out and snagged an old magazine from one of the waste bins. Idly he began flipping through it.

On the tenth floor Ames entered a hallway and looked left and right. With some effort he walked to the right, looking at room numbers on the doors he passed. The first door he came to had no number so he continued to the next. Again no number. "Blast it," he muttered. "Doesn't anybody mark their doors anymore?" Finally he came to a door with faded gold digits reading 1456. "What the heck is that," asked Ames. "The stupid building only has 12 floors."

The following door made a little more sense. It had 1006 written in yellow magic marker, barely visible against the old dark wood. With a curse the agent turned around and headed back to the stairway. There he continued down the left hand hallway, checking doors as he went.

He spotted 1021 and stopped with a sigh. Leaning his head against the door he pulled a key from his pocket and thrust it into the lock. The effort of the thrust caused the unlocked door to fly open and he stumbled into the room, tripped over a box and fell to the floor, smacking his head against the arm of a chair on the way down.

With a ding the elevator arrived in the basement and the door slid open. Ben flipped the magazine back into the bin and stepped in, his gloved index finger pushing the 10 on the ancient control panel. The door slowly hissed closed and the elevator started to rise.

In the room Blond groaned and stood up, using the chair to brace himself. The arm came loose and he staggered forward banging his knee against a coffee table. Hopping backward while holding his knee he banged into the doorframe. Swiping his hand along the wall he flipped on the lights and looked around. Cheap furniture was scattered around the room, a sagging orange couch, a blue and white-striped chair, now missing the arm rest, two scarred end tables with mismatched lamps, the coffee table with peeling veneer and a huge iron safe that sat in the corner brooding over the room.

Ames staggered over to the safe and began turning the dial.

With slow but steady progress, like an overweight lady headed for a sale, the elevator passed the fifth floor. Forte whistled as he waited.

With a thump the door of the safe came unlocked and Ames grabbed the handle and pulled. Ponderously the old safe opened. Inside were stacks of money, files of paper and a small wooden box. With lifting spirits the agent grabbed the box and slipped it into his pocket. For a moment he rifled through the papers. Most were stock certificates for companies like the "East India Trading Company" and the "Computing Tabulating Recording Company." Idly he wondered what those were. The money was all engraved with, "Confederate States of America."

In the hallway the elevator dinged and the door started to slide open. Hearing the sound Ames glanced at the doorway to the hall and went over to the window. He jerked it open, which was rather unnecessary since there was no glass in the window, and stepped out onto the fire escape.

Forte dashed out of the elevator and ran down the hall. He slid to a stop at the open door and looked into the room. With a quick glance he spotted the open safe and the wind blowing the curtains at the open window. He charged over and peered out. Below him he could see a shadowy figure clanking down the stairs two flights below.

Hurrying, he stepped through the window and tripped, falling face first onto the metal grill floor of the landing. He pushed himself to a sitting position and put his hand to the blood oozing from a scratch on his cheek.

"Drat," he muttered as he stood up and started down the metal stairs.

At the bottom Ames leaped from the final landing and lit onto the concrete sidewalk, bending his ankle over and falling to the ground. Pain lanced through his leg. With effort he climbed to his feet and hobbled toward the black car, but stopped when he spotted the gray machine.

Above him he could hear the ring of leather on metal as Forte hurried down the fire escape. Ames reached into his pocket and pulled out a large jackknife, yanked the blade open and jammed it into the front tire of the black car. With a blast of dry air the blade was forced back out nicking the agents palm as it skittered loose. Air began to hiss out of the tire while blood began to hiss out of the palm.

With a cry of pain and an evil grin he pulled out a handkerchief and wrapped his hand. Turning away from the car he hurried to his car, pulled out his keys and slid into the seat, or attempted to. The air bag was in the way.

Yanking out the knife again, he flipped it open and stabbed the silvery-white spheroid. He received a blast of air and a spray of white particles. Snapping closed the knife and putting it back in his pocket he slammed the door and snapping the lock

Forte jumped carefully from the last landing. The Black American landed lightly and spun around as he heard the car door close. He straightened and ran for the black car, only to have the engine roar to life as he reached it. He tried to pull the door open, but barely spun out of the way as the car leaped forward toward the dead end. Before hitting the wall again the car spun and rocketed toward the alley entrance.

As the black car accelerated down the road and surged around the corner, Forte ran to his car and opened the door, only to see the flat tire. He threw the door closed again and slammed his fist into the roof with a grunted, "Drat!" He watched as the taillights of the black car rounded the corner and disappeared.

CHAPTER ONE

General "Manystars" Tenstars, code name N, the unfamous and unknown head of the Department of Reconnaissance and Knowledge, was talking to another person when Ames Blond entered the office and stopped in front of the huge teak desk. Ames was mildly surprised to see the other person in the room. The General rarely allowed one visitor to see another. It was N's way of making sure that one hand did not know what the other was doing. It also provided for good job security.

The athletic and trim brunette Blond was an agent for the ultra-secret department and his job was to, uh, was to, uh . . heck, I don't know. He's some kind of spy or investigator or agent or some dumb thing or other.

Anyway, Ames was a government employee following in the footsteps of his father who had been a good government bureaucrat who instilled in his son the many traits required for government service. Such as; low work for high pay, a penchant for lots of bennies, and a desire for an office with a window. At present Ames had none of those, but he had dreams.

The two men had ceased speaking when Ames entered and the portly General now turned to Ames.

"Did you get the box?" he asked without preamble.

"Yes sir," replied Ames reaching into his pocket and setting the small wooden box on the General's desk. "If I might ask sir, what's in there that's so important? Does it have something to do with national security?"

The General looked grimly at Ames. "You didn't look in it?" Ames shook his head. "Well go ahead and look now. You'll never see anything like it again. Be careful though."

With trepidation Ames picked up the box and slid the catch open. Carefully he lifted the lid and peered inside. Sitting in the box was a brownish gray substance. It had a shriveled look and there was a white crust spotted on it. It exuded a slightly rancid odor.

Pulling his head back and looking up with an alarmed expression Ames asked, "What is it? Is it some kind of bacteriological agent for germ warfare? Should I be this close to it?" His voice became shriller. "Should I be breathing the fumes? Am I going to die with a really horrible skin rash? Will I have two headed babies? Why did you let me open it? Are you seriously insane?" He started sweating and dropped the box onto the desk. The gray-brown thing rolled out onto some papers. Ames crouched down in front of the desk with his hands over his head. "Oh, my god, we're all going to die!" The visitor took a step backward, his bespectacled head twitching back and forth from the General to Ames to the brown thing, rather like a three person tennis match.

The General's mouth dropped open and he quickly scooped the thing up and put it back in the box, snapping the lid closed. "What the heck's the matter with you, Ames? What the heck did you drop it for?" he demanded while wiping his hand on his pants. "It's only dog crap!"

With a quizzical expression Ames dropped his arms, stood up and said, "Dog crap? I risked my life for dog crap? What the devil is that all about?"

"Maybe I'd better explain," sighed the General. "Have a seat."

The General dropped into his large emu leather chair and started rolling the box back and forth from hand to hand. There was as soft "thunk" each time the turd hit the sides of the box. Ames took a seat in one of the straight back wooden chairs that lined the office wall. The visitor simply leaned against the map on the opposite wall.

"Back in the late sixties me and a friend of mine, Ben Forte, were in Los Angeles prior to shipping out to Vietnam. We were just cruising the street in a rented car, looking for girls, when we passed the Palladium in Hollywood. There was a Jimi Hendrix concert going on and the place was crowded. Broads all over the place. Well, we're looking for a place to park and we spotted this alley behind the concert hall. There was no one around so we pulled in and parked the car. Just as we're getting out these two guys come out of the theater, big heavy-set guys. They looked like wrestlers. They eyeball us for a second or two, but we're wearing our uniforms so I guess they figure we're okay. One of them waves at the door. A second later Jimi Hendrix comes out. I mean, it was him! You know, Afro, headband, the whole shmear. And he had this dog with him. Little bitty thing. Ugly as hell all covered with long mossy looking hair. It looked like a cross between a Chihuahua and a really bad wig that got caught in a ceiling fan.

"So Jimi drops the dog," he continued excitedly. "And the mutt runs around for a few minutes sniffing at everything in the alley and then it drops its butt and takes a dump. This one little turd. The thing turns around and sniffs the turd for a second and then goes over and wags its tail at Hendrix. Jimi pats its head like it did something great and then snags the dog and they all go back inside. Well, Ben looked at me and I looked at Ben and then we both ran over to the crap. I got there first and grabbed it. I mean this was Jimi Hendrix's dog's crap! It had to be worth millions! Or at least a buck or two, good for a couple of beers."

The General looked a little wistful and sad. "The next thing I know we're in this big fight, with Ben yelling the poop is his and me yelling it's mine. At one point he makes a grab for it and I tell him to leave the crap alone. I'm trying to make him understand that I was going to offer to share it with him when he hits me upside the head and stalks off down the alley, madder than a pit bull on steroids. He's yelling that he's going to get even with me if it's the last thing he does."

N looked between the visitor and Ames. "What was I supposed to do, give it to him? Anyway, I got back in the car and I put the crap in a cigarette pack I found under the seat. I drove around for a couple of hours looking for Ben, but I couldn't find him. He had disappeared into the crowd. The next day I was supposed to ship for Nam and didn't see him again for a couple of years." He paused and set the box on the desk, then took a deep breath and continued.

"Then one day he shows up demanding the crap. I was still a little peeved about him hitting me so, just to yank his chain, I told him to go to heck. Before I could tell him I was kidding he stalked off again. Since then he's been trying to find the crap. I think he's got private detectives or something, he keeps finding my hiding places. Well, I figured enough is enough, so I had you get it so I can sell it on eBay. I figure I'll share the money from the auction with Ben as a way of atonement." He glanced back and forth between the two and then looked down at the desk with the small box on it.

"So you had me risk my life for dog crap," Ames said again with a stunned look. "I'm racing all over town. I've got this madman chasing me and I darn near have a heart attack climbing those effing stairs, just to save your dog poop. I bang the heck out of a company car and R is going to have a fit when he sees it." Ames turned and walked over to the wall and banged his head twice. "What a bloody moron!"

"That will be enough of that!" shouted the General pushing back his chair and standing up. "I won't have you talking about a superior officer that way!"

"What officer?" asked Ames walking back to the desk, rubbing at the red spot on his forehead. "I'm talking about me. I should have looked in the stupid box!"

The General shook his head and waved his hand at the other visitor. "Forget that for now. This is Ned Oliver Wrights." Ames took the man's hand and shook it. N.O. Wrights was a thin man in a slightly rumpled brown suit. He had brown hair tending toward bald on top with watery brown eyes peering through thick-lensed brown wire frame glasses.

"NO is the head of Petroleum, Oil and Other Propellants for the Department of Homeland Security. As the head of POOP, NO is responsible for ensuring that our access to vast amounts of oil and other energy stuff are free and unfettered. He's also responsible for ensuring the ragheads don't make too great a profit while our oil companies get a huge return on their investment. All in the interest of national security you understand"

At that point NO Wrights butted in, causing the General to frown. "POOP has been having trouble lately with missing oil tankers," he said in a high nasal voice. "The ships leave the terminals in the Middle East, make their deliveries and then, on the return trip, disappear. They turn up a couple of weeks later with empty holds that smell like used toilet paper and crews with amnesia. We've tried tracking the ships, but they just drop off the map. No sightings, no GPS, no signals, nothing. It has Homeland Security and the presidents of the oil companies going ape. They want to know where the tankers are going, why they smell so bad and the truth about Roswell"

"So you want me to investigate?" asked Ames frowning. "The first two I can work on, but I thought Muldoon and Scurvy from the FBI were working on the last one."

"That's Mulder and Scully and no, I don't want you to investigate," said the man from POOP with a scowl. "I want you to sell that dog turd on eBay! Of course I want you to investigate! What the heck do you think I'm here for?" The little man's excitement caused his glasses to slide down his nose. He pushed them up with his middle finger, causing Ames and the General to both frown at him. N.O. saw the frowns, glanced at the offending finger and put the whole hand into his pocket.

Ames gave the General and N.O. both a puzzled look. "You did say the tankers were empty?" N.O. nodded, his bobbing head looking like the tippy cup bird. "So what's the problem? The oil gets delivered and the ships show up again a few weeks later. It's not like they don't show up at all. Just adjust the shipping schedule to take the disappearances into account. Heck, the crews are probably just having a small unpaid vacation or loaning the things out for Caribbean cruises. I imagine you can cram a lot of cheap tourists into the holds of one of those things. Just chuck in some cots and a few baloney sandwiches and you're good to go. For that matter maybe they're smuggling Mexicans. You know pick up a few in Vera Cruz and drop them at Miami on the way back to the gulf. Might explain the smell."

"That's not the point," said N.O. with conviction. "We can adjust the schedule, that's not that big a deal. It's that smell you see. When the ships come back their tanks smell like used sewage. That makes the oil smell and we're starting to get cars with really rank exhaust. I mean you can't tell in LA or New York, but in Littleberg, Iowa, the smell is really bad. I mean, imagine a couple of hundred dogs having a poop party on your front lawn."

Ames thought a moment. "Have you tried putting tracers on the ships, or maybe following them with war ships or dinghies? You might use a submarine or an airplane. You could also use a tracking device like they use in Singapore to track all the boats and ships they have in their harbor. It puts out a continuous signal and would let you know instantly if, when and where the ship disappeared."

They both looked at Ames like he was nuts. "Uh, Ames," said the General softly. "Do you have any idea what it would cost to do those things?"

Ames nodded his head. "Sure, but what's the cost of an oil tanker or the time lost on deliveries? Not to mention the smell in Littleberg."

The General and N.O. both shook their heads and N said, "Ames, first off, nobody gives a rat's tail about the smell in Littleburg. It's not like it's an election year. The problem is we have a budget that really sucks. Why, how would I be able to afford paper clips and those nifty fluorescent pens or more of that great imported coffee if we spent money on such non-essentials as war ships, tracking devices or GPS locators? Nope, we'll have to come up with a better plan."

Wrights nodded his head in agreement. Ames imagined him as the thin bird dipping his bill into a cup. "We don't have any leads and we, the General and I, thought it might be a good idea if you were aboard one of the ships, sort of as crew or a passenger or maybe a stowaway. Then when the ship disappeared and comes back you could tell us what happened to it."

With a puzzled look Ames glanced at N and then at Wrights. "If I'm on the ship and it disappears, won't I get amnesia like everybody else?"

The head of POOP glanced at the general and then at the wall. The General looked down at his shoes and then brushed at an imaginary piece of lint on his uniform. Wrights stuck his hands in his pockets and began a tuneless whistle while rocking back and forth on his heels. Finally N spoke up. "Uh, we hadn't thought of that. Let me give R a call. You head down to dirty tricks. By the time you get there R should have thought of something."

CHAPTER TWO

Ames stepped off the elevator and walked briskly down the hall toward the group of rooms where the Advanced Special Sciences and Hidden Office of Laboratory Studies were. As he reached out to pull open the door to ASSHOLS he suddenly pulled his hand back, remembering the last time he had gripped that doorknob.

R, the head ASSHOLS, was constantly thinking of new inventions and one of his projects was to make a spy proof door. The last time Ames had come to R's office and tried to pull the door open, it had slammed open on springs, crashing him into the wall and putting a large goose egg on the back of his head. He had also done a Roger Rabbit and seen stars, birdies and other toonish characters floating in the air.

Reaching into his pocket the man from DORK pulled out a handkerchief and carefully wrapped it around the doorknob. Leaning back and to the side Ames slowly pulled on the knob, gently easing the door open. With relief he saw that the door was opening without incident. With a sigh he released the handkerchief, letting the door slide closed again. Smiling he grabbed the knob with his hand. With a crash the door slammed open and plastered the agent against the far wall. He slid to the floor as toonish characters again appeared over his head and a large goose egg began to sprout where the head and wall had met. On the head and not on the wall..

"Bloody moron," he muttered climbing groggily to his feet. He staggered slightly as he walked through the still open door. He had just put his hand to his head to feel the rising lump when the door slammed shut, smacking him in the butt and sending him flying into the room. His waist struck a desk and his upper torso slammed down onto the desktop banging his head on a coffee cup. Slowly he slid off the desk and sank to the floor. The cup rolled off the edge and smacked him in the temple, bounced off his chest and hit the floor with a dull "tonk".

From what seemed far away he heard a cackle and a voice saying, "Did you like that one? Did ya? Did ya? That suckers great ain't it? It gets you coming and going. That has to be my best one yet. But it still needs something. Oh, yes, needs something. Ah well, I'll keep trying. Now get off the floor and come on. And pick up that cup before it gets broken. That's a special souvenir cup from the Amish music festival in Blue Balls, Pennsylvania. That suckers really rare." Ames felt a foot nudge him in the ribs.

With a groan the agent reached up and grabbed the edge of the desk. With effort he snagged the cup and pulled himself to his feet. Through bleary eyes he saw a skinny man with frizzy white hair and a purple polka dot lab coat grinning at him. Ames shook his head to clear the cobwebs and carpet lint. With a wave of a hand the purple polka dots walked through a door on the far side of the room.

When his eyes cleared the agent found himself in a large room with an expanse of bright green lawn taking up most of the space. The grass was beautiful, with evenly spaced bright green blades. It looked like it belonged in suburban heaven instead of an ultra-secret lab.

Blond set the cup on the desk and with slightly shaky legs, started across the lawn toward the door the polka dots had gone through. Behind him the cup wobbled for a moment then fell over, rolled to the edge of the desk and fell off, shattering into multiple pieces, shards, chips and slivers.

As he walked he could feel a slight tug at his left shoe. Stopping, he glanced down at the lawn. Blades of bright green grass were weaving themselves around his left shoe. Startled, he tugged his foot upward, yanking his foot out of the shoe that was now firmly attached to the green sward. With a yelp he ran across the room to the doorway. Grabbing the doorframe he glanced back in time to see the back of the shoe rise into the air like the stern of the Titanic and slowly slide downward, to disappear into the grass trailing shoelaces behind it. In a moment even the laces were gone. "What the heck was that?" he muttered.

"That's poo grass," said a voice in his ear, causing him to jerk his head around, nearly colliding with a wizened face under a thatch of unruly white hair. The face cackled and a trickle of saliva ran down the chin. A polka dot clad arm reached up and wiped at the slime.

"Blast it, got'ta stop that cackling," muttered R, the infamous head of ASSHOLS. With a "swook" sound he sucked the remaining saliva into the side of his mouth. Ames blanched and pulled his head backward. With a "clonk" he knocked his already sore head into the doorframe.

The ancient inventor pointed at the grass and said again. "That's poo grass. I designed it to react to dog poop. When a dog tries to poop on the lawn the grass reaches up and grabs the dog poop and pulls it underground where the poop is slowly eaten. The more the dogs use the yard for a toilet, the greener the grass. I figure people will pay big money to get rid of stray dog poop on their lawns and, with the budget so tight, we can make some money on the side. You must have had some dog doo on your shoe."

R turned and walked over to a table, as Ames remembered handling Hendrix's dogs poop in N's office. He shivered and wiped his hands on his pants. The grass expressed interest by leaning toward him.

Ames stared at the venerable inventor and then out the door at the grass. The shoe was completely gone and the grass sat there looking beautiful and malevolent. "What about my shoe? Those were an expensive pair of Dockers," he asked as he hobbled over to the table, his grass stained left sock leaving a slight smear on the tile floor.

R glanced down. "Forget the shoe, it's gone. Grass fertilizer. I hear they're having a sale at Picway. And stop leaving grass stains on the tile."

With an exasperated expression Blond looked at R. "Wait a minute. If it's supposed to eat the dog crap, why did it eat my whole shoe and not just the stuff on the sole?"

R shrugged his shoulders. "It's not quite perfected yet. For some reason the grass likes a little meat now and then."

"You mean it could have eaten me?" asked the agent with alarm.

"Nah," replied R. "It doesn't go for big stuff, just little things. However we have lost a couple of Chihuahuas and a Pekingese. Oh, and there was that Labrador, King was his name, that sat in one place for too long. They call him Queen now."

Ames shuddered and changed the subject, "Okay what do you have for me?"

R grinned, looking rather like an insane Keebler elf with dental problems. "This is going to be a tricky one. From all accounts no one has any idea why the crews of those ships don't remember anything, so we're going to have to assume that the perpetrators – gee I love that word. Say it with me, per-pe-tra-tors. Perpetrators, perpetrators. Has kind of a ring to it don't you think? Per-pe-tra-tors."

"Give it a break will you!" said Ames through gritted teeth.

"Alright, alright," replied R, slightly miffed. "Where was I? Oh yeah, since no one has any idea why the crews don't remember anything, then we have to assume that the perpetrators, heh heh, used some form of knock out gas. Since we don't know what kind of gas it was I can't give you anything to counteract it. You're on your own there."

"Well that's real helpful," muttered Ames. "What am I supposed to do to stop the gas from affecting me?"

"Try holding your breath," replied R.

"So I'm supposed to hold my breath from Galveston to Basra? Does the word blue come to mind? How about rigor mortis? That's the best you've got? You have dog eating grass and I have to hold my breath for three weeks?"

"It eats dog poo not dogs and no, actually it would be closer to two weeks, but I do have some stuff for you," answered R. He picked up a wallet and handed it to the agent. Ames opened it and started leafing through the papers as R continued, "That's your new identity. There's a seaman's license, a driver's license, some credit cards, the usual junk. Just don't try to use the cards, I maxed them out last Christmas and haven't paid the bill yet."

Ames looked dubiously at the wallet, a folded strip of leather dyed a shocking pink with an embossed picture of

Britney Spears on the front. "What the heck's with the wallet," he demanded. "This looks like it belongs to some little teeny bopper or an acne covered nerd with social problems."

"That the best I could come up with on short notice," explained R. "I got it at the local thrift shop just as they were closing. It was a grab and run deal."

"I can't take this on a ship with me! The entire crew will think I'm either very strange or be finding room in my bunk with me."

"So replace it with your own wallet for crying out loud. Do I have to do all of your thinking for you? You're supposed to be this super smart secret agent, capable of overcoming all obstacles, able to leap tall buildings in a single bound, smarter than all the rest of us. Bull puppy! Just switch wallets, but remember any damage to your personal wallet is not covered by our insurance."

"Okay, okay" said Ames looking up. "I'll switch the flipping wallets. This gets me aboard a ship, but what do you have in the way of gadgets to help me out?"

R looked surprised. "Gadgets? Gadgets? We don't got no stinking gadgets! You still owe me for a watch and a car. You want gadgets? Go to Wal-Mart."

"Wait a minute," replied Ames hotly. "I covered the cost of that watch and Hassim found the car."

"The car was a mess," stormed R. "We had to completely rebuild it after you were done with it. The thing was full of bullet holes, the suspension was shot, the windows were broken and the hula girl wouldn't jiggle."

"Bull crap. That's what the darn thing looked like when you gave it to me!"

"Yeah, but you didn't sign off on the pre-inspection checklist, so now you're stuck with the damages."

"Pre-inspection checklist? Whose idea was that?"

"You're friendly US government and Hetrz rentals."

"That was a rented car?"

"Certainly, you don't think the government uses cheap used cars did you? Only the best and newest for our bureaucratic flunkies."

The car in question was a 1974 blue Ford Pinto that Ames had used on a previous mission. During the course of that mission, some Middle Eastern thugs had misplaced the car, only to return it in seriously bad shape. That was notwithstanding the fact that it was in seriously bad condition when Ames had gotten it.

"All right so I don't get any gadgets," said Ames with sadness. "So all I have to go on is this stuff in the wallet?"

"No, I've got some other things here for you." R pulled a bright red carryall across the table. "Inside you'll find some clothes suitable for a seaman on an oil tanker, deck shoes and so on. It should set you up nicely, but remember you're responsible for this stuff."

Ames unzipped the bag and reached inside. He pulled out a pair of much soiled white boxer shorts with a picture of Scooby Doo on the front and a rather large brown stain on the back. He hurriedly dropped the shorts and briskly rubbed his hands on his pants. "What the heck is this nasty stuff," he exclaimed pointing at the shorts!

R peered into the bag and gave a sheepish grin. "Sorry, that's my laundry to take home to mother." He reached under the table and pulled out a second red bag and placed it on the table.

With trepidation Ames carefully unzipped the new bag and looked inside. He could see a new package of under shorts still in the wrapping. The collar of a blue shirt and the toe of a black shoe peered out from under the shorts.

Satisfied he zipped up the bag and placed it on the floor beside himself.

"Here, try this on," said R lifting his laundry off the table and setting it on the floor. With the other hand he handed the agent an unruly mop of dirty brown hair. Ames took the thing and looked at it while turning it in his hands. It crinkled when he handled it. "What's this?"

"That's a wig," said the inventor.

"Really? I thought it was the remnants of one of your dogs. What do I need a wig for?"

"It's not the wig, it's what's inside that counts."

Ames found the opening and looked inside. The entire inner surface was coated with a metallic substance.

"What's this stuff?" asked Ames fingering the metal.

"Aluminum foil. It is conceivable that the perpetrators are using some kind of mind-altering ray. The foil is in there to keep your mind from being affected."

Ames looked dubious. "What do you think we're dealing with here, space aliens?"

"You can never tell," muttered R as he glanced upward at the aluminum lined ceiling. Ames pushed the wig into the bag.

"So that's it?" asked Ames.

"No I've got one more thing," replied R. He pulled a packet from his lab smock. "These are your travel tickets from here to Basra with connections in Paris and Baghdad. There are also some meal tickets suitable for McDonald's or Burger King. I'd suggest staying with the dollar menu since the tickets are only worth two and a quarter each and you've only got four of them."

Ames examined the tickets. "Hey, these are second class tickets! Can't I get an upgrade to first class?"

"Not hardly, why do you think we're developing poo grass. The budget's tight."

CHAPTER THREE

The flight to Baghdad was pretty much uneventful. Ames had worn a modest business suit and his passport and seaman's papers had gotten him through customs without any problems. The only semi-event was in Paris when he was singled out for a complete strip search by the French customs people. The security people at Orly had allowed a party of Arab looking men with bulky carry-ons to pass before tapping him on the shoulder and directing him to a small room near the customs gate.

The agent tried to explain to the gendarmes that he was only passing through, but they insisted. The search had required the better part of an hour and included disrobing all the way down to his socks and shorts. The two security guards had grinned at him the whole time. One even went so far as to smile coyly as he dropped his pants.

The two officers then proceeded to paw through his clothes, turning his pockets out and dumping his stuff on the floor. One of them produced a knife and slit the soles of his shoes open and knocked the heels off. After wadding everything up and tossing the remnants into a corner, they finally appeared satisfied that he was not a terrorist, or interested in either of them. They indicated he should get dressed and then left the room, the shorter one looking at Ames wistfully over his shoulder.

After redressing, the agent headed across the concourse for his flight to Baghdad, the soles of his shoes making "thwapping" noises as his loose soles flapped up and down with each step. He barely avoided tripping when one loose sole caught in the junction of the floor and the people mover at the end of the boarding tunnel.

As he walked he noted that the "thwapping" came not only from his shoes but from various other people around him. While the others seemed oblivious to the weird noise, he inspected his fellow travelers. Some were missing the soles of their shoes; other had only their soles slit open. One woman waddled by, rocking back and forth on high heels with the spikes removed. She looked extremely annoyed. She also looked extraordinarily silly.

After he had boarded the plane and was seated the agent tied up the loose soles with some string obtained from the stewardess. She had a number of large balls of twine, in various shades, to somewhat match shoe colors. Apparently this was becoming a common problem on flights. He noted that the teenager in the seat across the aisle had his shoes wrapped up with little leather collars with silver spikes to match the leather collar with silver spikes he wore around his neck. The kid nodded at Ames, causing his blue and orange spiked hair to bobble from side to side.

The agent nodded back and spent the flight studiously reading the in-flight magazine. By the time the plane reached Baghdad he had memorized the recipe for Borscht with peanut butter noodles.

Ames disembarked the 747 at Baghdad International and scanned the airport concourse looking for Muslim Airlines. Apparently it was fairly new since he didn't see a kiosk for it and did not remember it from his last visit to Iraq. Finally giving up in frustration he stood in line at the Air France counter and waited while the line shuffled slowly forward. After a fifteen-minute wait he finally reached the counter.

Smiling at the cute dark haired attendant he asked, "Could you direct me to Muslim Airways, please?"

The girl frowned. "Where are you headed, sir?" the girl asked, poking some keys on her computer terminal.

"Basra," replied Ames. "I have a flight on Muslim Air in one hour."

The girl's frown deepened and she glanced down at the computer screen. "We have a very nice flight leaving in thirty minutes direct to Basra. That includes an in-flight movie and a complete meal with steak tartar and cabbage leaves. I'm sure you'd enjoy the flight."

"No thank you," said Ames with some misgivings. "My flight is on Muslim Air."

She poked at the keys on her computer. "Oh, look, sir. We have a special today. I can give you an upgrade to first class at no extra charge and we'll throw in ear-phones and our in flight magazine, "French Fried Flying." It would be no problem to book that for you sir." She looked hopefully into his eyes.

With a sinking sensation Ames responded. "No, I really have to take Muslim Air."

Dropping her shoulders the girl said, "All right sir, I tried. To get to Muslim Air, go to your right down the concourse and look for a green door on your left. Go through there and down the stairs . . . ."

Ames interrupted her, "Take a left and then a right through a brown door and go down the stairs. You'll find Muslim Air on the left."

"Oh, you do know where it is?" she asked with surprise.

"Did Muslim Air used to be called Iraqi Air, by any chance?"

"Why yes!" she exclaimed. "They changed the name when they consolidated with the Baghdad Taxi Company. They are now owned exclusively by Ali Baba."

"Ali Baba? Didn't he used to be an olive oil thief or something?"

She glanced nervously around. "Please keep your voice down, sir. Mister Baba is a good friend of the Baghdad police chief who is also an investor in the venture."

With a shrug and a wave Ames left the counter and went in search of the green door.

Within minutes he had wended his way down the stairs past the brown door and confronted a counter made of old planks and piled up date crates. A seriously obese Arab with a dirty beard sat in a dilapidated armchair behind the makeshift counter. He had a small portable television perched on his enormous belly and was watching the Playboy channel while munching on a Twinkie. A carton of the chemically improved desserts sat on the floor beside him. A pile of discarded wrappers indicated the demise of a host of previous Twinkies. Ames had dealt with the crooked ticket agent before.

As Ames put his hands on the counter, the Arab looked up and smiled. "Ah, my secret agent friend," he said while placing the television on the floor. He stood up and extended his hand, allowing a mass of Twinkie crumbs to shower onto the floor. Various insects and one large centipede emerged from cracks in the walls and hurried over for the feast. "Chew are flying wid us again?"

"Looks that way," muttered Blond taking the hand with trepidation. "I've got a flight to Basra."

The Arab carefully scrutinized Ames' watch before letting go of the hand. "Ah, chew will be taking de express! It only has six stops before Basra. Chew in luck, de plane leaves in one hour. Dat will be two hundred dollars American."

"I already have a ticket," said Ames pulling the packet from his pocket. "All I need is a boarding pass."

The Arab took the ticket and peered at it. "Ah, I am sorry. Dis ticket was issued before de price hike. It is no good now. Der is an-add on fee to use it. I am sorry." He handed the ticket back to Ames. The ticket felt slightly sticky.

"How much is this bull going to cost me?" asked the agent indignantly, wiping at the ticket with his handkerchief.

The Arab looked confused. "Bull? Der is no bull. Maybe de put one on airplane, but no bull here. But we got cow out back. Maybe chew want dat? It cost chew extra."

Ames scowled. "I don't want any cow. I'm talking about the crap I get every time I try to use your airline."

"Crap," exclaimed the Iraqi. "Der no crap on de airplane. De toilets not worked in years."

"Oh, for Pete's sake," exclaimed Blond. "How much is this gouging going to cost me?"

"As I say before, de price hike is not dat bad, only two hundred dollars. But for chew, since chew frequent flyer, I can gib to chew for one fifty." The fat man grabbed a Twinkie and took a healthy bite.

"This is highway robbery,' said Ames. "I can go upstairs to Air France and get the same flight for a hundred and ten. And the airplane isn't falling apart!"

"Ah, but de don't give duck tape with frequent flyer miles," suggested the obese clerk.

"They don't need duck tape, you twit. Their airplane doesn't fall apart!"

"But we have added many new airplanes to our fleet! Some of dem are close to brand new. Besides, de'er flight doesn't leave for seven hours. Ours takes off in one hour."

Ames thought for a minute. If he waited for the Air France flight he would miss boarding the ship at Basra. That would put a serious kink in his mission. It was Muslim Air or nothing. With a sigh he reached for his credit card.

The clerk glanced at the card. "I'm sorry dis is Visa, we only take American Express."

"Wait a minute, last time you took Visa and not American Express."

"We have had a policy change. Do you have an American Express card?"

"No I don't. I suppose you want cash, right?"

"We are pleased to accept cash, but none of that Iraqi stuff. Only American dollars, French Francs or Russian rubles." Ames noted that the Arabs English improved dramatically when he was talking about money.

"I'll give you fifty bucks," said Ames.

"I must have at least one hundred," said the agent.

"Seventy is my final offer or I go up to Air France," stated Ames with conviction.

The clerk reached for a pad of Post-It notes and started scribbling Arabic on the top page. When he was finished he handed the note to Ames and accepted three twenties and a ten in exchange.

With a smile the clerk stuffed the money in his pocket and said, "Chew plane leaves from gate ten. Hab a good flight and tank chew for choosin' Muslim Air." He dropped back down into the chair and hoisted the television back into his lap as Ames headed up the stairs to the main concourse.

After walking the length of the concourse for ten minutes looking for gate ten, he finally stopped at the Air France counter again. The same cute dark haired girl gave him the same sad smile. Before he even said anything, she pointed toward the main door. "If you are looking for gate ten, you have to go outside and get on the bus. It will take you to gate ten."

With a wave the agent pushed through the glass doors and stepped out onto the sidewalk. Looking left and right he did not see any bus, just two women sitting on the concrete and one leaning against the building. The two sitting on the curb were in chador with the heavy black burqua, but the one leaning against the building was wearing jeans and a bright white blouse.

Keeping a close eye on the two in chador as if fearing they would jump up and accuse him of apostasy, he casually walked up to the one in jeans and asked, "Excuse me, do you speak English?"

She pushed herself up from the sidewalk and said with a slight accent, "Why yes I do. Are you an American?"

She was blond and trim with gorgeous blue eyes and a figure that would do a Weight Watchers ad proud. There was no way this one had ever used a weight tracker.

"Hi," said the agent through a slightly thick tongue. "I'm Blond, Ames Blond and I'm looking for gate ten?"

Her face lit up like an aircraft beacon. Ames tongue dropped onto his shoe. "You're that British secret agent! I've always wanted to meet you! I think you're so adorable in all those movies. Do you really get to drive all those nifty cars and do all those neat things?"

With a slight scowl Ames reeled in his tongue and responded, "I'm Blond, Ames Blond. You're thinking of the other guy. He's the Brit. I'm an American, although, come to think of it, we do have some things in common."

She looked confused. "But you're not a blond. I'm a blond, see." She pulled a wisp of golden hair in front of her nose. "We have more fun," she continued.

Ames let out an audible sigh. "No I'm not a blond, my name is Blond. And, yes, I can see that you're a blond. Is this gate ten or can you direct me to gate ten?"

She looked closely into his eyes, making his stomach flop. He could feel her breath on his face and he had the sudden urge to grab her. Then she said, "Do you like goats? I think every place I go over here, all they have is goats. I get tired of goats. Do you have anything to eat on you besides goat?"

Ames stepped back from her with a blanched face. As a result of a previous mission the agent had a serious aversion to anything goat related including cheese and kid gloves.

"Sorry," he stated. "I don't have anything, but there's a McDonalds in town. I suppose you could get a hamburger there."

She sighed. "No, I stopped there earlier and all they had were McGoat burgers." She brightened, "So you're not a secret agent? I'm a reporter over here covering the war for CNN."

Blond looked at her dubiously, his eyes dropping to her chest. "You're a reporter? What do you report, fashion news?"

She laughed a tinkling laugh. "No silly, I go out with the Marines and report what they do. It's really interesting!"

"I'll bet the Marines love that," muttered Ames. "Listen, this has been fun, but I really need to find gate ten and catch a flight on Muslim Air."

She glanced around, "But this is gate ten. The bus will be here anytime now."

Ames frowned, pulling his eyes upward with some difficulty, "Gate ten? Bus? What does a bus have to do with it?"

She took his hand sending a thrill up his arm. "The bus takes us to gate ten."

The urge to grab here had come back. With an effort he disentangled her. "Where does the bus take us?"

She gave him a strange look. "To gate ten of course. Weren't you listening?"

At that moment an ancient bus turned in from the main road and chuffed its way toward the curb. Black smoke billowed from the exhaust and the back of the vehicle was dark with soot. The engine rumbled and wheezed, sounding as though it would die at any moment. The bus ground to a halt in front of Ames and the girl. It seemed to settle lower on what few springs it had left. The door opened and the girl grabbed his hand pulling him up the rusty stairs. He barely had time to grab his bag as they pushed their way into the crowded machine.

CHAPTER FOUR

Inside the bus it was as crowded as a Texas truck full of illegal aliens. There were people sitting four to a seat, people in the aisles, goats, chickens, bags, boxes, luggage and three dwarves. Somehow the young males found space to jump up and make lewd gestures at the blond. Some made lewd gestures at Ames.

The two women in Chador pushed onto the bus behind them forcing Ames into close contact with the girl, provoking an immediate masculine response. Glancing down and then back up at his face she beamed and said, "I see you like me."

"Ugel drp," Ames responded with conviction through his tied tongue. He cleared his throat and tried again. "Uh, I like you fine, um, uh, miss er um, what is your name?"

"Oh," she said brightly. "I'm Goody DeLay. Nice to meet you Mister Blond." She wiggled her hand up from between them and placed it under his chin. It smelled like lavender soap. With effort he extricated his hand from where it was trapped between a seat and his hip. He brought the hand up and they shook. Her hand was soft and warm, causing an increase in the masculine response.

At that point the bus jerked forward and the coupled hands smacked Ames in the chin knocking his head back into a woman behind him. There was a "thunk" of bone on bone and a grunt of pain from the woman, causing a growl from a man standing next to the woman. Almost instantly a sharp pain appeared at the lower extreme of Ames' butt crack as the male companion of the woman applied the point of a knife. With a yowl Ames' masculine response rapidly disappeared.

Goody leaned forward and peered over his shoulder, forcing his autonomic system to make a choice. The male response began to increase thereby increasing the pain at the end of his butt crack. He decided the opposing sensations made for an interesting experience.

With surprisingly good Arabic the girl yelled something at the man and the pain in the butt went away. "Thank you," muttered the agent as the passengers around him laughed. The girl shrugged but stayed pressed against him.

The bus jounced along a driveway and turned right onto a main road, swaying back and forth on non-existent springs. Every once in a while the chassis would bottom out on the tires, creating a lurching motion followed by a heavy screech. Sparks dribbled from the rear of the bus. The motion caused Ames to rub against the girl producing a very pleasant feeling. He smiled broadly at her, but conversation was impossible with the loud rattling and groaning of the bus. When the bus went around corners the passengers groaned as well. Ames and Goody rode face to face staring at each other with really stupid grins.

While Ames enjoyed himself, the bus traveled north through Baghdad passing a canal on the right. Most of the land they passed was taken up with olive groves and a few scattered warehouses. When the highway started to curve to the west the bus turned left onto a dirt road. The bus continued north, jouncing and bouncing the passengers as the bus dipped in and out of ruts and depressions. Occasionally the bus would hit a particularly deep hole and the passengers would get a brief spell of weightlessness. The chickens particularly enjoyed this, being normally flightless, and expressed their pleasure by spraying white globs onto the passengers, most of whom ignored it.

With a lurch the bus turned right and then, a few minutes later turned right again. With a final wheeze and a loud bang, followed by a cloud of black smoke, the bus came to a stop. The bus door opened and there was a mad dash for the exit. Goats, chickens and people spilled out onto the dirt track surrounding the bus.

Ames staggered out with the rest of the crush and looked around. He was standing on the edge of long dirt runway with a whitewashed building at one end. An ancient Ford Tri-motor airplane sat on the runway near the building. Looking around, the agent could not see another plane. With a sinking feeling he glanced back at the Tri-motor. There was already a long line of people and animals near the entry hatch. "Oh, drat, not again."

The girl, who had been forced out next to Ames, looked at him. "What was that?" she asked.

Ames looked at her and attempted a smile. It came out as a cross between a leer and a frown. "I've traveled on Muslim Air before, back when it was called Iraqi Air. Make sure you get your duct tape."

"Duct tape?" she asked with a quizzical expression.

"Yeah," said Ames. "With frequent flier miles you get duct tape."

"Why duct tape?" she asked as they walked over and joined the line at the airplane.

In response he pointed at the airplane.

The airplane was a relic of the 1930's and looked its age. There were patches all over the once beautiful aircraft. Some made of aluminum and others made of cardboard or goatskin. The port tail wing seemed to be held on with rope and wire. There was duct tape wrapped heavily around the right tire and a sheet of plastic, held in place with tape, covered one of the side windows. The side of the plane had "Muslim Air" scratched in black Magic Marker with, presumably, the same thing in Arabic underneath. A whitewashed rectangle on the side barely covered faded red letters spelling, "TR NS WO D AIR IN S."

A man with a brimmed cap with an anchor on the front, who Ames guessed was the pilot, came out of the white washed building, walked over to the plane and yanked open the door. It came off in his hand and he dropped it on the ground. He nudged the door with his toe before climbing inside. The plane swayed back and forth as the pilot moved forward inside.

A stout woman in a blue chador with silver wings pinned to an expansive bosom waddled over to the plane and took up position at the door. She nudged the broken door under the plane and called out something in Arabic. Passengers started handing her Post-It notes and climbing in. Ames glanced at Goody. "By the way, where are you headed?"

"Oh, I'm going to the Marine base at Mosul. There has been a rash of camels using the goat crossings and the Marines are mounting an offensive against the camel herders."

Ames laughed. "I think you have the wrong plane. This one is an express that goes to Basra."

"Yes, it does," she said as they climbed in. "This plane goes to Basra after stopping in Mosul, Irbil, and a couple of other places. I think it gets to Basra in about six hours." They pushed a goat and two chickens out of a pair of seats and sat down.

There was a loud thud and a wheeze followed by the roar of an airplane engine. "Blast it, that goofy Arab lied to me again," said Ames with disgust. "I'm going to miss my ship."

"You're a seaman?" asked Goody breathlessly. "I love seamen."

Ames gave her a strange look and started to say something when there was second thud and finally a third as the last two engines started. Conversation became impossible with the roar. They were pushed back into their seats as the plane rumbled forward and ran down the runway. With a series of bumps and groans the plane hopped into the air, its left wheel scrapping a tree on the way up. A couple of bolts from the back wing fell off, described a perfect arc over the tree and clonked a farmer and his goat in the head. The farmer dropped with a thud while the goat looked around angrily for something to butt back at. After whipping its head back and forth a couple of times it settled on the prostrate farmer. Lowering its horns the goat slammed into the agriculturalist's nether region, skidding him two feet forward.

Back in the plane, a stewardess in a black chador with silver wings on her chest walked down the aisle passing out multicolored rolls of duct tape from a box. Passengers held up their Post It notes and received, or didn't, a roll of tape. Ames got a nice roll of red tape, but Goody didn't get any. Apparently she wasn't a frequent flier with Muslim Air. To make her feel better he passed her his roll, much to the annoyance of the stewardess. The invisible female in black kept grabbing the tape from Goody and handing it back to Blond. Finally Ames settled the matter by unwinding a couple of feet of tape and wrapping it around Goody. The stewardess glared at him with barely seen brown eyes, turned and flounced back to the front of the cabin. Ames sat there for moment and tried to figure out how one flounced in a tent like over-garment.

Goody struggled to get loose from the wad of red, but only got it tangled in her hair. Ames tried to carefully pull it loose without taking hunks of blond hair with it. He only partially succeeded. The sticky red stuff lived up to its name of "Hundred mile an hour tape", meaning it took a wind moving at one hundred miles an hour to break the adhesive loose.

Amidst screams, curses and really erotic looking wiggles and squirms, from Goody, not Ames, although the agent did do some squirming, the man from DORK slowly pulled the crap loose. Eventually the last of the stuff came free leaving the girl panting and gasping with a real bad hair day. When the stewardess came by, Goody kicked at the aviated waitress two or three times without success. Her foot kept getting hung up in the voluminous black burnoose.

The flight from Baghdad to Mosul took less than forty-five minutes and Ames was sorry to see Goody go, although she did leave the agent her contact number in Baghdad. He had hoped to join the Mile High Club, but they barely got above a thousand feet. Thinking back on it, as he watched her get off the plane, he decided he would like to ride the bus with her again sometime, even if she did pile two feet of red duct tape on his head before leaving.

The flight to Basra without Goody seemed interminable, with pit stops at every city, town, village, oil well, oasis and camel pit in the country. Twice the passengers were forced to deplane and wrap some critical part, such as the engines or wings, with duct tape to get the beast back into the air. And once they were forced to land when the air in the plane became too thick smoke to see or breath. A quick application of duct tape, and the sacrifice of one chicken, solved the problem and they were back in the air in no time.

With a loud thump the Tri-motor landed at Qasr Tall Mihl airfield outside Basra. The landing was immediately followed by a loud bang and the "thumpa-ta thumpa-ta" of a blown tire. The airplane slewed across the runway knocking out two camels and scattering a herd of goats, finally coming to rest with one wing on the ground. There was a general rush for the door followed by a rush of the privates and other passengers. The intrepid secret agent waited for the rush to cease before making his way leisurely to the door only to trip over three chickens and thump down the stairs on his butt.

Climbing to his feet, and dusting the seat of his pants, he was suddenly grabbed by a monstrous Arab with a long black beard. "Ames my dear friend," the Arab shouted in his ear. "Welcome to the jewel of the east, the beautiful city of Basra."

Ames pulled his head away from the greasy bush of hair and looked at his accoster. Then he smiled. "Hassim! What are you doing here? I thought you were working full time for the CIA?"

"Shh," whispered Hassim, dropping Blond to the ground. "I am undercover as a junk jewelry salesman. I am trying to find the people who are selling fake camel dung and threatening national security."

"Are you sure you're not trying to find the people who are selling fake camel dung and interfering with your selling fake camel dung?" mentioned Ames with a smile.

"Ahh, but if I sell fake camel dung then it is in the interest of the country. If others do it, who knows for what nefarious purposes they do it?" Hassim had previously worked as an independent contractor for DORK and assisted Ames on another mission. His major claim to fame was knowing just about everyone in the

Middle East and selling them fake silver jewelry. He had been so successful in that mission that the CIA had taken him on full time to sell fake silver jewelry. Oddly, now that the government was involved, much of the fake silver jewelry was real silver and priced below market value, but with government subsidies to help make up the difference.

"So what brings you to Basra?" asked Ames pulling himself from Hassim's grip and ducking as a chicken flew, squawking, from the door of the plane. The chicken ricocheted off Hassim's head, leaving a large white spot.

"I am here to pull your bacon, may Allah forgive my use of the heathen word, from the fire." He dabbed at the white spot, smearing it down his forehead and onto his rather large nose. Ames wriggled his head and shoulders in disgust. "You have missed your ship. I will have to take you down river to catch it at Abu-al-Hasib. That is a number of miles down the Shatt al-Arab waterway. Come I have the car waiting."

Hassim grabbed Ames' carryall and led the way to the parking lot, a dirt track next to a white washed building. As they walked into the lot they passed ancient Fords and Chevy's, with an occasional low slung Citroen. Suddenly Ames stopped dead. His hand came up to point and his mouth dropped open. "That can't be!" he exclaimed pointing at a car.

The car was a faded blue Ford Pinto with a broken windshield, bullet holes in the side and a plastic hula girl standing on the dashboard, her hips lethargically swaying back and forth. "That can't be the same stupid car!"

Hassim beamed. "Yes, my friend that is the same lovely car from our last mission. R sent it over especially for you. Is it not great?" The Arab waved his arms expansively at the car.

"Bull puppies," said Ames angrily. "The darn thing is falling apart and makes three miles per hour wide open. Even the hula girl doesn't work right. Say, did you sign for that thing?"

"No my friend," said Hassim. "I signed for you. It is your car."

"Oh toe fungus," muttered the agent. "I hope the heck you completed the pre-inspection checklist."

"There is a pre-inspection checklist?" asked Hassim with his eyebrows raised. "I thought that was only for rental cars."

"It is a rental," said Ames in disgust. "R says the budget is tight again."

"Ah, that would explain all the forms I, you, had to sign." The Arabs frown brightened into a smile, "But I did do you a favor and selected the no insurance box to save you some money."

"Terrific, we'll probably slam into a camel in the next five minutes and I'll get sued for everything I don't own," muttered Ames, glancing over at Hassim. "Maybe I can claim the signatures are forgeries or possibly mental exhaustion. I hear suicide works."

"Not so," said Hassim. "To clear government debt they sell your corpse for scientific study, or fertilizer, whichever is getting the lower price at the moment. In some cases they go after your progeny out to the third generation." He hefted Ames' bag into the back seat through the broken back window. The car groaned slightly as the bag hit the seat. That caused dust to fly up and fill the interior. Ames stifled a cough as the thick air came out the window.

With deep misgivings Ames slid into the front passenger seat as Hassim climbed in and spent the next five minutes trying to get the car started. Finally, with a belch of black smoke, the Pinto roared to life and settled down to a weak grumble, with an occasional hiccup.

CHAPTER FIVE

Catching the ship had proven to be a tad more difficult than Hassim or Ames had imagined it would be. For reasons no one could explain, the Shatt al-Arab waterway was clogged with capsized and sunken ships, some dating from the 1930's. Everything from freighters and tankers to dhows, scows and rowboats lay on their sides creating a complex maze along the twisting river from above Basra to below Al-Faw, the last town before reaching the Persian Gulf.

As a result, the ships speed through the waterway was considerably hindered, allowing a passage of no more than 3 knots headway. Unfortunately for Ames, the Pinto, spewing black smoke from its exhaust, made a top speed of 6 miles per hour, just under twice the speed of the ship. This would have allowed them to eventually catch the ship, sometime in the next century, if the road were straight. It wasn't. The road meandered as much as the waterway. It was also crowded with camels, goats, sheep and poorly maintained automobiles, some in even worse shape than the Pinto (if that were possible). With each mile they fell a little bit more behind, and they only had slightly less than ten miles to Abu-al-Hasib where the ship would stop to take on a pilot to take them the rest of the way through the Shatt al Arab and down to the Gulf.

Finally, unable to make sufficient headway, the two agents were forced to stop at a roadside diner and make a call to the ship. Hassim found that the boat had already passed Abu-al-Hasib and their next best bet was to try and catch up at Al Faw, another fifty miles down the waterway.

After grabbing a couple of quick camel pies the two jumped in the car and sped off down the road, further blocking traffic as other drivers tried to pass them. Fortunately for national security, the ship had not been able to get a Gulf pilot in Abu-al-Hasib and would be forced to remain in Al Faw overnight until one could be procured.

At six in the morning, two miles outside Al Faw, after driving all night, the front of the car began swaying back and forth. Hassim pulled the car to the side of the road to find out what was wrong. He almost turned the engine off, but Ames grabbed his hand and stopped him before he turned the key. "That might not be a good idea," said the agent. "The way things have been going it might not start again."

Hassim nodded and they both got out to inspect the front end. Ames poked at the tire on one side while Hassim kicked the one on the driver's side. With a "thump," the tire on Hassim's side fell off, followed by a second "thump" as the front left side of the car dropped to the ground kicking up a small cloud of tan dust. Ames rushed around to the driver's side as Hassim bent down to look at the damage. With a thick finger he pointed at the front disk and looked up at Ames. "It seems that all of the lug nuts have fallen off."

"Well that figures," muttered Ames. "How the heck did the lug nuts fall off? Weren't they tightened properly the last time the tire was put on? Who was the schmuck who put the tire on and didn't tighten his nuts?"

Hassim quickly looked down and gave a sheepish smile.

"How the heck are we supposed to get to the ship now? How far is it to the dock?" asked Ames.

Hassim sat down on the tire and looked around. "We are about two miles away. I think we may be able to hitchhike, if we are careful not to get into a car bomb."

Ames glanced around with a worried look. "Car bomb? That's just what I need, get my butt blown all over Iraq. Can you fix that thing?"

Hassim stood up and grinned while dusting off his hands. "Actually, yes. I recall a joke I heard once." Ames made a come-on gesture with his hands.

"It seems this guy had a flat tire and pulled over to the side of the road. Next to the car was a fence and a sign that said, 'Happy Dale Lunatic Asylum'. That made the guy a little scared and he rushed to get the tire changed. In his haste he kicked the lug nuts into the bushes.

"As he was searching he heard a voice say, 'Take one lug nut from each of the other three wheels and put them on the fourth tire. That will get you to a service station where you can get more lug nuts'. Looking around the man saw a face looking through the fence.

"Startled, he said, 'That's a pretty good idea. What are you doing in a nut house?' The voice answered back, 'I'm in here for being crazy, not stupid'."

The agent laughed as he proceeded to pull out the jack and lug wrench. He hooked the jack under the bumper and started ratcheting the thing upward. At that moment the engine died with a blat of black smoke. Ames threw down the tire iron in disgust.

Hassim stoically picked up the wrench and continued ratcheting. Within minutes he had one lug nut off each of the other tires and the tire remounted. Ames tossed the jack and wrench into the trunk as Hassim twisted the key to restart the car. The car chugged and blew black smoke through the exhaust, creating a black smudge on Ames' trousers. He hurriedly got out of the way as the Arab pressed on the gas and turned the key again.

The car burped, hiccupped, chugged and started, the motor rumbling like a cat in heat. Smoke drooled out the exhaust, creating a very low-lying cloud near the ground. Hassim jammed the car in gear and tore off down the road. Ames ambled along beside the car, opened the door and slid into the seat.

An hour later the blue car rattled to a stop at the gate to the crew pier in Al Faw. They could see a number of ships going east and west along the waterway and a few that were anchored in the small bay. Ames looked around and asked Hassim, "Which one is the ship I'm supposed to be on? Is it here or did we miss it?"

Hassim pointed to a tanker with a dark green superstructure and white hull that sat at anchor a hundred yards from the end of the pier. "I think that is it. It is called the *Exxon Valdez Two*. It used to have the route from California to Alaska until it ran aground one night and spilled its cargo of gin into the ocean. I understand there were two hundred thousand gallons slated to warm up the cold Alaskan nights. The spill made the Alaskans highly upset, got a lot of sea birds and fish drunk, and annoyed the environmentalists, who don't like the idea of fish and birds partying together. There were apparently some purists who didn't believe in extra specie mingling. Anyway, the *Valdez* was relegated to hauling oil from Basra to Gulf City."

"So I get to ride with a bunch of drunks?" asked Ames.

"Yeah, but not as much as they used to be. Oil doesn't mix as well with tonic water as gin does."

As they watched, a boat moved away from the side of the ship and angled in toward the shore. It's rough direction was toward the pier, but it kept weaving back and forth, going left for a space and then back right again. At one point it made a complete circle before getting back on course.

As it neared the pier they could see that the boat held four men, one of who was hanging over the stern with his face almost in the water. Two others standing on the seats and looked like they were fighting with oars while the fourth sat in the back guiding the boat with a small outboard motor.

With a thump the boat hit the pier and bounced off while one of the men dropped his oar and tried to grab the mooring post. He missed and fell into the water. The boat turned back in and barely missed hitting the guy in the water.

With a grind of wood on wood the boat jammed against the pier and the second man with an oar tossed the thing up onto the pier and grabbed the mooring post. Using his other hand he quickly wrapped a rope around it, connecting the rope securely. The boat promptly rotated back out to sea leaving the man hanging onto the mooring post. The opposite end of the rope he had tied slipped lightly from the boat and dropped into the water. The man with the motor slewed it around and pushed the boat back into the pier. The fourth man pulled his face out of the water long enough to grab the rope from the water and tie it to a stanchion.

The man at the back fumbled with the motor for a moment, first revving it higher, making the boat's nose dig into the water, then throttling back and finally shutting it off. The person hanging off the stern stood up and shook water from his arms. Together they grabbed the guy in the water and pulled him aboard. The man on the mooring post climbed up onto the pier.

As the other three climbed up onto the pier Ames stepped closer to them and asked, "Are you guys from the *Valdez Two*?"

The four of them stopped and the one who had been operating the motor stepped forward slightly. He was a dark skinned older man, rail thin, wearing a dark blue shirt open at the collar. His tan pants were held up with a thick belt from which roughly ten thousand keys hung from a short chain. "And who are you?" he asked.

"I'm Blond, Ames Blond," said the agent.

The man's mouth dropped open and the others stared. "Holy smokes," he gasped. "The guy from the movies? Bloody heck, I didn't think you were real! I love your movies! Do you really get to diddle all them broads?" He stuck out his hand to shake.

"Sorry," said Ames. "But I'm not that guy. My name is Ames Blond and I'm not British. I'm supposed to join your ship here as an ordinary seaman." He reached out to take the hand and then stopped. The hand was not a hand, but a metal hook that curved upward to a sharp point. With a start he jerked his hand back.

The man looked down and pulled his hand back. "Oh, sorry," he said as he transferred the boat hook from one hand to the other. "Darn near skewered you there." He put the hand back out. "Names Smee, Thomas Smee. I'm the second officer."

Ames shook the man's hand as he continued, pointing to each of the other men as he spoke. "That there is Mike Ratlung, ordinary seaman same as you. The short fella's Bob Cratchet, the ships cook and that there with all the chains is Joe Marley, the store keeper. He's gon'na take them chains over to the shipwright and exchange them for some other ones."

Mike was a tall man with a scarred and pock marked face wearing sodden clothes from being in the bay. It looked like he had had no access to Clearasil when he was a teenager. Marley was stout and broad across the chest while Bob was a somewhat diminutive guy with long blond hair pulled back into a ponytail that extended down his back almost to his waist.

Ames let go of the hand and said, "Are you guys okay. I mean you guys aren't drunk or anything are you?"

Smee frowned. "What do mean drunk?"

"Well, you were all over the harbor coming in and I heard what happened to your ship in Alaska, and you know. . . ." Ames faltered to a stop.

The four guys looked a little uptight. "Darn it," said Smee with disgust. "I wish people would stop bringing up that Alaska thing. We haven't had any problems like that in at least a week. Why do they keep harping on it! We were all over the place because the rudder on the boat is broken and Joe had to control it by leaning over the stern board."

Ames glanced at the boat, "So what was the thing with the oars? It looked like those guys were fighting."

"Nah," replied Smee with a wave of his hand. "They were using the oars to balance the boat. For some reason the darn thing leans to port side and tends to sink if you don't get it balanced right."

"Why don't you just get another boat?'

"What? Are you nuts? That boat belongs to Exxon. Do you think they want to cut into profits by paying for boats all the time? We're lucky they feed us."

"What about the new chains you're getting?"

"We're not getting new chains. Marley takes them to the shipwright who fixes the broken links and cleans them up. When we stop back here the next time we'll trade em back again. You just wait here. We'll be back in no time and head out to the ship. You got your papers on ya?"

Ames tapped his pocket. "Yeah, right here. Say, how come you guys are still here? We were running late and figured we'd miss you"

Smee glanced back at the ship. "We're running late as well. Captain's got a hair up his butt about some white whale. That's this broad he met in Basra and she is one seriously big woman. Got a butt that would flatten a truck. She took a shine to the skipper and said she'd follow him to Al Faw.

"Since we couldn't go fast down the waterway, he's been going a little slow hopin' she gets tired of waiting and goes home before we got here. Anyway, you wait here while we go and drop off these chains, then we'll head out to the ship."

With a wave the four started up the pier, Marley dragging his chains and moaning about doing all the work.

CHAPTER SIX

The *Exxon Valdez Two* was an NV class crude container carrier with a DWT of 100,000 tonnes. She was double hulled with a stern superstructure and bridge with B&W 6L70MC diesel engines that could produce 13,176 horsepower capable of driving the ship forward at 13 knots. She was 243 meters long, had a beam of 42 meters and a draft of 19 meters. The ship could carry 26,600 tonnes of crude oil, which is about 292,000 barrels of the stuff. And I have no idea what any of that means. It was an oil carrying ship painted green and white. It's really big and really long and when it goes by the whistle goes "tweet," "tweet."

Ames left Hassim at the dock when the four sailors from the *Valdez* returned, shaking his hand and admonishing him to get the darn car back to R in one or at least a half a dozen pieces. Hassim promised to have it back in a couple of days or months or whatever.

The five of them rode out to the ship in the motor dinghy, weaving and yawing all the way. Also turning, tipping and bobbing. Mister Smee seemed to have a pretty good handle on controlling the wayward boat and they only went in four circles for the short trip. Bob and Mike held up the oars and swayed back and forth trying to time their movements to the rocking of the boat.

Joe spent the entire trip with his face hung over the stern board trying to keep the wayward rudder on course.

Every once in a while he would surface and blow water into the air. After spitting and sputtering he would take a number of deep breaths before plunging his head back over the side. As he plied a Planters Peanuts can to the water in the bottom of the boat, Ames wondered how long Marley could keep that up before he drowned. Strangely, they arrived safely at the ship with everyone still alive, in reasonably good condition and only eight inches of water in the bottom of the boat.

Smee tied the boat to the gangway and the five of them hustled up the boarding ladder (actually a staircase, but it would not be nautical to call it that) to the main deck. Halfway up, Ames stopped to change his grip on his duffel bag. Looking back down he saw that the dinghy was now full of water and only the bow was visible, tied to the gangway. Seat cushions floated in the water. Behind him he heard a yell and Cratchet went screaming back down the ladder yelling about saving the cushions.

At the bottom he slid to a stop, tripped on the bow of the dinghy and went head first into the water. Resurfacing he started grabbing seat cushions and chucking them onto the boarding platform. Mike arrived at the bottom just as Bob tossed the last cushion aboard. Mike helped Bob out of the water and the two of them connected the bow of the boat to a gantry line. Ames turned and continued his way upward.

At the top of the gangway Smee was waiting for Ames to catch up. He took Ames' arm and pointed him toward the stern. "Come on," he said, "I'll take you up to the bridge and you can get your papers logged into the manifest." At that moment Joe began operating the gantry, raising the dinghy up to the deck.

Smee dropped Ames' arm and the two men headed aft toward the towering aft superstructure. The deck was neat enough, although the paint was peeling and rust streaks spread like fungus under pipes, pumps and up the gunwales. Trying to keep from tripping over odd and unidentifiable equipment, Ames followed the second officer down the broad expanse of deck and waited while Smee opened a hatch in the foreface of the huge deckhouse. Looking back Ames saw the dinghy rise above the gunwale, Cratchet's dripping form kicking and screaming as he was lifted into the air with his pants hooked on an oarlock.

Ames lost track of the odd tableau when they went inside and secured the hatch (door, whatever). They went up three flights of metal ladders (more stairs), their footsteps reverberating off the steel bulkheads (walls). At the top Smee pushed through a steel hatch and Ames stepped onto the bridge (where they drive the ship, not a thing for cars to cross water). He had based his expectation on what he had seen in old movies, with gray colored controls and panels here and there with possibly some old guy with a beard and crushed nautical cap standing at a huge steering wheel. What he got was totally outside his understanding.

His feet landed on a deck (floor) carpeted in a pale blue, the deep pile cushioning his feet. Glancing around he was pretty sure he had entered the bridge of the *Star Ship Enterprise*. A long console, painted pleasant light beige, and with a leather-covered dashboard, ran under the forward (front) ports (windows). There were various gauges, dials, and flashing colored lights set into the leather covered surface. Just behind this console sat a control island that curved slightly to the left and right with two deep padded command chairs behind it and within the curve. The face of the control panel had a dizzying array of lights, radar and computer screens, dials, buttons and levers. Overhead lighting came from softly muted fluorescent fixtures. The walls had nautical paintings interspersed with red fire extinguishers, multi-colored maps, and odd-looking boxes and conduits in a variety of colors. A coffee service sat on a small table to the left of the hatchway. It looked like it belonged at the Kennedy Space Center instead of an over used oil tanker. All in all it seemed a very pleasant place to work.

There were two men on the bridge, both dressed in white shirts with dark blue ties. Both had dark blue boards with gold stripes along the shoulders of their shirts. Neither of them had a beard or a crushed cap. They looked like businessmen rather than sea and wind hardened sailors. They both looked up as Ames and Smee came on deck.

The older of the two handed the other a clipboard and walked over to Smee and Blond. He held out his hand. "Welcome aboard," he said. "You must be Blond. I'm Captain Blie."

'Yes, sir. Thank you, sir," said Ames taking the hand.

The captain pumped once and dropped the hand, gesturing for Ames to follow. "Come into my cabin for a minute Mister Blond. We need to discuss some things. Smee, take a look at the pressure readings on the number two piston, if you would please. They seem a little high."

Smee touched his hand to his forehead and ducked back out the hatchway. Ames followed the captain to a door set in the aft (rear) wall of the control room.

They entered a beautifully decorated office stateroom combination. The walls were done in glowing dark wood paneling with pictures of ships and seascapes. There were the usual fixtures such as clocks and weather gauges done in brass mounted here and there. A huge oak desk dominated one corner and a four-poster bed with deep green hangings stood in the opposite corner. The bed was piled high with pillows and cushions whose principal color was pink. Ames gave the Captain's back an odd look.

The captain moved behind the desk and settled into a large over-stuffed command chair and gestured for Ames to take a seat in a padded leather chair. As the agent sat the captain said, "As I said, welcome aboard. Now, how much experience do you have on commercial ships?"

Ames pulled his seaman's papers from his pocket and set them on the desk. "Absolutely none, sir. My greatest experience with boats was this plastic tugboat that sailed around the bathtub when I was seven. It usually sank within the first two minutes of the bath."

The captain looked down at the papers. "Swell. They send me useless supercargo. You're supposed to be replacing an able bodied seaman who was on the engine detail. We lost him in Basra when he was elected to the religious council. He was a pretty good engine man, but I guess the lure of power and graft was too much for him.

"The government says I have to have you on board, that you're some kind of secret agent who's here to solve some hinky problem for the Department of Homeland Security and some agency called POOP. I think that describes this whole business pretty well and that all this is pretty much bull turds, but I do what I'm told and so will you. You will not get in the way of the operation of this ship. If it comes to you and your mission and the safety of this ship, I will throw you overboard in a heartbeat. Do I make myself clear?"

Ames nodded.

"I have no idea what the problem is supposed to be," continued the Captain. "They say that some ships have disappeared and then reappeared, like David Copperfield and his stupid mirror tricks. There have been no problems on this ship and I will see that there are none in the future. I expect you to have a pleasant working vacation while we head for Galveston. The question remains, what do I do with you?"

The captain swiveled his chair and looked out through the brass-rimmed porthole. Ames sat and twiddled his thumbs. His left thumb seemed to be winning so the agent put extra effort into the right. The left fought back furiously and Blond was forced to twist his body left and right to prevent the capture of the thumb. At one point he banged his elbow on the desk. Just as the agent finally trapped his left thumb with his right, the captain turned back and asked, "Can you cook?"

"Yes, sir," the agent nodded, disentangling his thumbs which were glaring at each other. "I can boil water and I do this really good corn chowder with potatoes and ham. You add in onions sautéed in butter and . . . ." He trailed off as the captain's face darkened.

"Okay," said Blie, taking a deep breath and looking back at the porthole," What I'll do is assign you to the galley and move Midge to the deck. That will move Smith over to engines to take Da'uud's place." Blie glanced back at Blond. "He's the one who left the ship at Basra. Smith likes to get dirty, and that gets to be a problem when he's mucking about cleaning the crews quarters. He gets them dirtier than when he started, so his working on the engines won't be a problem."

The Captain scowled at Ames, "Bear in mind, if you can't cook, tell me now. There are eleven men aboard including yourself and we all like to eat. Well, I'm not sure about you, but the rest of us do. We have enough supplies aboard for the two-week trip. You burn stuff and have to throw it away and we end up on half rations. That annoys the crew and worst of all, it annoys me. You don't want to do that.

"You'll be working with Bob Cratchet." He stopped and looked at the ceiling before continuing. "Do us all a favor while you're here. See if you can keep Bob's hair out of the stew. That blasted ponytail is a pain in the butt."

Blie pulled Ames' papers over in front of him and began to idly paw through them. He glanced up. "You're dismissed. Go see Mister Smith, the first officer. He'll tell you where to go and get someone to help you stow your gear."

Ames went back out onto the bridge and looked around. The second man in a tie was now seated at the curved console, switching switches and buttoning buttons. He had a phone tucked under his chin. Under his feet Ames could feel the throb of the engines getting stronger. Glancing out the side ports he could see the riverbank slowly slipping by. They were underway. Ames wasn't sure if he should be seasick or not. After a moment of checking his stomach's reactions he decided he'd put that off for later.

The first officer hung up the phone, glanced around and spotted Ames. He lifted a hand and beckoned the agent over.

As Ames stopped in front of him the officer said, "I'm Felipe Manuel Ortega de Vega de las Montigo con Chili de Favor por Mucho Dineros de Rivera. The crew calls me Mister Smith. I'm the First Officer of the Valdez. The Captain tells me you'll be working with Bob in the galley? That's great. We're all getting tired of sliders and bug juice." He stopped as he saw the confusion in Ames' face.

"Burgers and Kool-Aid," said Smith with a smile. "I used to be in the Navy. Go out that hatch you came in and go down two levels. You'll find the crew quarters at the end of the passageway (hall). The second room from the far end is Cratchet's. He should be in there changing his clothes. Go on down and he'll show you your room and where to stow your stuff. Welcome aboard."

CHAPTER SEVEN

The trip the rest of the way down the Shatt al-Arab waterway and through the Persian Gulf was pretty much routine, marred only by two incidents. Ames spent the time establishing his culinary skills by burning water and deep frying hamburgers. As an added taste treat he made bologna and squash sandwiches with a macadamia nut sauce. Within days he had the entire crew on a healthy diet and each crewman had sworn to reduce weight during the voyage, or, as Marley said, "I ain't eatin' anymore of that garbage!"

Ames was pleased that he had made friends with the crew and even had a number of requests to hang around the yardarm, whatever that was.

The first incident was in the Persian Gulf off Bahrain when an old Chris Craft motorboat edged up to the side of the tanker and the occupants tried to board the ship. Smee had the con when the boat showed up and he quickly spread the word. Crewmen rushed to arm themselves as they dashed to the deck rails. The bad guys would have a tough time boarding this ship each man thought as they held their weapons. There was one ball bat, a broken pogo stick, two wrenches, a beach ball and a ping-pong mallet. There would have been a ping-pong ball, but someone stepped on it during the rush. Cratchet held the squashed remains in his hand just in case.

There were six people in the boat, three men and three women. The men were dressed in jeans and T-shirts and were waving lit fireworks sparklers claiming that they had come to inspect the holds. The three women wore bikini bathing suits with thong bottoms and had veils across their faces and scarves on their heads. The girls seemed more interested in waving their, ah, chests at the crewmen looking down from the deck than in assisting their boyfriends in the takeover.

After a tense five minutes, they were finally chased off when Marley used a bullhorn to read passages from the Bible to them. One of the would be taker-overers gunned the motorboats engine and yelled something about witches and demons as they fled back up the gulf. To make matters worse one of the veiled women fell out of the boat as it sped away. The crewmen of the *Valdez* were very insistent about assisting the over-busty creature, but she refused to be helped by heretics and unbelievers. As her bra floated away she cried that she was deeply ashamed that they had seen her face when her veil came off.

The crew did the only decent thing and left her there floating in the water. But only after Cratchet took a dozen picture of her for his "collection."

Ames later learned that the people in the small boat were picked up by a US warship off the coast of Bahrain and transported to a secret CIA torture camp in Cincinnati, Ohio. There they were subjected to a fourteen-hour a day marathon of old Gomer Pyle, USMC television shows while sitting naked in a hot tub. They cracked in less than twenty hours and gave up a complete list of boat rental and tanning salons in Bandar Abas. One of them even recommended a couple of good restaurants. They were later released in downtown Los Angeles where they thought they were back in Teheran after finding many of their missing relatives suspected of being imprisoned by Saddaam Hussein.

Later that year the Senate would hold hearings into the mistreatment of prisoners by making them strip naked. The prisoners, not the Senators, although making the Senators work in the buff might not be a bad idea. It would certainly keep them from dealing from their sleeves.

The second incident was a little more disturbing. Just days after passing through the Strait of Hormuz the *Valdez* had angled right (is that port or starboard?) and headed for the coast of Africa. During the night of the fifth day the ship's cat went a little bonkers and started running up and down passageways, leaping from lockers, hissing at mirrors and yowling at the top of its lungs. There was a mad scramble by the crewmen to catch the cat and throw it overboard, but in the middle of the chase the thing disappeared.

Although they searched for three days the cat was not see for a while. However, that did not mean it was gone. Little presents began appearing here and there; cat poop in a shoe, a really rank urine stain on the captain's bed, a dead mouse in the meatloaf, a hairball in Cratchet's comb. Oh, wait, that's what Cratchet's comb always looks like. Sorry, Bob, my mistake.

The problem did not go away until Smee finally discovered that the cat had mistaken Cratchet's marijuana stash for catnip. Apparently the cat had been rolling around in the stuff and went a little more ape than is normal for a catnip high. The cat was finally captured just days out from Galveston, inbound to unload, and slowly weaned from the marijuana using oregano and tuna fish. As a side benefit Bob said he was getting a better toke from the addition of the cat fur.

Other than that the ship had a pretty good cruise.

Oh, wait a minute. Hold it. I forgot the third incident. It was not much. Just that the crew went to sleep on the third day out from Galveston, after unloading their oil, and woke up a month later in downtown New Orleans.

The ship was parked next to a Woolworth's across the street from a still broken levee. Some late Mardi-Gras attendees had spray painted caricatures of naked women on the hull using Day-Glo orange and strung beads from deck railings. Three naked women were found sleeping in the captain's bed and a naked guy was found in bed with Cratchet, although he did not seem to mind. Cratchet that is, not the guy.

Some hurricane leftovers had taken up residence in the number three hold, claiming that FEMA had arranged for them to live there until their homes were rebuilt. The government finally evicted them by offering them fifth floor condos free of charge on the beach in Miami.

The subsequent investigation determined that the empty holds smelled like urine, sewage and old sweat socks, but no one had any idea what happened. The ship's cat stalked around the deck sniffing at every corner and piddling in odd places, which was not unusual since Cratchet seemed to be doing the same thing.

The ship was boarded by the New Orleans Police who stole three televisions and a stereo, the FBI and an odd looking man in a black suit with a really weird looking pen. The entire crew was doused with coffee and questioned for three days straight, then shipped off to Cincinnati. A team of specialists was called in to examine the ship thoroughly. After a two-day examination they determined that the ship was empty and the holds smelled like sewage. They were shipped off to Cincinnati.

As the crew was hustled to the airport for the trip to Ohio, Ames was singled out and placed aboard a G-IV Gulfstream and flown to Washington. The plane landed through gusting wind and blowing snow. The gusting wind would ease up once Congress let out, but the snow was another matter.

Upon arrival he was whisked to DORK's ultra-secret headquarters across from the Treasury Building, in back of Fatboy's Pizza, down two flights of stairs and behind the third urinal on the left.

As the man from DORK entered General Tenstars office, that unbemedaled luminary looked up from the report he had been reading on an outbreak of psoriasis in Kansas. Tossing the report down he stood up and walked from behind the desk.

"Well, Ames," he said holding his hands with the palms up.

"Deep hole in the ground with water at the bottom," replied Ames with a straight face.

Nonplussed the General scowled and continued. "So what the devil happened aboard that ship?"

"I have no idea," said the agent with a shake of his head. "One minute I was making this really terrific spinach soufflé, the next I woke up in the captain's bed with three broads. The captain was really upset. He ended up naked in bed with Cratchet."

"Didn't you use that stupid wig that R gave you, the one with the tin foil?"

"Yeah, I had it on, but it didn't do any good. There was this guy in a black suit who said that those only work for Gremetikins, whatever the heck those are."

"So you think it was maybe some kind of knockout gas or something?" asked the General as he sat down on the edge of the desk. The desk gave a loud creak, but held - barely.

Ames thought a minute. "Yeah, it could have been, but it would have to have been awful fast acting. Like I said, one minute I was cooking, the next I was in bed, although that seems a little odd to me. Out of all the crew I was the one in bed with the girls. Not that I'm complaining mind you, but I think we missed something there. Maybe I ought to go back to New Orleans and question them. I could get real close and work on them until they, er, talked. Yeah, the more I think about it, the more I think I should head back there!"

"Forget it," said the General, shaking his head. "Those girls have been questioned thoroughly by the FBI, the New Orleans police, and four guys from Mike's Pizza. I think the mayor talked to them too. Also the head of FEMA, ten Democrat Senators and that guy who defended Michael Jackson. No, we have to come up with a better clue. Have you ever heard of Maude Silverpinky?"

Ames thought for a moment. "Isn't she the head of some do-gooder outfit? Save the whales, burn a bra, hump a dog foundation or something? Supposedly as rich as Croesus."

"Close. She's a billionaire many times over. She was married to some shipping tycoon until he dumped her for the former wife of a dead president. She parlayed her alimony on the stock market with shares in Microsoft and UNO cards. The reports say she's the richest person, man or woman, on the planet. I gather she owns four or five small countries and half the Senate. Now she heads the Coalition to Lose Oil Dependency. Those CLOD's are responsible for trying to push through legislation to put through two-thousand percent surtaxes on oil and oil products. So far only the French have done so, but they are pressuring our Congress. In her statement before the Urban Grandmother's Environmental Society she told the URGE that we should be withholding oil from industrialized nations and giving it to third world countries. The URGE fell into the urge and threw rocks and SUVs at her. She left the gathering swearing revenge,"

"When did this happen," asked Blond. "I've been at sea the last week or so and didn't get much news. We only had the Internet, television, radio, iPods and TiVo. It was tough to get the news."

The General scratched his head and thought for a minute, then reached down and snagged a sheet of paper from his desk. He blew dust off it and scanned the page. "Oh, yeah, here it is. That was seven years ago."

"Seven years? What makes you think she'd do anything now? She probably forgot all about it."

"Well, she's apparently making good on her threat. She bought out the hairdressing salons at three thousand nursing homes and instructed the staff to do only beehive dos. She's got two million old ladies out there now with sore necks. We think that makes her a prime candidate for this plague of missing ships."

"Well you can't beat information like that," muttered Ames. "Where do I find this loony toon?"

"She's giving a gala bash tonight at the French embassy to commemorate the signing of the Kyoto Accords. At least she's supposed to if her guests can get the through this blizzard long enough to talk about global warming."

"Hey, no problem," said Ames. "I'll pick up some snow shoes from R."

"Better pick up a dogsled while you're at it. It's really blowing out there."

CHAPTER EIGHT

The soirée at the French embassy was supposed to have started at seven in the evening, but the weather presented a few problems and the majority of the guests did not start arriving until after nine. In typical French fashion the chefs pulled their hair, yelled and screamed about ruined truffles, flattened soufflés and burnt poulet en sauce de salete.

Most of the guests, having no idea what this stuff was supposed to actually taste like, thought the meal was wonderful, even as they scrapped blackened flour from the bottom of the dinner rolls. Only those of some discernment felt that the chicken in dirt sauce needed additional salt or maybe some ketchup.

Ames looked resplendent in a white tuxedo with black polka dots, a red paisley sash and a green and yellow striped bowtie. The fact that everyone else was wearing black - black suit, black dress, black tux or black jeans - did not bother anyone, although the French minister of culture did raise an eyebrow and wiggle his hips slightly.

Many of the guests had arrived in large Suburban Utility Vehicles, although there were one or two fanatics who showed up at the reins of dogsleds. One diehard insisted on parking his Sno-Cat himself, thereby preventing the valet from collecting a much needed tip. The owner later came out to find the treads on the Sno-cat had been slashed. The young valets, all of whom were carrying steak knives they said were used to remove ice, were questioned and later released as having no knowledge of the crime.

During the meal, and the presentation of a paper entitled, "The Effects of Hydrocarbon Emissions on Polar and Sub-Polar Greenhouse Gas Production as Initialized within Urban Environments Surrounded by Managed Industrialized Management Systems in Third World and Post Third-World Economic Models," Ames tuned out the emaciated Vegan giving the lecture and studied those at the tables around him.

Most of these high-powered, moneyed people seemed to be normal, average, every-day people with a penchant for gullibility. The charts and graphs that the Vegan was projecting onto the front wall, ignoring the film screen on the rear wall, had them all spellbound. Some were so spellbound that they hit themselves in the eyebrow with pommes frites or a dribble of potage d'oignon as they tried to convey interest while eating. Glassy eyed stares seemed to predominate. One hearty gentleman was scrambling rapidly through a "Harvard Edition of the New World English Dictionary" as the Vegan uttered each long and incomprehensible word of his dissertation.

In this clutter of bovine acceptance there were a number of people who were standing in a small group off to the side of the room, ignoring the Vegan and chatting in low tones. Careful to be circumspect the agent shifted in his chair and slipped off his jacket. Twisting the jacket inside out he examined a 16 x 20 color glossy taped inside the back of the coat and compared it to the chatterers.

The picture was of an old, aged woman, chubby to the point of obesity, getting out of a stretch limo while being assisted by two exceptionally handsome young men dressed in white beach towels, slippers and sunglasses.

The woman at the center of the chatterers bore a striking resemblance to the woman in the photo, including parallel lines of wrinkled flesh hanging from her jowls.

The two young men at her side, dressed in black beach towels, appeared to be the same two as in the picture, but it was hard to tell since they were not wearing sandals or sunglasses now. Each of them had on elegant shiny black shoes with Argyle socks held up with black garters attached to their towels. Silver tassels hung from their nipples. Ames thought the tassels were somewhat gauche.

Just as he was making up his mind as to the identity of the female chatterer, the woman on his right plucked the coat from his hand, twisting the fabric to examine the photograph. Startled, Ames looked at her and made a grab for the print. She held it just out of his reach.

"Well looky here," she said in a loud voice, with just a trace of a Southern accent. "You got yerself a picture of Silverpinky! What've you been doing, honey, stalking her?"

"No, maam, I have not," said Blond to the blue haired dowager with a trace of indignation "I am merely an admirer. Could you give me back the photo please?"

She glanced at the image and then held it down by the side of her chair, out of reach. "Well, honey, you can stalk me anytime." She gave his thigh a squeeze causing him to jerk backward in the chair. His hand pulled on the tablecloth and flipped a tray of bouf ebreche into the air.

The beuf hit the dowager squarely in the face causing her to fling her arms up, slapping the gentleman on her left. That personage stabbed himself in the cheek with a fork and kicked the table sending a gravy boat sailing down the length of the board slopping white sauce on anyone within range.

At that moment someone yelled, "Food fight," and began flinging asparagus tips around the room. Within minutes the air was filled with plates, spoons, various foods and a couple of waiters. Someone threw a platter of roast beef at the Vegan and hit him square in the chest. The Vegan staggered back and swiped at the mess on his shirt. With a wail he dashed from the room screaming about dead animals. Flung copies of his voluminous dissertation and three steak knives followed him from the room.

The group of chatterers, led by Silverpinky, sidled over to the wall and watched the spectacle. There was a sudden scramble as the group dodged a short stack of buttered pancakes and a tray of bacon rolls. Money traded hands as various bets were made on the outcome of the fight.

Ames carefully lifted himself from the floor and crept toward the wall on hands and knees. He reached the barricade with only minor splatters and stood up. Glancing to the left, he moved over to stand with the chatterers. One of them looked over at him and then returned his attention to the flying food, ignoring the agent.

The agent carefully crept along the wall until he was beside the dowager. Stepping forward slightly he faced Silverpinky and said, "This is better than a Broadway show, and a little more tasty, don't you think?"

The aged dame twisted her head to peer at the government snoop, her jowls quivering. She gave Blond a withering smile. "And who might you be?"

Ames moved closer to her and put out his hand. One of the towel draped Adonis' stepped in the way to prevent the touch. The agent countered by reaching out and whipping the towel away. The startled kid looked down and then ran from the room, pink cheeks flashing, both on his face and his posterior. The French Minister of Culture smiled in admiration, then hustled out of the room behind the youth.

The other Adonis scooted behind Silverpinky, peering fearfully over her shoulder. His hands gripped his towel tightly.

"I'm Blond, Ames Blond," said the agent, again extending his hand.

Ignoring the hand, Maude asked with some surprise, "What does a British intelligence agent want with an American environmentalist movement? Don't you have enough troubles with the labor movement, the falling pound and an overflow of foreigners?"

Ames dropped his hand and said, "No, you're thinking of the other guy. I'm American. I'm just a believer in the environment, the same as the rest of these good people here."

The rest of the good people were becoming slick and slimy with food waste. The French ambassador was running in circles dripping brown gravy, trying to stop the conflagration. He stepped into the remains of a carrot quiche and slid to the floor, bumping his head on a table. Three men in black jeans immediately stooped over him and extracted his wallet, Rolex watch, change purse and his underwear.

Silverpinky eyed Ames warily. "So, as an environmentalist you must be highly concerned about the carbon dioxide emissions from industry, automobiles and lawn mowers that are causing problems with global heating, stagnant water temperatures and a rather strange hockey stick graph that is pretty much indecipherable?"

"No, actually, I'm not," stated Ames. "I'm much more concerned with the carbon dioxide problem caused by people in general."

Ah," smiled Maude. "You have concerns with all human endeavors then?'

"No actually, it's the breathing that concerns me. Do you realize that there are seven billion people on this planet all sucking in oxygen and spewing out carbon dioxide? My God, the total output of human breath must exceed all the greenhouse gases put out by industry and cow farts combined. Why if you add in human farts and belches, I predict that we don't have much more than four or five minutes left for life on the planet."

Silverpinky frowned. "Are you trying to make a fool of me?"

"Why, no ma'am," Ames answered earnestly. "I think you and the entire environmentalist cause can do that fine on your own. No, I'm just real concerned about being able to breathe without inhaling tiny microscopic particles of cow and human crap. You do know that farts are the deadliest plague to ever hit mankind?"

Maude stared at Ames and blinked. At that moment a miniscule "brrrrip" sounded from one of the gentlemen accompanying the hag and an odd aroma mixed with the scent of Swedish dough balls. He immediately pointed his finger at the lady beside him and an argument ensued. Within minutes the two were on the floor kicking and straining at each other while slopping in brown gravy. A waiter discretely threw a tablecloth over them.

Ames smiled and pointed at the heaving fabric. "There you see the kinds of problems digestive gases produce? By the time they sort this out there will be at least one more person farting his or her way through life."

The woman looked Ames up and down, her frown increasing. "You seem to be very ill informed Mister Brunette. I . . ."

Ames interrupted her, "That's Blond, like the hair color."

"Say what," she blurted slightly confused.

"The name. It's Blond, like the hair color."

"But your hair is dark. That's a hair color."

"Good observation. Yes, my hair is dark. No, my name is Blond. The two are selectively variable. But, then I notice your pinky isn't silver. It's more of a drab grayish death tone color tinge, whatever. How about I call you Grayfinger or Deathcolorlittlefingerwoman?"

She harrumphed and started to turn away.

"Say, Grayfinger," Ames said to her back. "How're your oil interests? I here you made a killing during the seventy two embargo and amassed quite a fortune when Iraq grabbed Kuwait?"

She turned back toward him. "I don't own any oil interests. Oil will be the downfall of man," she said with conviction.

"Certainly it will, every time you slip in it," said Ames with a grin. "I understand you've been accumulating a considerable stock of oil shares."

She looked him up and down again, then forced her way out of the room without replying while trailed by sycophants and chatterers. The tablecloth humped its way across the floor and disappeared around the corner.

Ames was grinning at them as a pecan pie slapped into the side of his head.

CHAPTER NINE

It was late when Ames knocked on N's office door after coming straight back to DORK from the soiree at the embassy. He had to bang on the thing four or five times before he heard a muffled grunt from somewhere inside. Taking that as permission to enter, he pushed open the door and walked into the semi-lit room. A brass lamp with a tiffany shade sat on the long ornate desk provided the only illumination, throwing the room into shadows and creating odd colorful patterns on the ceiling.

At the desk a large lump perched next to the lamp, casting a weird humped shaped shadow on the wall. As Ames peered at it the hump twitched and made odd blowing and groaning noises. Papers on the desk fluttered from the breeze from the blowing. The shadow on the wall moved back and forth looking like a whale in heat.

Assuming the lump was his patron Ames took a step into the room and softly called, "General? General Tenstars?" The only response was an increase in the grunts from the hump.

"General Tenstars," the agent called a little louder. The puffing ceased for a moment leaving the room in deathly quiet. Ames took another step forward. There was a sudden loud grunt and the blowing and wheezing restarted.

"General?" asked the agent. The hump twitched. "Well phooey," muttered the spy.

"General!" yelled Blond.

The hump jerked upward knocking the lamp onto the floor creating strange shadows on the ceiling and moving the colorful patterns to the sidewall. Ames saw an arm sweep upward and then a flash of light followed by a loud bang. A bullet whizzed past his head and thumped into the door sending splinters into the air. The agent dropped to the floor with wood shrapnel in his cheek as the gun fired four more times.

"Son of a female dog in heat!" yelled Blond crabbing backward toward the door. "Sir, it's Ames! Stop firing. Blast it you're going to put holes in me!" He slapped his hand upward at the light switch. A bullet spanged into the wall inches from his fingers.

The agent jerked his hand down. He was counting his fingers as the gun silenced and the overhead lights flickered on. The General sat at the desk holding a 9mm in one hand and rubbing his face with the other. He dropped the hand from his face and peered blearily at Blond.

At that moment the door banged open again and someone yelled, "Freeze!" Ames twisted his head to see two security cops in pink and blue coveralls standing in the doorway. The cops wore silver kepis with gold trim and had large bronze badges affixed to their coveralls. The writing on the badges identified them as the Police of Overt Forces. The POOF's each had a broad black belt around his waist that supported numerous pouches. A black earphone, with a silver antenna, protruded from each of their ears. Brown cowboy boots with tan stitching completed the ensemble.

One of the comic cops held a silver 9mm pistol with an extended magazine. The other had a LAWS rocket on his shoulder, one eye peering through the plastic sight glass. The other eye looked upward at a weird angle.

Ames rolled onto his back and put his hands up or along the floor or, well, heck, they were upward above his head, but not in the air. More along the same plane as his body, I think, but pointing toward the back wall. Are you understanding any of this? If you do, explain it to me.

There was a growl from the General and both cops lowered their weapons. "Sorry sir," said the one with the pistol. "We didn't realize you were sleeping in here again. We really wish you would notify us when you do this so we can have a team standing by to fix the holes in the walls."

The General muttered an apology and slid the gun into a desk drawer. The two security officers pulled the door closed as they left, both shaking their heads and whispering. One of them was spinning his finger near his forehead. Ames assumed that was some kind of cop sign language.

The General looked around with bleary eyes. "Ames is that you?"

"Yes, sir," said the agent, getting up off the floor and brushing the carpet lint off his trousers. A couple of pecans dropped from his hair and a truffle slid off his shoe.

"What the heck are you doing here?" N asked while rubbing his eyes and glancing at the pink watch on his wrist. "It's after two in the morning!"

Blond walked over to the desk and stood in front of it. "I just got back from that environmental conference at the French embassy and I figured you would want a report right away. I got to watch a really good food fight and made contact with Silverpinky."

The General stood up and walked over to a coffee machine. He filled a cup with some cold, stale looking brown stuff, then turned and lifted the carafe, offering

Ames some. Blond blanched and shook his head, sprinkling more pecans on the carpet. The General took a sip and grimaced through brown stained lips. "So what did Silverpinky have to say and did you bring me a doggy bag?"

"Sorry, sir, no doggy bag, but I think I might have a truffle or two here." The agent picked at a smear on his jacket and pulled a half chewed bagel from his pocket. He rubbed the bagel in the smear and offered it to the General. The officer dipped the bagel into the rancid coffee and took a bite.

Tenstars sat back down at the desk and took another sip of the brown stuff. A glob of something dripped off his chin and landed on his uniform jacket adding itself to a spot of ketchup, two mustard stains and a glob of what looked like grape jelly. The colorful stains seemed to add additional awards to the General's unbemedaled chest.

"No problem. Tell me about Silverpinky," muttered N taking another bite of the bagel.

Ames pulled a chair from the wall and sat down. The General scowled. Ames stood up and put the chair back. "Well, she's an older broad with dark red hair, but that was probably dyed since I could see strands of white where the dye didn't take. Or she could be dark haired broad with streaks of white added for contrast. I saw that once in Cosmopolitan magazine. Not that I was reading the magazine. I mean that ain't macho. I happened to see it at the doctor's office. It was sort of setting there on the table with the pages open and there was this picture of this broad with a white streak in her hair. You know what I mean?"

The General growled, "Get on with it and forget the stupid magazine."

"Yes sir, no problem sir. As I was saying, she had on this really nifty gold lame dress with blue ruffles, probably designed by Dominique or, at least in his style. It could have been one of his students. There was a matching lame clutch with silver clasps and a bronze tiara studded with pink diamonds that sat in her hair. It looked like an Alexander, but might have been Kolkachev. He does nice work. She was . . . ."

"I don't give a rat fart what she was wearing," yelled the General. "Did she say anything about oil?"

"Oh, well she asked for vinegar and oil for her salad and she mentioned that she does not have any oil interests, except for what she puts into her SUV and her Lear jet. She also mentioned using oil to heat her six homes, three summer cabins and the Mediterranean villa not to mention the New York townhouse and the Fishing cottage in San Francisco. That's the small one with twelve rooms."

"She seemed to be really into this environmental stuff. I mean she really wants people to stop using oil and oil products. She said she thinks everyone ought to be using ethanol even though there is that minor problem with formaldehyde poisoning and that thing about using up all the land to grow the corn needed to produce the alcohol to mix with the gasoline. She wasn't too concerned about the lost taxes or the cost of the government subsidizing ethanol. I guess once people really start using the stuff the subsidy will go away and the price will drop below six dollars a gallon. She didn't think starving people for fuel would be a real problem. She mentioned something about letting people eat cake which I thought was rather nice of her."

The General frowned and began digging through the pile of papers on the desk. "Wait a minute. I think I saw something here." He pulled out a dog-eared sheet and examined it. "Nope, wrong one. That's from Studio Adult

Rentals." He tossed the paper back down and kept digging.

Ames reached over and surreptitiously snagged the Adult Rental paper and looked at it while the General pushed papers onto the floor.

There were some catchy titles. "Blond Vixens in Love," "Three Loves in Two Rooms" and "Horror of the Monster Breast." Ames thought that one might be pretty good. He really liked those old horror movies.

"Aha," the General exclaimed, looking up from the mess on the floor. He stood up clutching a file covered with Post-It notes.

"I knew I saw something," he said scanning the notes. "It says here that Silverpinky owns two shares of stock in Rawhide Motels who, in turn, own the Anything Money Holding Company. Anything has interests in the Plaque Toothpaste Company who own a piece of New Jersey Waste Disposal and Landfills. NJWD and L own some of Doggy Diapers Inc. They have a small part of Phil's Suburban Lawncare and Phil happens to own a share of Exxon that he got as a Christmas present when he was six years old. I knew something was wrong here. Silverpinky does have oil interests!"

The General waved the file as an exclamation point, sending papers and Post-Its in an arc across the room. They fluttered to the floor like blue, yellow and pink confetti, sticking to chairs, desk, Ames and the floor.

Ames pulled a blue Post-It from his forehead and said. "That pretty much proves that she's involved in this right up to the tip of her pink tiara. I knew there was something funny when she had those two guys in towels escorting her. Neither of them was wearing bow ties and their garters were on the wrong legs."

The General flopped back down into his chair. "Now we're getting somewhere! You're going to need to go back over there again.

Ames blanched. "You want me to go back over to the French Embassy? That place is still a mess from the food fight and I don't think they've had time to clean up yet. Plus I don't think Silverpinky is still there. She hot-footed it out of there pretty fast when I started asking about oil. And I think the Minister of Culture still wants that date with me. I blew him off the first time by telling him I had to wash my hair, but I don't think that will work again."

"I didn't mean the embassy," said the General. "Although you might go back and see if you could get that doggy bag. I meant you should go back to the Middle East and try again to track a ship. Since you've been gone seven tankers have reappeared and four more have gone missing. That's a total of thirty-two ships that are accounted for or unaccounted for and they represent a huge volume of crude oil carrying capacity. Not to mention the odd smell of the ships.

"The Navy has tried just about everything to locate the missing ships; homing devices, satellites, dolphins. They even tried trailing one with a submarine by staying underwater just behind her rudder. They lost her during one moonless night. Never heard a word and didn't see anything. The sun went down, the ship was there. The sun came up. The ship was gone. The only clue that the ship was ever there was a yellow rubber ducky floating in the ocean.

"I want you to go down to Dirty Tricks and have R set you up to go on another ship. This time I want full protection for you so you'll remember everything that happens. Make sure he includes some type of taping and tracking device so we can keep track of where you're at."

"Ah, sir," Ames said quietly while looking at his Star Wars watch. "Could this wait until morning? It's after two in the morning. I don't think anyone will be down there and it's been a long day. I could sure use some sleep."

"Nonsense," said the General with a wave of his hand. "That screwball R never sleeps. I think he invented something that props his eyelids open. Whatever. Get down there and get started. And turn out the light when you leave"

Ames walked to the door, snapped off the light and glanced back before going out the door and pulling it shut behind him. The General had pulled the gun back out of the drawer and was lowering his head back onto the desk.

CHAPTER TEN

Ames carefully approached the door to ASSHOLS and gingerly reached out to turn the doorknob. The infamous head of research was attempting to develop the perfectly secure door and had been experimenting using the door to his lab, and the people who came in the door, as lab rats. More than once Ames had stumbled into the testing ground, with disastrous results, usually in the form of twirling stars and birdies.

With quick movements the agent twisted the knob, jerked the door and rapidly stepped back toward the opposite wall. Nothing happened. The door remained solidly closed.

After waiting a couple of minutes to be sure there would be no delayed response from the door - a distinct possibility - he reached out and tried again. He attempted to twist the knob, but it did not move. He pulled on the door, but it remained firmly shut. With a sigh he turned around and glanced up and down the hallway. The only sounds were the ghostly creaks and groans that inhabit old buildings. It did not look like anyone was home. He started to turn to head back upstairs.

With a crash the door flipped upward smacking Ames in the butt and driving him head first into the opposite wall. His head hit with a solid "thunk," causing a small shower of plaster. The agent rebounded and landed on his face on the floor. Birdies and stars appeared over his head. With a vague motion of his hand he swiped at them to make them go away. They just got bigger.

Behind him the door dropped back down and closed with a click. The hallway returned to its previous innocent appearance. Ames stared blearily at the double doors in front of him and wondered how come there were two knobs on each door. As he stared, the doors resolved back into one door with a single knob.

Groaning Ames rolled over and pulled himself up to a sitting position against the wall. He put his hand up and felt the beginnings of a large noodle in the middle of his forehead. He checked his hand and was gratified to see that there was no blood. He would have a fair lump but no scar so he wouldn't look like an older Harry Potter.

As he started to stand up the door opened normally and the white shocked head of R peered out. "I thought I heard something," he stated in a high nasal voice. "Don't you ever go to bed? I see you have been checking out my latest anti-intrusion device. I think this one is the best by far." He gave a quick high-pitched cackle. "Yep, no one is going to figure out that you have to pull down on the doorknob to get in. Yep, this sucker is going to make me rich! Yes siree Bob, I'll be able to get off this miserable government salary and live properly with real food and a real home with a real bed instead of the crappy cot at Mom's house. I might even be able to finally meet girls." He disappeared back inside.

Ames staggered across the hall and reached for the doorknob. He almost turned it again, but stopped himself at the last second. With a grimace he followed a hunch and pushed down on the knob. There was a click and door popped open. Carefully he stepped through and into the lab.

The beautiful expanse of bright green "poo" grass was gone. In its place was a round disk of shining blue plastic around twenty feet in diameter and about a foot thick. It sat on a number of plastic tripods spaced evenly around the perimeter. Along the outer edge were hundreds of metal clips, spaced equidistance apart, attached to wires that led to a huge electrical consol. Red, blue, green and yellow lights played across the face of the consol. The arrows on dials wiggled back and forth and a heavy hum filled the room. Ames watched the disk for a few minutes to see what kind of maleficent activity it would get into, particularly that activity that would damage one secret agent named Ames Blond. After five minutes of watching the disk did absolutely nothing.

Shaking his head the agent walked around the disk and headed for the other room. As he passed the disk his clothes started to feel odd and he noticed that his shirt was sticking to his skin. He passed a screwdriver on a table and it rotated toward him as he passed. He kept a careful eye on the bluntly sharp instrument until he was through the doorway into the other room.

R was at a table with his back to Ames, the movement of his arms indicating that he was working on something out of sight. Blond walked up behind the scientist and extended his hand to tap R on the shoulder. As his hand came close to the elderly potential genius, a bright blue spark jumped from Ames to R striking the older man in the left ear and producing a dark smoke ring. The old man gave a loud yelp and jumped a foot into the air, his white shock of hair standing straight up.

The small white radio that he had been working on flipped into the air while making a sizzling sound. Blue sparks flared around it and a voice similar to Elmer Fudd issued from the speaker. Elmer ran up and down the scale before fizzling out. The radio began giving off white smoke as it reached apogee and started a rapid descent toward the floor. It hit with a loud crack and broke apart sending smoking parts skittering across the floor. Elmer instantly shut up.

R landed back on the floor next to the radio, staggered for a moment and then turned on Ames with a ferocious snarl. "What the devil is wrong with you, you twit! Didn't you read the sign in the other room you illiterate moron?"

Ames held up his hands. "Whoa there fuzzy, what sign?"

"The sign next to the contra-gravity plate," R growled some more. "You're not supposed to go near it or you'll pick up a heavy dose of static electricity."

"There was no sign," said Ames shaking his head.

"Sure there was! You just missed it – as usual." R pushed passed the agent and disappear into the other room. He was back a moment later wearing a sheepish expression, six paperclips, twelve thumbtacks and the screwdriver. His hair was standing even straighter, if that were possible.

"Sorry," he said. "The sign fell over when the disk sucked the staples out of the support easel."

Ames backpedaled away from the old man as he reached for the table. There was a loud snap and a spark ran from R's hand to the table. The air smelled like ozone and R's hair dropped back onto his skull. The screwdriver and paperclips fell to the floor. The thumbtacks rattled against the table like miniature machine gun fire.

As R let out a sigh, Ames asked, "What was that all about?"

R brushed at his hair with his hand as he explained, "I'm working on a contra-gravity device, you know, to defy gravity. Sort of like anti-gravity without the not. An electrical charge is caused to spin across the surface of the plate creating a massive static charge that does not have a fixed north south axis. Since there is no fixed axis the magnetic field of the earth cannot act on it and the disk rises into the air."

"Hey, that sounds like a great idea!" exclaimed Ames. "How's it going?"

"It's not! The darn thing just sits there magnetizing everything that comes near it. I'm pushing two mega-volts through that sucker and it doesn't do anything."

"Oh, I don't know," said Ames, brushing at his shirt. "It might be a good way to iron clothes, except your electric bill would probably be through the roof."

R waved his hand and leaned against the table. "What do you want? Why'd you come down here and bust up my radio? I just got that thing. It's supposed to have the truest sound in the world without a huge speaker system. Now I'll never know!"

Ames toed a piece of broken plastic. "Ah, sorry about that. N sent me down to see what you have that can help me out. He's sending me back out on a ship again."

"Didn't the wig work?" asked R, his foot crunching a circuit board as he walked around the table.

"Not really. I got knocked out just like everybody else. But on the plus side, for a while there I was getting some really good radio stations. The sound and clarity were awesome. It sounded just like a big band was right next to me. Truest sound I ever heard."

"So where's the wig at? I need that thing back for my inventory."

"Well, it kind of went missing what with all the hullabaloo when we were found again. I think some guy in New Orleans is using it as a pet. He takes this wire and hooks it to the wig. Then he holds the wire down by the ground and it looks like the wig is on a leash. Kind of neat looking."

"Oh, so you've misplaced more government equipment! I'll make a note of that so I can dock your pay. And where's the car? Did you misplace that thing again?"

Ames looked at the floor. "No, Hassim has it. He's the one that signed for it."

"No he didn't. I have your signature on the receipt."

"I didn't sign those," cried Ames defiantly. "Hassim forged my signature!"

"Bah, they all say that. Your pay gets docked until either the car shows up or you prove it's not your signature."

Ames let out an exasperated sigh. "Okay, I'll get a hold of Hassim and find out where the car is. In the mean time what do you have to keep me from losing my memory?"

R went over to a closet and began pulling items out and stacking them on the table. It took him close to five minutes to get all the junk out. Boxes, containers, bins, bags, and jars all littered the table. Ames looked at the pile and could identify nothing.

Finally R set the last box on the table and turned to Ames. "Okay, I couldn't be sure what the bad guys were using to take away your memory, so I came up with a bunch of different options."

Ames looked aghast. "I can't take all that stuff with me! I'd need six suitcases! And I'd never remember what does what."

R glanced at the pile and back to Ames. "You don't get this stuff, you twit. That's stuff that has to go out to the auction in the morning. Come on, your stuff is over here." He led Ames to another table.

Ames glanced back at the mess on the table. "Just out of curiosity, what auction are you talking about?"

R looked at the table and sighed. "Federal law requires that all excess equipment be sold at auction and the money used to reimburse the federal treasury for part of the original cost. Unfortunately those twits in the GSA have decided that means everything from used string to unused tomatoes, broken shoestrings, wilted cabbage leaves and any other kind of trash. Oddly, everything seems to be selling. I got twenty five hundred the other day for two used pencils. The guy that bought them sold them on eBay as having once belonged to Leonardo Da Vinci. I guess he got a pretty good price. Here's your stuff here."

R picked up a small plastic box and opened the cover. He took out two small flesh covered pills. "These are anti-gas filters. You stuff them up your nose and breathe through them. The filters are good for sixty days, but you have to clean them daily to get the boogers and crud off them, here, let me show you." R took one of the pills and stuck it up his nose and sniffed inward. Then he pulled it back out and stuck it back in the box. "See, real simple." Ames gagged.

Snapping the box shut he set it down and picked up a thing that looked like an iPod. "This is an anti-noise device. You hook it to your belt and put the earplugs in. Once you turn it on you won't hear anything that goes on around you and nothing will distract you."

"Did you modify the iPod to do that?" asked Ames as he picked up the device to look at it.

"Nah. It's a standard iPod off the shelf. Teenagers use them to ignore their parents. I figure it will work just as good for ignoring bad guys."

Ames nodded as he put the iPod back on the table and picked up a pair of glasses. He turned them in his hands and then slid them onto his face. The world promptly became very blurry. "What are these for, to protect the eyes from invisible rays or something?"

R snatched the glasses from Ames' face. "Not hardly, dippy! Those are my reading glasses. I wondered where I put them down."

"So what else do I get?" asked Ames hopefully glancing around the room at the nifty gadgets hanging from the walls and filling cabinets.

"You still have your seamen's papers?" Ames nodded. "Then you're all set to go. Here sign for those things."

Ames picked up the pen and bent over the receipts. As carefully as he could he signed Hassim's name.

CHAPTER ELEVEN

This time, as Ames' plane descended toward Iraq to join a ship, he considered himself lucky. He had caught an Air France flight out of Orly in Paris, direct to Basra. He would not have to fool around with commuter flights on Iraqi Air or whatever they were calling themselves this week.

The flight from France had been pleasant enough, except that they had made an unexpected change to the in-flight meal. Instead of frog legs they had had toad feet, which were in no way as tasty as the decimated amphibian stubs he had been expecting. As he munched on the minuscule muscles he had visions of toads hopping around on really small crutches and pushing tiny wheelchairs.

After leaving the customs and immigration area in Basra, where he had been stripped naked and thoroughly searched for explosives, weapons and any loose change in his pockets or carryall, the agent had entered the airport concourse where he expected to be met by Hassim. Instead a small Arab wearing a blue business suit and slate colored turban was standing in the center of the concourse holding a bright yellow sign that said "Mr. Blond" in blue letters. The thing had small red light bulbs around the edges that flashed on and off and a big black arrow that pointed downward. As if that were not sufficient he was also yelling the name, in really bad English, at the top of his lungs.

The passengers from a number of airlines had stopped to watch the diminutive demons antics. He was alternately moving the sign up and down and swinging it back and forth. There must have been some kind of remote control for the lights. Sometimes the red lights would rotate on and off around the sign, other times they world flash on and off in weird sequences. But that could have been a short in the wiring as a small cloud of smoke hung in the air and there was the heavy scent of ozone.

Ames moved quickly through the staring crowd, grabbed the small person, putting his hand over the guy's mouth. "Shut the hell up, will you! This is supposed to be a covert operation!"

The little man dropped the sign, creating a flurry of "pops" as light bulbs broke and pulled Ames' hand away. As the sign burst into flames he continued the movement by rotating his body and flipping Ames through the air over his back. The agent let out a croak and slammed into a fat lady in a chador, knocking her over, before landing on the floor. The lady staggered back into two more people and the crowded concourse began to look like a domino set, people staggering and dropping right and left. A few even went left and right. Packages and suitcase flipped into the air.

A goat went sailing through the air as its tether was caught by a ceiling fan, the animal suddenly became airborne, rotated six or seven times and then went sailing off into oblivion somewhere past the Air France counter. Four chickens followed it apparently believing the goat was making a break for freedom.

Eventually all movement ceased and the groans of the wounded could be heard throughout the terminal. The airport looked like a battlefield with no survivors, except for a few wayward chickens who had escaped the massacre flapping loose from personal baggage.

Ames pushed two people off him and struggled to his feet. He almost grabbed the little man, but stopped just in time. Around them other people were picking themselves off the floor, regaining luggage or chasing chickens. The goat staggered back into view with three of the chickens on his back.

Ames frowned at the small Arab. "What are you nuts? This was supposed to be a covert mission, you dip. Now I think everybody in the Middle East knows I'm here including Saddam and all six of his wives."

"Chew mus'be Mis'er Blond," said the little guy with a huge grin, ignoring Ames' anger. "I here to meet chew and take chew to da chip."

"Who the heck are you?" asked Ames with a growl. "And why are you trying to wreck my life? And what the devil is a chip?"

"Ah, I am Ahmad Jabar," said the short one with a bow. "I sent by chore fren Hassim to get chew." He tugged on the agents arm and they started walking toward the door.

Ames frowned. "I'd say you got me pretty well. I suspect I'm lucky you didn't get me arrested for starting a riot. Where is Hassim and why isn't he here?"

"Hassim do spetial CIA work to in Mosul. He also do sale on camel chit and not able to away get. He appoint me honorary CIA man and sent me here." The little guy reached into his suit and pulled out a wallet. He flipped it open to disclose a hand drawn card that said CIA, had a circle with a chicken and a four-pointed beam of light in it, and listed his name in English and Arabic. It also had a coupon for a free McGoat burger attached to one corner. He flipped it closed again and stuffed it away.

"Hassim say I get official card when I have nuff points."

They walked out the door and headed for the parking lot. A police cruiser with flashing red lights passed them headed for the terminal. It was followed by three armored cars, two Abrams tanks and a battalion of troops from the 101st Air Assault force. The cruiser skidded to a stop and a khaki clad cop jumped out and began to string yellow tape all over the place. The tape stated, "Terrorist Crime Scene – No Entry Permitted." Followed by a bunch of squiggles that might have meant something to an Arab – or could have been an advertisement to Honest Horem's Used Cars.   The assault troops began handcuffing passengers, chickens and goats and hustling them into closed vans.

"So how do you get points?" asked Blond, flipping out his sunglasses and putting them on to block the bright afternoon sunlight. He looked back briefly at all the activity in front of the terminal.

"It not hard corden to Hassim. I get one point for simple mission like dis one. I get five points for stealing state secrets and ten points for offing 'nother spy." He frowned. "Hassim not clear on whose spies I to off, ours or theirs." The little guy looked up at Ames and spotted the sunglasses. With a huge grin he wiped out his own glasses and put them on. They were neon pink with bright red lenses. A small goofy looking yellow bird's head decorated each upper corner of the lenses. Ames glanced down and then did a double take at the way the glasses brightened up the little person's features. They made him look like a slightly demented seven year old.

"Well I'm sure you'll figure it out," said Ames brightly. "Where are you parked?"

Ahmad pointed across the street. Ames could see a number of cars parked in the lot, as well as two or three camels. There was also a bus parked at the curb to take people into town. The bus had a line in front of it, but no one was boarding. The driver was guarding the doorway with a Nerf bat that he used to swat anyone attempting to get on the bus, although he did take fares and pocket them. A sign proclaimed something or other in Arabic.

"Which car is it?" the agent asked as they started across the road.

"Oh, it is not a car," said Ahmad. "I do not have a driver's license."

Ames felt a sinking sensation as Ahmed guided them away from the bus and taxis. "Oh, no," he muttered. "Not camels again!"

Ahmed grasped a camel's halter and clucked at it until the beast knelt down into the dirt. The beast looked at the two men while chewing on some undefined substance in its mouth. Ahmed went to the side and scootched himself up into the saddle. Sitting there he bore a great resemblance to a lawn gnome on an anthill. With great reluctance Ames followed suit, straddling the animals hump behind Ahmed.

The Arab pulled out a stick and lightly tapped the beast on the shoulder. With a heave the camel extended its back legs to stand up, throwing the unprepared Blond forward. The agent flipped over the hump, his head going down and tossing his legs into the air. He bumped into Ahmed with his crotch around the small man's head and both men fell onto the ground as the camel jerked its front section upward. The animal looked around at the two people in the dirt and calmly spit at them.

Ahmed looked up from where his nose was attached to Ames' zipper, pulled himself loose and stood up to give Ames a really dirty look, while brushing dust from his suit and rubbing his rather large nose. "What, chew stupid or just totally uncordated? Chew never ride camel before?"

Ames stood and brushed at the dirt on his trousers. "I'm an American! We ride Chevies, Fords and Subarus. We don't normally go riding around on hump backed fertilizer machines. There are no bucket seats and its tough trying to make out. There's no back seat. Is there any chance of getting a cab or maybe taking the bus?" He looked back wistfully at the driver with the Nerf bat.

"Da buses not run 'cause suspect suicide bombers maybe hiding 'splosives in da lunch bags and da cabs be spected for possible bombs in dere headlights. I tink it plan by da unions to 'crease wages and benefits. Take da buses and cabs off da street for few days and people be okay to pay anyting to get a ride."

"So we go by camel?" asked a disheartened Blond looking at the cud chewing beast.

"We go by camel," stated Ahmed firmly as he jerked on the camel's tether. Once more the beast lowered itself to the ground. With a swift motion Ahmed leaped into the saddle and held out his hand to help the agent aboard.

With some misgivings Ames took the small Arabs hand and slid his leg up and over until he was seated on the backside of the hump again. He grabbed tightly onto Ahmed's robe with one hand and to the saddle with the other. At a click from Ahmed the camel heaved itself upward rocking Ames back and forth.

Just as he was congratulating himself on keeping his seat, the agent felt himself sliding backward. He grabbed Ahmed's robe with both hands as his butt slid off the camel's backside until he was dangling with his chest straddling the camel's butt. He could feel the ropelike tail twitching against his chest.

Ahmed made gurgling noises as the robe tightened around his throat. The Arab let go of the tether to pull the robe loose and he flipped through the air as Blonds weight pulled him backward. Ames let go and landed on his bottom next to the rear legs. Ahmed did a beautiful full gainer before landing with a thump on his face in the dirt.

At that moment the agent looked up with horror as the camel raised its tail. He scrambled rapidly to the side and just missed being deluged with camel urine, although a few drops managed to hit his leg and jacket. The rather smelly puddle soaked into the dust until only a damp brown stain remained. Ames scuttled further from the camel's rear.

Ahmed climbed to his feet muttering unholy words in Arabic. He slapped Ames in the head as he stalked back to grab the camel's tether again. The camel gave a loud groan in protest as the Arab yanked hard downward on the line. The camel retaliated by jerking its head upward causing the small person to flip back into the air, over the hump and back face first into the dust, again. The large man's nose was becoming decidedly red and even more prominent.

Ahmed stood up again and staggered back toward the animal's front. He took a half-hearted swipe at Ames, missed and fell to one knee. He knelt there for a moment shaking his head and rubbing his nose. Finally he once more stood up and walked to the front of the camel. Taking a firm hold of the tether the animal was once more pulled down to his knees. Pulling a rope from his robe the little Arab grabbed Ames by the ear and shoved him toward the animal.

"Chew get into da front saddle dis time," he said angrily. "Chew are too damn clumsy to have behind me."

Carefully Ames slid into the front saddle. Rapidly Ahmed tied the rope around the agent's waist and connected it to the saddle. He then climbed up onto the hump and grabbed the reins from Blond. With a click the animal jerked forward and back, rising to its feet.

Ames bobbled back and forth, hitting his head on the camel's neck, but managed to stay in place. Ahmed grunted and the animal began plodding forward. Within minutes Ames felt his lunch rising into his throat. The camel's shuffle forced the men to sway back and forth, back and forth with each step. It was worse than being in a dinghy on a rough sea. With a cry of "Ralph," the agent lost his lunch over the side, spattering the camel with amphibian remains.

The camel looked back and gave Ames a dirty look. Ames felt that he had gotten even for the urine. Ahmed laughed heartily. The camel spit again.

CHAPTER TWELVE

The *Exxon Valdez* II was working its way northeast following the African coast just south of the horn. The *Valdez* was following the same route that it had taken when she had been hijacked the first time. Captain Blie was not pleased with the concept and only the payment of a hefty bonus had swayed him to follow Ames' suggestion. But he was happy that DORK had been able to get his crew released from Cincinnati even though they acted very strangely for the first few days.

The crewmen tended to twitch a lot and their eyes tried to go in two or three directions at once. Some had a tendency to walk sideways. All except Cratchet who looked as normal as anyone could, which was really scary since Cratchet had never been normal.

The plan called for the Captain to take the ship to Galveston and return to the Gulf by following the same path that it had before, southward along the African coast inside Madagascar to the cape and then northward to Texas. The return trip would be the opposite with the ship running south from Texas to the cape and then north past Madagascar to the horn and then eastward to the gulf. Somewhere along that route, hopefully, the ship would again be seized by whoever was taking the ships. Since no one had actually been injured in any of the hijackings it was hoped that this condition would continue.

Unfortunately, no one was real sure that the ship would be taken. While ships were continuing to be hijacked, the hijack locations were everywhere from the east coast of Africa to Sumatra to Australia to Japan. In a very brazen attack, one ship had been taken just three miles off Gulfport, Mississippi.

Ames stood on the port bridge wing watching the stars in the clear African sky hoping that an attack came so he could clear up this mystery.

He was deep in thought when he felt a shadow move up to his side and he flinched away, throwing his arm up to protect his head. He looked over from under his arm to see the dim figure of Cratchet leaning forward against the railing, his ponytail fluttering in the breeze. "Kind of nice out here at night, but you seem a bit edgy," Cratchet said.

"Yeah, it is," said Ames putting his arm down and gripping the rail as he glanced out at the ocean where the stars reflected off the waves and twinkling lights in the sky seemed like a velvet carpet lit up for Christmas. "It sure can be beautiful out . . . ." He stopped when he noticed that Cratchet was slumped on the deck by the rail.

"What the heck," he muttered, bending down to check the seaman.

Cratchet was letting out soft snores and twitching slightly in a deep sleep. Ames grabbed him under the arms and pulled him away from the edge and against the forecastle wall. He looked rapidly around to see if anything could have caused the little man to fall asleep that quickly. The agent bent down and sniffed the seaman's face but did not smell anything odd, which was odd, since Cratchet generally smelled odd.

Then a thought struck him and he quickly checked the filters stuck up his nose. Although somewhat booger encrusted, they were firmly in place. He sniffed at the air but didn't notice anything unusual. The agent then ran to the after forecastle door, went through it and pounded up the stairs toward the wheelhouse.

There he found First Officer Smith slumped in a chair by the control console. Marley lay on the floor almost under the console. Both were snoring and twitching slightly. Ames idly wondered what the heck Marley was doing under the console.

Ames bent down and checked the pulse on both men to see if they were okay. He tried slapping them, but there was no reaction.

As he turned to go into the Captain's cabin he felt, rather than saw, a shadow cut across the big bridge windows. He changed course and looked out. The night was dark and moonless and it took him a moment to figure out what he was seeing. It was the reflection of the lights off the inside of the glass.

Realizing he could not see a thing, he rushed through the door out onto the bridge wing. Looking upward, he could see that the stars were going out. He checked his watch and, sure enough, morning was hours away. He looked up again and the stars were still disappearing.

The stars were vanishing in a straight line that led from the port side of the ship to the starboard side (left and right to you non-nautical types), and there was a heavy feeling to the air. The line of vanishing stars moved forward from the stern toward the bow. Somewhere toward the stern he could hear an odd thrumming sound that seemed to get louder and stronger as the minutes passed. He had the odd feeling he was in the movie, "Independence Day." He glanced around to see if there were any green aliens with big silver eyes.

At that moment a flash of light came from the bridge.

He turned his head and looked through the bridge wing window into the bridge. The agent saw someone coming through the door on the other side of the bridge.

Ducking down he peered through the corner of the window. A man dressed in black moved casually across the room to the control console. He leaned over the controls and punched buttons and poked at switches. Ames could feel the engines of the Valdez slowing, the vibration in his feet tapering off until it was gone.

Ames ducked down so he would not be seen, his eyes looking upward to follow the blackness as it moved steadily toward the bow. As he watched he could feel the Valdez slow to a stop, but there still seemed to be some motion. Then he realized what it was.

The blackness was another ship, a ship big enough to gulp down the Valdez like a minnow. The black line must be the forward edge of a huge opening that allowed that ship to bring the Valdez into its maw.

"That's how they did it," Ames muttered to himself. "They use a big ship to eat the smaller ship. That big ship must use some kind of stealth technology so radar and sonar can't hear it. And, with the smaller ship inside, it would look like the Valdez has just disappeared."

Ames was agog with the thought of how big that ship must be. It would have to be over a thousand feet long, two hundred feet wide and a hundred feet tall. That was one big ship! How the heck could anyone, satellites or aircraft, miss something this big?

As Ames watched the man in black bent down, checked Smith and Marley and then left the bridge. A moment later the black line in the sky reached the bow of the Valdez and began to drop rapidly toward the water, as though a giant door were closing. Within minutes there was a low thumping sound and the area around the ship became very black, with only the running lights fore and aft and the lights from the bridge permeating the blackness.

Ames was straining to see into this when a host of large lights flashed on, pinning him to the bridge wing deck. His eyes watered from the sudden onslaught of light and he rubbed at his eyes with his fists. It took a few moments for his vision to clear and then he lay down on his belly to peer over the side of the deck.

Below him the hull of the Valdez swam in a pool of water that had been gulped up with the ship. A number of hydraulic arms, faced with what looked like rubber, were extending outward from the sides of the bigger ship. These moved toward the Valdez until they thumped against the ship's hull. A sucking sound started and the water level began to drop. At that moment Ames heard a voice holler something unintelligible and he realized that there were a number of people on a catwalk just above the hydraulic arms.

The people were all men dressed in deep brown coveralls with silver belt buckles. Each of them wore a yellow hardhat except for one who had a red hat. He was the one doing the yelling.

The men in brown were doing something by each of the hydraulic arms. As they completed this task they would head down the catwalk toward the stern of the Valdez. Ames watched until they were all out of sight somewhere behind the ship.

Moving carefully he slid across the deck of the wing toward the door into the bridge. Reaching up he grasped the door handle and pulled it open just enough to slip onto the bridge. He raised himself to a squatting position and duck-walked to the door of the captain's cabin and slipped inside.

After pulling the door closed he rapidly glanced around the room. Everything was the same as when he had been there before except for the captain who was lying on the deck next to his overturned chair behind the desk, and there were no broads in his bed. Blond shook his head in sadness at the lack.

Quickly the agent checked to see that the captain was alive and well, if totally unconscious, then moved to the radiotelephone set into a desk on the back bulkhead. He flipped the switch on and moved through the frequencies trying to find some station that he could send a warning to. He got only the white noise of static and some dude talking about black figures crossing a river.

When Ames tried to talk to that individual he was loudly cursed as a "wetback pinko trying to jam the circuits of patriotic peoples and he should get his Chicano fanny off the radio."

Ames decided that someone was using that message to jam the ships radios. He sarcastically thanked the guy," gracias usted fornicador malo de madre," and switched off the radio.

Giving up on that, he left the cabin and worked his way to the after hatchway, opened it and stealthily headed down the stairs to the crew quarters, his footsteps "tinging" and "clanking" on the metal steps. It sounded like a herd of tap dancing rhinos in a hailstorm. Keeping a sharp eye, as well as his lazy eye, open he checked the berthing area and the mess, only to find the remainder of the crew were all sleeping in various poses, except for Ratlung who was sleeping in only one pose. Seeing that none were in immediate danger Blond headed for the hatch to the main deck.

Peering out the hatch and along the massive expanse of metal plates he reasoned that the man in black had to have had some way to get aboard. That meant either a rope up the side of the hull or possibly the boarding ladder on the port side.

Moving cautiously he left the forecastle and slipped across the deck to the edge where he could look left and right along it. He did not see any rope or other means to gain access to the Valdez, so he went back into the forecastle and used the internal passageways to get to the port side. There he did the same thing, carefully looking along the edge of the deck for the means of access. He spotted a rope hanging from the after deck. Below him, the water had been completely drained and the Valdez now rested suspended by the hydraulic arms as though in an enclosed graving dock.

He had just started moving toward the stern when there was a grinding noise. Looking around he saw that two of the men had returned and were operating a control panel on the catwalk. Ames flattened himself on the deck and could see that what he had thought was a large beam extending upward was in fact a moveable gangway that was slowly being lowered to the deck of the Valdez, creating a bridge between the deck and the outer catwalk.

The gangway came down until it clanked against the deck of the Valdez, giving access between the tanker and the larger ship. Along the outer catwalk a line of black clad men ran forward and turned to cross the gangway. Ames scuttled backward along the forecastle and across the deck to slip behind one of the deck hatch covers. Scooting down he peered around the edge of the hatch.

The men in black headed for the forecastle hatches and started entering the tanker. One man stopped when he noted the body of Cratchet resting against the forecastle wall. He rushed over and grabbed the diminutive mate, picked him up and promptly dropped him again. He then proceeded to do a rather strange dance, swinging his hands in the air and then brushing at himself, hopping on one foot and then other and then waving his hands in the air again. This went on for a couple of minutes until a dark shape flew from the black clad man and Ames figured it out.

The ships cat had taken the opportunity of Cratchet's condition as a perfect time to make a contribution to the sailor's wardrobe. The man in black had arrived just as the cat was making the deposit and the cat was, perforce, furious at the intrusion and quite willing to take out his anger in trade. Idly Ames wondered why the cat was up and about and not sleeping soundly somewhere.

With the cat no longer a problem the MIB again picked up Cratchet as though he had no weight and carried him back across the gangway and down the catwalk. Minutes later other men in black reappeared, each carrying a crewmember. All were taken down the catwalk to disappear into the gloom at the back of the ship. The brown clad men followed them, leaving the gangway in place.

After waiting a few minutes to see if there was going to be more activity, Ames slipped from behind the hatch and ran to the gangway, across it and down the catwalk. As he headed aft he slowed and began to move stealthily toward a door set at the end of the catwalk. A red light blazed beside the door.

As he moved closer the red light turned to green and the door began to open. Hurriedly the agent slipped over the edge of the catwalk and hung by his fingers, the dark drop to the lower deck beneath his feet. He glanced down at the darkness and then up again as he heard footsteps above him.

A man in a blue coverall stood above him holding a machine pistol in his hand. With a grin the man said, "Welcome aboard. The next time you try sneaking around you might check for cameras. We have been observing you for the past fifteen minutes. Why don't you climb up from there before you fall?"

CHAPTER THIRTEEN

Ames sat on a couch in what looked like a typical living room. There was a television in a pink multi-sectioned entertainment center flanked by a pink stereo and a quad of pink speakers, a DVD player and an old VCR. A digital plasma television hung on the wall, which made Ames wonder why there was a regular TV in the entertainment center.

Various knickknacks adorned the other shelves; A complete set of Chinese year figurines with a goat, a dragon, an ass, and the rest of the menagerie. There were six unicorns and a dusty green elf that had apparently missed the Christmas box. A few books on sex, intimacy and poker loitered here and there looking dejectedly unused.

A pink wingback chair sat next to the entertainment center and a small pink end table, with a brass lamp and pink lampshade resting on the pink surface, sat next to it. The pink overstuffed couch that Ames sat on was in the middle of the room with a long pink table behind it. A coffee table in front of him held a pink candy dish containing pink macaroons and pink Christmas candy and a pink vase with slightly wilted pink roses. Various pictures, mostly of "Pinky," by Thomas Lawrence, with pink frames, hung on the wall.

When the agent got up to look at them he determined that they were all prints that had probably been purchased at Wal-Mart or maybe some Christian thrift store. Two of the pictures were photographs of some chubby little girls in pink leotards and pink tutus. The agent assumed that those pictures were of whoever owned the overly feminized room.

Ames wandered across the pink carpet and brushed his hands lightly at the pink walls. There were two pink doors out of the room, both locked when Ames tried to open them.

Sitting back down on the couch, Ames absent mindedly reached for a piece of candy as he thought about his predicament. He was locked in pink hell aboard a ship that did not exist. He idly picked up a piece of hard candy and lifted it, bringing the entire bowl into the air. He looked at it briefly and set the bowl back down. Holding the bowl with one hand he used the other to pull on the candy. It didn't move. He pulled harder and the bowl skittered across the table leaving a deep scratch. Saying to heck with it he let go of the bowl and candy. The candy didn't let go of him.

His fingers were stuck to the sugary mess. He held the bowl to get his hand loose and when he pulled, the bowl skittered again leaving another deep scratch. He put his other hand on the mess to pull his first hand loose and found both were now stuck. "Well, phooey!" he muttered.

He lifted the bowl and brought it close to his face where he could lick at the mess with his tongue in an effort to loosen the fingers. His tongue got stuck. "Tham it!" he stuttered, jerking on the bowl. "Ow, thit," he stated as his tongue tried to leave his mouth.

He worked up a glob of saliva and worked it out of his mouth and along his tongue. Slowly the candy started to loosen and he jerked his tongue back into his mouth. Using more spit he worked his left hand loose and, when it came free, swung the bowl to the right to dislodge the candy. The bowl slipped free and spun across the room striking the entertainment center and cracking the plasma television screen. The bowl shattered, raining glass particles on the deep pink carpet. The TV dropped off one of the screws supporting it and dangled from the other, one corner pointing at the floor.

The candy remained firmly attached to his hand.

"Dad blasted thing," he muttered as he flipped his hand up and down. "Get the heck off me you stupid thing!" The candy wobbled up and down with his hand.

"Maybe if you left your hands off things that don't belong to you, you might not have that problem," said a voice behind him.

Ames leaped up and spun around to find Silverpinky standing behind him. As he had jumped his hand had brushed his slacks and he now had the candy, and his hand stuck to his leg. He surreptitiously tugged at the mess as he stared at the aged maven.

She stood with one hand on her hips and the other holding a pink dyed hairless Chihuahua dog. "So how come you're awake and the rest of your crew is asleep where they're supposed to be?" she asked as she raised a hand and rubbed the small dogs head. Her hand came away with a pink coloration. The dog bared its teeth at Ames. Ames bared his back.

"A natural immunity to knock out gas, I guess," said the agent while wiggling his hand back and forth. The dog's head bobbled up and down while watching the agent's leg.

"I doubt that," she responded. "It's more likely that you have some kind of filter in your nose. That makes you some kind of spy. Who are you?"

"I'm Blond, Ames Blond," said the agent. He stuck his tongue out at the dog. The dog piddled on Pinky who dropped the animal and looked disgusted. Pinky looked disgusted. The dog didn't care.

A frown creased her already creased face. "Why are the British interested in what I'm doing?" She brushed her pink slipper at the dog that stood quivering and shaking.

"I'm not British," said Ames. "I'm American. The name is Ames Blond. You're thinking of that other guy. He's not real, I am."

"You say you're blond, but your hair is dark," she said quizzically.

"Well buggers," muttered Ames darkly. "Don't start that stuff. My name is Blond, not my hair color. What is everybody, a bloody moron?"

"Take is easy Mister Bland," said Pinky looking closely at Ames. "Haven't we met before?"

"Yes. I met you at the environmental conference at the French embassy a few weeks ago."

"Oh, yes," she said nodding her head. "You're the guy with the linguine on his suit and a green bow tie. You had a problem with breathing. That problem might get worse." She frowned again. "Didn't we go through that hair routine before?"

"Yeah," muttered Ames, "Try and keep up would you?"

She glanced down at his wiggling hand. "You know, that candy is just for decoration. It's been there since two Christmases ago. Nobody's messed with it until now."

"Don't cuss," said Ames.

"Say what?"

"Christmas. You get hounded from here to Afghanistan if you use that word. I believe its use is now classed as a hate crime by seventeen supposedly civilized nations. I understand that it has worse connotations than damn or hell. I think the F word is more acceptable."

"Whatever, I celebrate Chrisakwanzachuka anyway," said Silverpinky. "What are you doing here besides breaking my TV, scratching my coffee table and busting my candy dishes?"

"Actually I'm just a simple seaman who happens to be unaffected by sleeping gas. Just what are you doing here anyway? I think you violated some kind of law by stealing this ship."

"Yeah, right," said Silverpinky, glaring at Blond. "If you're a simple seaman then I'm simple Simon."

"Hi Simon. How ya doing?" said Ames with a smile and a facetious wave.

Silver glared some more. The dog piddled again, earning it a glare from Silver. "You won't think this is so funny when we get where we're going." She pulled a small plastic box, like a television remote, from her pocket and pressed a button.

Ames winced, expecting some horrific result. Instead there was a click as the lock on the door came undone. At the same time a small-wheeled robot scurried from a hole in the wall and snagged the dog. The dog howled as it was dragged through the wall and out of sight. For a couple of minutes afterward the muted sounds of dog whines could be heard. Then they suddenly stopped.

After the door lock clicked, almost immediately one of the doors opened and a slender blond in a pink coverall came in. The newcomer glanced at Ames and then over to Silverpinky. With a start she spun her head back to Ames. "You!" she cried.

Ames grinned. "Hey hot pants, how's it going? When did you get hooked up with this old broad and her ship stealing scheme?"

"You stay away from me you crooked woman hating Dork, you." The girl held up her hands as though warding off evil, the forefinger of her right hand crossing the forefinger of her left, making an odd cross symbol.

"Careful there, sweet shorts," said Ames still grinning. "I heard you could be locked up for showing a cross, something to do with racism and or religious freedom." The girl quickly pulled her hands apart and looked carefully around.

Silverpinky looked from one to the other. "What's going on here?" she asked. "Do you know this guy?"

"This is the son of a female dog who defamed me and made me lose my job! He's an agent for DORK and he's a real dork as well!"

The old gal creased her brow, which was hard since it was already pretty creased. "What's going on here Sheila? You mean he fixes screwed up computers? So he's like with the Nerd Squad or something? What's that have to do with you losing your job. Did you hack in a bug or a really stupid bit if adware?"

Sheila glared angrily at Ames. "This son of a dog defamed me and when I filed a sexual harassment suit against him the government said he didn't exist and dropped the case. A week later I was relieved of my duties with DORK! They said my leaving had nothing to do with the suit. When I tried to file a suit against DORK for firing me as the result of a harassment suit I was told there was no such thing as a DORK."

With a puzzled expression Silverpinky asked, "What the heck is DORK other than a very odd kid in high school?"

"It's the Department of Reconnaissance and Knowledge," replied Ames. "It's the organization I work for." He turned to the girl. "Nice to see you again Miss Bitz. What's a good looking broad like you doing with wrinkles here? Oh, and what color are your panties this time?"

If looks could kill, the daggers coming from Sheila's eyes would have chopped Ames into hamburger or even a nice pate. She started sputtering and only stopped when Silverpinky gave her a couple of good slaps on the back. The robot peeked it antenna out of the wall to see if there was something more it could grab.

Ames had had a run in with Miss Bitz during the course of a previous investigation. She had met him at National Airport, to drive him to the DORK offices. He had made a simple comment to her and she went ballistic, filing a sexual harassment suit against him that was eventually dropped when the government refused to acknowledge that Ames even existed. It was at that time that Ames found out he really did not exist. No driver's license, no paycheck, no apartment, no plants, no life, no status. Even his sneakers were not his. For a while it gave him something of an inferiority complex until he found out the one advantage. No income taxes. If you don't exist there are no taxes to pay and no audits. Now each April 15th he walked by the IRS office and gave them the finger.

Silverpinky looked thoughtful. "So you are a spy. We have ways of dealing with spies." With a wave of her hand she waved at the girl. "Sheila, take this person and throw him into the brig!"

"But we don't have a brig," said the girl, carefully eyeing the robot which was now completely out of the wall and tugging at the leg of her jumpsuit. She kicked at it with her foot. It scurried back to the wall while making rude noises. Ames and Silverpinky watched it until the door over the hole snapped shut.

Miss Bitz shook her head and continued. "At least I've never seen it. Then again it might be someplace in that icky smelly place with all the noisy stuff in it. You know, where all the noise comes from? I hear people say that things like gearies or whatever gets locked up down there. Somebody might be able to lock him up with those geary things."

The aged crone gave Sheila a withering look. "How the devil did you get through college?"

"My boyfriend was the dean of students," said Sheila with a bright smile. "He was always telling me I could go all the way!"

The head distaff shook her head. "Just take him and lock him in one of the cabins! And don't forget to take the key with you!"

CHAPTER FOURTEEN

Ames lay on the bed staring at the ceiling. For some time he had been trying to figure out the gurgling sound that he could faintly hear through the walls. It almost sounded like water flowing past the hull, but he knew that the cabin he was in was above the waterline near the upper decks or, at least, he thought so.

Sheila had taken him from the pink living room looking place and up two flights of stairs to another deck, then down a short hallway, through an archway and down a flight of stairs. Opening another door they had gone across a hall and through an empty ballroom with hanging multi-colored crepe paper, a dozen over-turned tables and a few cases of empty beer bottles rolling around, making it look like Cratchet's room, only bigger.

Out the back door of the ballroom and through a galley that smelled vaguely of burnt toast and rancid bacon, up a flight of stairs, down two flights, up one, down two, along a hall, around a corner and through a small room, up two flights, down three more, then down a hallway to one of the doors that were spaced along it. Opening one of them she told him to go in.

"This was Mike Federowski's room so don't mess with his stuff," she said as she motioned him inside.

Ames glanced around. The room had a single berth mounted against one wall, a small desk and a chair. The bed was untidy and the desk was covered with a pizza box and three cola cans. A pair of slacks was draped over the chair and heaps of dirty socks were scattered around the floor. There were a number of empty beer cans on the floor and some indefinable paper wads were dangling from the ceiling like crushed white bats. A pair of underwear, with suspicious dark stains, was hanging from the bedpost. The room smelled of mildew, sweat socks and old banana with overtones of something really gross.

"Where's Fred Owski now?" asked the agent twitching his nose and slapping the candy against his leg. It stuck again. "Doing his laundry I hope." He looked pointedly at the underwear.

Sheila ignored the direction of his stare while she held her nose. "That's Federowski and no, he fell overboard a couple of nights ago."

"So, you don't think he's coming back do you?"

"He might. He was a good swimmer and you never know."

"So putting me in here is like, some form of barbaric torture?"

"Not really. This is the only room available unless we chained you up in the sumps or stumps or whatever. That place were all the water goes in a ship. That place down near where the geary things are. You know what I mean?"

"Right," muttered Ames as she closed the door.

He had cleaned off the bed, including the somewhat stained sheets, and lain down. The mattress had an odd aroma and the pillow was worse. He got up and flipped the mattress over, but then flipped it back because the grape jelly stains on the bottom side made it sticky and that was worse than the smell of the topside.

Trying to ignore the rancid smell and the dark greasy spot in the center of the pillow he lay down and thought things through. Using the available information he tried to determine a plan of action.

Unfortunately there was very little available information. The *Valdez* was inside a larger ship, the crew was unconscious and stuffed somewhere else. He was locked up and out of communication. About the only good thing was that he was out of that ghastly pink room. At that moment something shifted and he got a good whiff of the pillow. He stood up, gagged three times and rubbed the back of his head to get rid of the smell. He decided that the pink room had some merits.

With a grunt he began looking around the room. Opening the desk drawers he found an odd assortment of unpaid bills, erotic magazines, children's books and rubber gloves. With a disgusted sound he slammed the last drawer closed. It seemed to him that the world might be a better place with Mr. Federowski somewhere under water.

He wandered into the bathroom and wished he hadn't. It might have been all right if only the toilet had been flushed at least once. I will not describe the brown and oozing mess dripping from the porcelain throne.

There were at least a half a dozen cakes of melted soap in the scummy looking shower stall and a really nasty looking sock hung from the shower rod. The sink was filled with some really icky looking red-jello like stuff. Ames poked at it with his finger, trying to figure out what it was. He finally decided it was a left over from the movie the "Blob" or the remnants of a washcloth that had soaked too long. The smell finally got to him and he rapidly decamped back into the bedroom.

Closing the door to the john tightly, he paced the room, opening closets, looking under the bed and, just for the heck of it, trying the door. It opened.

Ames stood for a moment in amazement looking at the slightly open door, his hand on the latch. Pulling it open all the way he peered out into the passageway. There was no one around. Apparently Miss Bitz had taken the key, but, not being instructed otherwise, she had not locked the door.

Listening for a moment to the sound of machinery, he left the room and pulled the door closed. Heading aft, moving carefully along the wall, he came to another doorway. He tried the latch, found it open and slipped into the room.

This was a copy of Federowski's, only much cleaner. The open closet revealed almost a dozen freshly cleaned blue jumpsuits. Taking one down, Ames held it against himself. Scanning it he decided it would probably fit. Quickly he slipped off his shirt and trousers and donned the coverall. The fit was a tad tight through the shoulders and a little loose in the hips. The chest bulged out somewhat as though the guy who owned it worked out with weights, but it would serve even though the legs were a little short and the crotch pulled in a little tightly against his.

He sniffed at the mattress and pillow and found a pleasant floral scent. With a grin he grabbed them both and dragged them down the hall to his room. He pulled the smelly bedding from the bed frame and installed the clean. He then dragged the smelly stuff down the hall to the other room. As an afterthought he went back to Federowski's room and grabbed a handful of beer cans and the pizza box. He tossed them into the other room with the mattress. He surveyed the scene and snapped his fingers.

He returned to his room and, using a pen, picked up the underwear and transferred it to the once clean room. Now satisfied, he nodded at the effect.

Feeling rather good about his deeds he also felt the call of nature. The rest facilities for this room were very pleasant, although the agent was somewhat in doubt about the character of the guy using the room. There were an assortment of eyebrow pencils and rouges next to the sink. A pair of pantyhose hung from the shower rod. The spy decided a Joe Namath wanna be lived here.

Nature required five minutes of his time and the agent stood up feeling much refreshed. He reached for the chrome knob, but stopped, grinned and left the room without pulling the handle.

He slipped back out into the hallway and continued heading aft. Coming to a stairwell he had a choice, up or down. Down would probably lead to the engine room or the *Valdez*. Up would go to the bridge or the deck. He chose up.

Moving cautiously he crept up the stairs being as quiet as possible. He tried to ignore the clanks and clunks of his footsteps on the metal steps within the metal confines of the stairwell and the echoes that reverberated from one end of the ship to the other.

There were a lot of steps. He was apparently not as near the upper decks as he had thought earlier. He had to climb up a total of eight flights of stairs until they ran out at a small landing and a door with a small round window inset at face height. He stood huffing and puffing from the climb. He leaned against the wall gasping until his heart rate returned to normal before carefully looking inside through the window. He saw no one, so he stepped through, banging his knee against the metal combing. Gritting his teeth he hobbled down a short passageway to another door. This one also had a small window inset in it.

Ames peered through the window into what seemed to be a control room similar to that in the Valdez. He spotted two men and a woman sitting at consoles manipulating controls of some kind. It was the window in front of them that gained his attention.

The window was a narrow strip less than a foot high that ran from one wall across the top of the consol to out of his view. The glass or whatever that made up the window must have been fairly thick, for through it the agent could see water where he expected to see air.

The water was greenish and semi-dark as though the light took some time to get through it. Occasionally various finned denizens would swim past.

Ames spotted a couple of sharks, a small whale and one guy in a suit with a concrete block attached to his feet. A wet suited guy peered briefly into the room before being swept backward by the current of the ships passage.

Since the window was near the top of the ship the obvious was clear. The ship was either underwater or had sunk and the crew were trying to pump it out and get it back to the surface. That seemed a little doubtful so the agent opted for submarine.

That explained why aerial and satellite imagery failed to find the missing tankers. The big ship would swallow the tankers then submerge. The hull must be made of some kind of sonar absorbent or sound resistant material making it stealthy. With quiet engines and screws the ship would be almost impossible to detect, rather like a nuclear missile submarine, only a lot bigger.

As Ames peered at the control room Madam Silverpinky hove into view walking behind the control console. Her gaze was moving from the console to the window to the door. Ames ducked down.

Above him the aged captain peered through the small window, flattening her face against the glass so that the wrinkles flattened out, making her look at least two days younger. Her eyes scanned up, down and sideways.

Ames scrunched himself into a ball against the door and stared at the wall. Silverpinky was hijacking oil tankers using a massive submarine, doing something that stunk up the holds, then setting the ship and its crew free. For what purpose? What the heck were the point of the hijackings and the expenditure of the massive amounts of money that it had probably required to build this sub? It did not make any sense. He had to figure it out and the only way to do that seemed to be to go where the submarine was going.

Looking upward he noted that the window was now clear of wrinkles, although it was over-laid and almost opaque with rouge, powder and bright pink lipstick. Keeping an eye on the multi-colored fresco the agent stood up and turned back to the stairwell.

With a sigh he headed back down the stairs and returned to the Federowski's room, but with a minor stop along the way to collect some clean toilet paper and a can of Glade.

CHAPTER FIFTEEN

Ames was sleeping when there was a knock at the door. He sat up and rubbed his eyes, looking around trying to figure out where he was. All the lights were off except for a small lamp on the desk. The stains on the lampshade threw eerie images on the wall and the bulb had a tendency to flicker. For a moment the agent thought he was back in Al Raini's cave where he had spent a previous harrowing mission. However there was no fat Arab sitting in the chair by the door so this had to be somewhere else.

Then the knock came again and he swung his feet out of the bed and padded barefoot to the door. He said, "Come in," as he approached it. The knock came again.

"Come in," he said a little louder. Another knock.

"Oh for Pete's sake," he muttered as he grabbed the latch and pulled the door open. Sheila stood on the other side balancing a tray in one hand as she started to knock again with the other. Her knuckles rapped on his forehead creating a hollow "clonk, clonk," sound. She gasped as she realized that he was standing there.

"What's this?" he asked, rubbing his head. "The last meal for the condemned man?"

She looked slightly startled. "Oh, no! This is dinner. We're not going to starve you, you know."

"Well thank you. Here let me take that." Ames lifted the tray from her hand and turned to go back in the door.

The tray clipped the edge of the doorframe, slid sideways and started to flip over. The agent made a grab for it, catapulting the thing into the air and flipping it backward at the same time. Dish covers, dishes, food and silver did a beautiful half-gainer through the air and splattered all over Miss Bitz. A dish conked her in the head, broke in half and headed for the floor leaving strands of tomato covered spaghetti dripping from her platinum hair. Two small loaves of Italian bread arced through the air like fresh roasted SCUD missiles. A wayward fork poked her in the arm and a water glass emptied its contents down her front, soaking her coverall and clearly indicating that she was braless. She gasped as the cold water slid down her front. The only item left intact was the cardboard container of milk.

Jerking his head and eyes away from her chest, Ames reached out and grabbed her as she started to fall to the ground. The sudden weight of her body pulled him off balance and they both landed on the deck with a solid thump, with him on top. The intact milk carton let go with a "pop, squish" as Sheila landed on it. Milk dribbled from under her behind.

Her eyes came back into focus while looking into his eyes. "Well you've got a heck of line. First you attack a girl verbally and make her feel like crap, then ogle her to death and when that doesn't work you beat her with food and physically assault her. What's next? Do you hit me with a club and drag me off by my hair?"

On an impulse Ames kissed her. She wrapped her arms around him and kissed him back. A few minutes later they came up for air. He looked down into her eyes. She looked up into his spaghetti smeared chin. "Well, that took you a while to figure out," she said with a grin.

"What?" he croaked.

"Didn't you know that when a girl hits or yells at a guy it means she likes him?"

He rolled over and sat up. "So by abusing me and trying to sue me for everything I own, you were trying to tell me you liked me? I thought that stuff went away when I hit puberty."

"Sure," she said, sitting up and raking pasta from her hair. "I thought you were really cute when you came up to me in the airport. And no, that stuff never goes away. We girls just make it more difficult for you to figure out."

Pushing himself up off the floor he gave her his hand and helped her up. "I hate to put a halt to the affair of the century here, but you're covered with spaghetti sauce and I'm the captive of a lunatic. You need to get cleaned up and I need to escape."

"Silverpinky isn't a lunatic," said Sheila as she started to unbutton her coverall. Ames couldn't keep his eyes off the movement of her fingers. "She has this all planned out. She knows exactly what she's doing."

Ames struggled valiantly and pulled his eyes upward. "What plan? What's she trying to do, besides make oil smell like crap?" His eyes lost the battle and dropped back to her chest.

She stopped unbuttoning, much to Ames' disappointment, and put her hands on his arms. "Why she's filling in the old oil domes." She turned aside and started walking toward the bathroom, the milk creating interesting patterns on the rolling muscles that Ames had trouble not watching.

Ames stood for a second, his mind a total blank. As she started to disappear into the bathroom he suddenly jerked back to reality and darted across the room. He caught up with her and grabbed her by the arm. "What? What do you mean she's filling in the old oil domes? What's she filling them in with?"

"Crap," she said slipping loose from his hand and pulling the coverall from her shoulders. She started to close the door, gagged and turned a few odd shades of green. She yanked the door back open and stumbled back into the bedroom.

"Oh, my god," she moaned. "That's horrible. Didn't your mother teach you to keep the bathroom clean?" She retched again.

Ames grinned. "Lovely isn't it? It appears our missing friend Federowski has some unusual toilet training. In this case a flat zero."

She wiped a hand over her mouth. "You mean you didn't do that?"

"Are you kidding?" said Ames with a frown. "I couldn't be that much of a pig if I tried."

"Oh, thank god," she muttered. "I thought I was going to have to completely retrain you." She took his hand. "Come On we'll use the shower in my room."

Against his will the agent was towed down the hallway to another room. They left a trail of spaghetti noodles and Parmesan cheese on the floor tiles. The agent had a bad moment when they turned into a room that Ames thought he recognized. The girl stopped with a start.

The room looked like a copy of Federowski's. The mattress and pillow were stained and rank. There were beer cans and a pizza box on the floor and the bathroom was emitting a strange odor.

"I knew it," the girl cried. "Federowski must have swum back to the ship. I told you he was a good swimmer. Look at this place. He must have been using my room because you were in his. Look at this, he trashed the place. The pig took a dump in my john. He even took one of my coveralls." She paused and looked at

Ames, her eyes running up and down his form. "Nah, couldn't be," she muttered shaking her head.

Stunned by his mistake the agent for DORK pushed at an empty beer can with the toe of his shoe. "Ah, why don't you take a shower and I'll try and straighten things up a bit here." He pushed her toward the bathroom.

"Well, all right," she said. "But if that slob Federowski shows up you give him a piece of my mind, okay?"

"Sure thing," said Ames brightly. "If there's any available."

She frowned at him for a moment as though unsure what he meant, then went into the rest area leaving the door slightly ajar. Ames caught a few brief glimpses of a bare shoulder, a trim hip partially covered by scanty red fabric and the toe of a left foot. After a few seconds he could hear the sound of water running in the shower.

He bent down to pick up an empty beer can when a thought occurred to him. He quickly stepped into the lavatory and pushed the chrome handle on the toilet. A satisfying flushing sound came followed by a scream from the shower stall.

There was a flurry of activity from behind the curtain and an unladylike voice demanded, "What moron flushed the blasted toilet?"

Ames again quickly decamped from the restroom and began to rapidly pick up beer cans and pizza boxes. Holding them he looked around the room and could not find anywhere to put them. The only waste container was a small metal cylinder next to the desk that might hold a half dozen used tissues if they were packed tight.

He rotated in a circle four times like a dog settling in for a nap, before going to the door and tossing the stuff out into the hall. Hurriedly he grabbed the mattress and pillow and dragged them back to his own room. He started to put the dirty stuff onto the bed, but shuddered and dragged the junk back to Sheila's room. Replacing the befouled nest he found some clean sheets and a pillowcase and used them to make the bed. As a final touch he sprayed the whole thing with half the can of Glade.

Leaning over he sniffed at the bed. There was a heavy scent of bayberry with a slightly rancid smell of used urine, sweat, hair oil and grape jelly. After thinking it over for a whole three seconds he used up the other half of the Glade. The empty can went into the hall with the rest of the junk.

At that moment a bare hand dripping water waved from the bathroom. "Ames, would you be a dear and hand me a clean coverall?"

The master spy pulled one of the blue suits from the closet and started to pass it across. He stopped and held it just out of reach. The hand extended itself further, revealing a well-turned shoulder. He pulled it back slightly. A face framed by wet dog blond hair glared out at him and a hand grabbed the material and disappeared inside. The hand returned a moment later giving him an Italian salute with one finger. The bird disappeared and the door slammed shut.

Thirty minutes later the blond bimbo bounced buoyantly from the bathroom berobed in blue, bobbing a bright bonnet of blond blocks before the befuddled brunette, bedazzling the Bashington BORK before beginning ba brading boyter ber be bang ba bad bing ber.

Ahem.

The girl came out of the bathroom - clean, bright and newly covered with face powder, eye liner, eye shadow, three layers of base, two of mascara and a rouge from a pear tree. With a little effort she could have passed for an extra in "I, Robot." Ames thought she looked sexy as all get out. Then again, Ames thought a clothes tree looked sexy as all get out. Ames didn't date much. Tough to do without a pay check.

With a cattish smile she passed in front of Ames and dragged her fingers across his cheek. His brain clicked off and he started drooling. His eyes followed her swaying hips as they headed for the door, the autonomic male response from Basra returning. Pain in his lower section, from the male response inside the too small area of the coveralls, caused the brain to click back on. He wiped the dribble from his chin, adjusted the middle portion of his garment and followed her out of the room.

She stood just outside the door looking at the hallway. She faced Ames and pointed. "See, he's been here too. That Federowski messes up just about everywhere he goes. What a slob!" She kicked the pizza box out of the way and headed toward Ames' room.

The agent started to follow, but stepped on a beer can. The can crushed into the shape of his foot and locked on. As the agent stepped forward the can clacked against the tiles of the hall. He walked a couple of paces with a "Clock, thump, clock, thump," before giving up. He reached down to remove the can and fell, over hitting his head against the wall. Toonish birdies fluttered into the air like startled grouse.

Shaking his head he twisted to grab the can. The too tight coveralls objected by tearing up the back with a loud "rippppp." The agent fell over on his side with his leg pulled toward his chest. The knee gave out with another "rip," followed an instant later by the suits crotch. A sleeve followed and three buttons popped loose.

Disgusted, Blond pulled himself to his feet, blue cloth dangling. He looked up to see Miss Bitz staring at him. Making a moue she shook her head. "So your cupids choice for me? I think there may be problems with this, possibly even major retraining." She walked off down the hall shaking her head.

CHAPTER SIXTEEN

For two days Ames sat in Federowski's room and wondered what the heck Sheila had been talking about. When the girl had come out of the bathroom the first night she had been wearing a towel and all thought of oil, tankers and crappy smells had slipped from Ames' mind. By the time she left he realized he didn't have an answer, or for that matter, dinner.

When breakfast came the next day it was delivered by a seriously ugly guy in a crappy looking brown jumpsuit that did nothing to hold in his overly-extended waistline. As he took the tray, and a clean brown coverall, Ames asked Ugly about Sheila.

"You mean da broad wit the great knockers?" asked the man. "She's got udder tings to do sides takin care of nosy spies. Jus eat cher brefast and mind cher own bidness." He pushed Ames back into the room and slammed the door. This time the agent heard the lock click shut.

Setting the tray down on the desk he tried the door and confirmed his suspicions. The door was now locked. He sat on the bed and ate the eggs, toast, bacon, ham, sausage, grits, homes fries, hash browns and bran muffin the kitchen had provided, while sipping on orange juice, tomato juice, coffee and tea. When he was finished he patted his well-fed stomach and decided that, if nothing else, they did indeed have no intention of starving him.

During the next two days, besides eating rather too well, the agent spent the time cleaning Federowski's mess and disposing of the rather large heap of soiled clothing from the closet, floor, bed and desk.

Using an old spy trick that may still be used by young spies, Ames got Ugly to open the door and then, surreptitiously blocked the door latch. Since he did not have any gum, the preferred medium for blocking door latches, he used one of Federowski's condoms. A new one, not a used one.

Keeping his eye glued to the peephole in the door, Ames was able to determine when Ugly left his post to answer nature's call. When the overweight, over-height dwarf was out of sight, Ames popped the door open and threw Federowski's junk out into the hall. The fat guy had yelled blue blazes when he found the hall a mess. He tried to blame Ames, but the door was now securely locked again.

With nothing else to do and needing a shower, not to mention a bowel movement, the agent reluctantly swamped out the bathroom with a plunger, six bottles of Lysol and a T-shirt used as a gas mask. When he was done he tapped on the door to the hallway. When Ugly pushed the door open, Ames again blocked the door latch. And he again tossed all the junk and waste out into the hall when Ugly wandered off. Ugly discovered this really bad crap and responded by trying to chuck the stuff into the room with Ames. Blond hooked a chair under doorknob and then spent a rather fun hour listening to Ugly complain and moan about the dirty hallway.

When the bathroom was completed and Ugly had quieted down, the agent twiddled his thumbs and stared at the wall for an hour or two until he became bored. It would have taken longer but his left thumb kept beating his right thumb, even when the right thumb cheated.

Seeking intellectual stimulation he pulled the porno magazines out of the desk drawer and actually read the articles and stories in them. A couple of times he tried playing tic-tac-toe with himself, but had trouble winning, so he gave that up and went back to the magazines. The magazines surprised him; the articles were in no way intellectually stimulating and, therefore, not in the least bit boring.

In the afternoon of the second day he could feel a change in the pitch of the engines and the gurgle outside the hull subsided. An hour or so later the ugly man in the brown coverall opened the door and gestured for Ames to come out. The agent considered jumping him and taking the gun he was holding, but decided against it. Better to see what was going on before causing hate and discontent.

As the agent left the room and started down the hall he noted a large stack of Twinkie wrappers on the floor next to a chair next to the door. Ames wondered briefly if Ugly were related to a certain overweight clerk at the Baghdad airport. Their eating habits, speech patterns and physical appearances were amazingly alike.

He was led back through the passageways and down stairs, up stairs and down stairs again, with Ugly muttering obscure threats, until they were back at the door to the catwalk near the *Valdez*.

When the door to the catwalk opened Ames was momentarily dazzled by afternoon sunlight streaming through the large opening at the front of the sub. The submersible appeared to be docked inside a large building and the front had been opened to allow the *Valdez* to be removed.

As he walked across the gangway onto the deck of the *Valdez* his theory was confirmed. He could feel the pulse of the tankers engines under his feet. When he came aboard the gangway was lifted out of the way and the big tanker began to slowly move forward.

He was led into the bridge house and up to the control room where Silverpinky and Sheila, along with a number of crewmen, were looking through the bridge windows as the hull of the sub slipped by. Sheila gave a small smile while Silver gave him a frown.

Silver was clad in a red jumpsuit with a silver zippers and green tassels. She had a large red bow in her hair, making her look like an overly-decorated Christmas tree. The old fart again held the small hairless dog in her arms. The dog looked slightly psychotic with round white eyes that jumped at each small sound. The animal seemed to be particularly observant of any small electronic noise. When those occurred the animal would twitch and dribble saliva. Silverpinky ignored the beast's odd behavior.

Sheila still had on the pink coverall and was apparently still braless. He could tell by the frontal exposure and by the fact that he knew her bra was still in his room.

With a sweep of her hand the aged dame gestured to the outside building using the dog as a pointer. "Take a good look, Mister Blond. This will be your home until the completion of our mission." She dropped her hand back down, causing the animal to thump onto the carpet. It promptly piddled and snuck under the control consol.

"Unlike the crew of this ship, who will be kept safe and unaware until it is time for their return, you will stay here. You have seen too much to be allowed to go back to Washington."

She looked at the ugly guy in brown. "Take Mister Blond to the guest accommodations and make sure he's locked in. I'll decide what to do with him later." The ugly guy grinned and poked Ames in the side with his gun.

"Miss Pinky," piped in Sheila. "Maybe I better go with them to make sure he doesn't forget the key."

"Hey," grumbled Ugly. "Watt chew tink? I'm stupid?"

Silverpinky looked back and forth from girl to the ugly guy and back. "Maybe you'd better. Between the two of you there might be one complete brain. Get him out of here."

By the time the trio had descended to the deck and walked toward the bow, the tanker had come to a stop outside of the submersible with its hull against a pier. They waited for a moment as the boarding ladder was lowered and the ship was tied off.

Blond took a moment to inspect the massive submarine. It was huge, with a massive pair of doors in the bow. The thing was an odd gray black color that made it hard to see any details, except for inside the big doors, which were slowly sliding closed.

Ugly poked Ames again and the three headed down the stairs to the quay. Ames was fascinated by what he saw. The tanker was tied to a pier inside a massive building that could house not only the huge submarine and the *Valdez*, but could probably handle two more tankers as well. A blocky looking group of pumps stood spaced along the quay.

A somewhat confusing array of pipes led from the pumps across the pier and through the side of the building. His examination was cut short when Ugly prodded him to climb into a green golf cart. Ames took the passenger seat while Sheila drove. Ugly sat in back threatening the agent with his pistol.

Ames glanced over at Miss Bitz. "Where are we? I mean what country is this?"

"This is Mozambique," she said. "We're up the Save' River just north of the village of Nova Mambone."

"Hey," butt in Ugly. "I don' tink chews supposed to tell im dat!"

"Oh, pipe down, Clarence," she muttered in disgust. "He's not going anywhere so it doesn't matter what I tell him."

"Clarence?" asked Ames with a grin at the ugly workman.

"Hey, chew watch chews mout. My mama gib me dat name and it a goot one!"

Sheila chuckled. "Anyway, the next closest real town is Beira to the north about hundred and fifty kilometers."

Ames glanced around. They were now outside the building on a dirt road. There were cardboard and tin huts spaced here and there with tall, poor looking Africans shuffling to or from someplace or other. Looking back toward the building he was surprised to see that it was barely visible. The structure was cleverly camouflaged with netting, green and brown paint and a scattering of broad-leafed trees, some of which grew from the roof.

"That's a pretty good trick," he said pointing a thumb back at the building.

"Yes, it's invisible to aerial and satellite imagery. The only thing that might find it is laser imaging and with the world economic situation nobody can afford that anymore. Nobody knows we're here."

Ames looked around the landscape. "This may sound dumb, but what are you doing here? I see these crappy huts and a whole lot of grassland. What are you using the oil tankers for? Is there oil here or something?"

"We don't pump oil here, silly," she giggled. "We're putting shit into the ground."

"What," interjected Ames? "What do you mean you're putting shit into the ground? What kind of shit and why? And why are you cussing so much? Shouldn't you be saying you're putting stuff in the ground, or, better yet, explaining what you're putting into the ground, rather than using an epithet to describe that or those items. My old English teacher and she was quite old, probably dead by now, but then English teachers seem to last forever, rather like really bad bubble gum. I once had a piece that lasted for at least three summers and part of a winter. It had a taste that . . . . "

She shut him up with a hand across his mouth. "We don't dump stuff onto the ground, dummy. We pump shit back into the ground."

Ames took her hand away and said, "Huh?"

She gestured at the grassland. "There used to be some oil wells here taking oil out of small oil domes. That was back in the fifties and they didn't last long before they ran dry. It was too expensive for the oil companies to use new techniques to get the last of the oil, so the wells were abandoned. We're filling those domes with crap."

"I hate to state the obvious, but, why? And what kind of crap?"

"To get rid of the crap, why else," she said enigmatically.

"So you're putting some kind of crap into the ground here and you need the tankers to get the crap from wherever it is to here. I guess that makes sense, but what kind of crap and where does it come from? And what does all of this have to do with oil?"

"Silverpinky is planning to use the crap to replace the fuel in cars and trucks and electrical plants and stuff."

"So she's trying to stop the use of oil?"

"We're not trying to stop the use of oil. We're trying to replace it with something better."

"And what would that be?" he asked.

"Shit," she said, reaching down by her foot. "Put your hands on the dashboard."

Ames lifted his hands and moved them forward as he asked, "Why?"

At that moment she slammed on the brakes and Ames was propelled forward with his hands and arms preventing him from smacking the dash. In the back seat, Ugly, unprepared for the stop, jerked forward. As he was jerked off his seat Sheila lifted a wrench and swung her arm backward, clonking the man in the forehead. With a grunt he dropped back into the seat, a nasty goose egg sprouting just under the hairline.

Ames raised his arms to fend off the wrench. "Whoa there girl! Drop the wrench and get your PMS under control!"

She looked startled and dropped the wrench on the floor. "I don't have PMS," she said. "I'm helping you escape."

Blond looked at her for a moment, then slowly scanned the countryside. Except for an occasional tree and small hill the land was as flat and bare as a baby's bottom. Off in the distance some small tree covered hills obscured the horizon. "Escape to where?"

"I already told you," she exclaimed in exasperation. "Beira is just north of here about one hundred and fifty kilometers. You go north along the coast and you should get there in about five or six days."

"And what do I eat while I'm wandering around in the bush? I'm not real good at bringing down an antelope with a rock. And I hear Africa has big cats called lions that like to eat small tender things like me."

"Here," she said, reaching down and grabbing Ugly's gun. "Take this and I have a packet of food and a canteen in my bag for you."

"If I run off you're going to get into trouble."

"No I won't because you're going to hit me with the wrench. I'll tell them we hit something and Clarence and

I got knocked out and you escaped." She handed him the wrench. "Here clout me in the head." She winced a little and closed her eyes.

Ames examined that lovely face and shining blond hair, then shrugged his shoulders and smacked her with the wrench. She dropped forward onto the steering wheel. He hopped off the cart and ran across the grass to a low hill. Ducking down he took stock of his situation.

Then he got up and ran back to the golf cart. Reaching behind the seat he pulled out Sheila's bag, patted her on the head and ran back to the hill. Ducking down again he pulled open the bag and looked inside. There was a compact , two tubes of lipstick, a small mirror, a bottle of rouge, two credit cards, seventeen dollars in cash, three pennies and a quarter. It also contained a small umbrella, two notepads, six pencils, three pens, two lint covered Certs tablets and some stale peanut butter crackers that were rather frayed at the edges. Except for the crackers, Certs tabs and maybe the lipstick, there was nothing to eat and darn sure nothing to drink.

He stuffed everything back in the bag and scuttled back to the golf cart. Chucking the bag into the passenger seat he rummaged around until he found a second bag under Ugly's foot. He jerked the bag loose knocking Ugly onto the ground. The agent scuttled back to the small hill and peeked inside the new bag. There were three bottles of Perrier, a ham sandwich, one chicken wing and four Oreo cookies.

"Well this is going to last all of about an hour," he muttered. "What did she think this was, a picnic?"

Hefting the bag he headed north across the grassland.

CHAPTER SEVENTEEN

The sun overhead was blazing hot, searing into his eyes as sweat dripped down his body staining his clinging jumpsuit creating dark splotches on the brown-cloth. Where the skin was exposed it had turned bright red from sunburn. He had Sheila's cloth bag stuck on his head like a cap to protect his brain from frying, making him look rather like a red paisley Smurf.

The remnants of the sandwich, chicken and cookies had disappeared down his throat a day ago and his stomach was now making hunger noises. The Perrier was also gone, but the water had been reluctantly replaced from local streams he had passed. Reluctantly because of the stories he had heard about parasites in African water. He figured he had a pretty good start on a tapeworm by now.

This unfortunately proved too true as his bowels began to express their dismay at his drinking habits. At first it was a slight pressure that he had to stop and relieve, but as the hours went by the pressure became greater until his stops were acts of strain and pain, crouching in the grass with his pants down.

By the end of the second day, he was feeling decidedly dehydrated. This led to drinking more water and that increased his distress. At times he felt like he could feel the suspected worm tickling his butt as he walked. It was not a pleasant sensation.

The land had remained flat and grassy for most of his trek. The first and second days he had to keep his eyes and ears open for pursuit. A couple of time he had heard helicopters roaring off to the east, but none came near his line of march.

But the land was changing. In just the last hour the land had started swinging upward and the trees were growing more and more dense. Unfortunately the trees and underbrush didn't diminish the heat. The air seemed to grow more humid with the increase in vegetation. For a few moments Ames considered heading eastward back toward the grassland. But Sheila had said that Beira was north, so he maintained his unsteady march in that direction.

He had also heard some unpleasant yowling sounds from the plains. At least in the trees he might have a chance of escaping should some tawny figure with lots of claws and teeth decide he would make a great dinner.

With each step forward the forest became much denser and it was becoming an effort to push his way forward, so it was with some relief that he brushed branches aside and found himself in a small clearing. For a few minutes at least, the going would be easier.

As he crossed into the clearing he stopped for a moment and took a swig of the suspect water from the Perrier bottle. The liquid was hot and metallic tasting but it did refresh, slightly. He stuffed the bottle back in his pocket and started across the open area.

He was half way across when he felt his legs yanked out from under him and his body jerked into the air. His head felt like a basketball as he bounced up and down at the end of a vine noose wrapped around his left foot. He became slightly dizzy as the ground came forward and then slipped back with each bounce. He could feel an up chuck coming on, which was rather a relief from having to squat. Slowly the oscillations settled down and he found himself hanging upside down from a rather large tree. The chuck syndrome went away.

The bag and gun dropped to the ground with a thump, one of the Perrier bottles slipping from his pocket and hit the ground breaking with a clatter. "Well, drat," he muttered with his head hanging two feet from the ground.

Twisting he tried to pull himself up so that he could reach his foot, but succeeded only in making the vine bounce around more. He felt the last of the cookies trying to get back out so he quit struggling. As the bouncing again subsided he heard a rustle in the bushes and looked over to see two very small men come into the clearing.

The men were a deep brown color wearing fur covered loincloths and carrying spears. Their faces were heavily wrinkled with light tan streaks down the cheeks. The odd thing was that they both appeared to be less than three feet tall, but that was hard to tell from the inverted position.

The two pygmies stopped and stared upward at Ames. One of them ground his spear and leaned on it and began haranguing his partner in grunting sounds. The other one glanced from Ames to his buddy and back again. With a shrug he dropped his spear and bent over. The first native put his spear on the ground and climbed onto the other ones shoulders. With a heave the second one lifted himself to his feet with the first one balanced on his shoulders. While the second one held his feet, the first one stood up creating a single person almost six feet tall.

With hesitant steps the bottom man shuffled toward the tree and the rope that Ames could now see wrapped around the trunk. As the native shuffled forward the native on top waved his arms to keep his balance – and failed. As they neared the tree, the man on top lost the battle and pitched forward smacking his head against the bark. He dropped to the ground and rolled, flipping the legs out from under the bottom man. Both ended up in a heap.

They both sat up and started jabbering at each other. Finally one of them stood up, grabbed a spear and started hopping up and down while swiping at the rope with the blade of the spear held above him. Ames could feel a headache coming on as the kangaroo with a spear kept hopping up and down and missing. Seeing all this activity with inverted eyeballs was somewhat disconcerting.

The other guy watched his pal for a couple of minutes then blew air in disgust. He turned around and looked at Ames and then up at the rope. Pulling a knife from his belt he ran at Ames. Blond started to scream as the little man jumped into the air and grabbed onto his legs, one foot landing on his chin, the other in an armpit. Holding the knife in his teeth the pint sized dwarf started climbing up Ames.

Ames tried to look up to see what was going on and had the misfortune to note that the native wore nothing under the loincloth. There must have also been a lack of toilet paper in this mini-jungle. With a disgusted sound he dropped his head back down and stared at the bouncing brown man.

The climber made steady progress upward by placing his foot into Ames' crotch and lifting himself up. This produced a groan from the agent, who started thrashing around to relieve the pressure. The climber ignored the movement and started sawing at the rope.

The climber parted the rope on Ames' foot just as the jumper finally found his mark. Both sections of the rope let go at the same time and Ames dropped to the ground with the climber still on him, and the foot still in his crotch. The 90-pound native fell with a thud and Blond yelled as the pain hit him. Trying to protect himself from further damage he curled into the fetal position with his hands gripping the area between his legs.

The climber ignored Ames' distress and pulled out a length of rawhide rope. Using it he flipped the agent onto his back and neatly hog-tied his arms. The jumper picked up the length of rope that had fallen out of the tree, formed a loop and pulled it over Blond's head. With a jerk he pulled it tight around Ames' neck.

The two stopped for a moment and surveyed their work while talking in their incomprehensible language. Satisfied, the jumper pulled on the rope and the climber poked Ames in the butt with the knife. Ames got the point and stood up, his body slightly bent from the injury to his privates. Jumper yanked on the rope and the trio marched across the clearing and down a well-hidden path, with Ames using an odd wide legged gait.

Half an hour later the three broke out of the forest into another clearing, this one occupied by about thirty individuals and a number of roughly made lean-tos. A small fire in the center sent dark smoke into the air as a seriously short and ugly woman pounded some kind of vegetation between two rocks. Another female, who could have almost been the first ones twin, was using a knife to skin a small animal. Most of the men seemed to be leaning against trees sleeping or talking quietly together. A number of children were playing some kind of game with sticks that involved a lot of chasing and slapping. All stopped what they were doing when Ames and his captors entered the clearing. Ames suddenly felt like the girl in the leotards and bunny ears who got the wrong word about the party at the dean's house.

Amid the stares of the company Ames was led across the clearing to an old man seated in front of one of the lean-tos. The old man could have been anywhere from twenty to ninety, his face almost lost in wrinkles. Close-cropped white hair ringed his head and ribs showed along his sides. If he had been a monkey he would have fit nicely into "The Lion King." He waved a hand as the trio stopped in front of him. While the three engaged in a long conversation that had a lot of pointing, poking and dancing around, Ames looked around.

The tribal area looked like it should have been the centerpiece for a National Geographic Magazine. Truly something out of the Stoneage. All of the people wore rough leather loincloths, except for the children who wore nothing at all. The lean-tos could barely be classified as shelter. They were made of two or three stripped branches pulled together with leafy branches tossed over them. A good wind would probably knock them over.

The people ranged from a baby who slept in a leather basket hanging from a tree, to the old man, with other ages mixed in. Most appeared healthy if somewhat skinny. As he watched one of the women finished smacking the plant with rocks and added the resultant fibers to a rock bowl sitting next to the fire. Craning his neck the agent could see water boiling in the bowl along with green and brown strands of something. He hoped it wasn't lunch.

His attention turned back to the threesome when jumper yanked on the rope. Ames looked down into the brown eyes of the old man.

"Vas ya doing in unser wald?"

For a moment Ames stared in incomprehension. The old man spoke the words again and the agent realized that what he was hearing was some kind of weird Afrikaans, a mixture of Dutch, English and Bantu.

He tried German, which was the closest language he knew. "Ich bin hier durch unfall. Ich versuche, an Beira zu gelangen." It was now the old man's turn to look uncomprehendingly.

"Well, phooey," muttered Ames. "This isn't going to work."

"Shet ma," said the old guy. "Why you no use Angliz first?"

"You speak English?" Ames asked with a startled expression.

"Corse I do. I work de house in Praetoria I yung. Me go der get job, earn rand. Goot peple, traet oaky. Speak Angliz." Ames could barely make out the words within the accent.

"Thank God! Look I'm an American and I need to get to Beira. Can you help me?"

"Shew go Beira? Shew mercan? We maybe help. Why we help? What want Beira?" The man wrinkled his nose. "Why shew stink?"

"I've got a case of dysentery. I need to get back to the United States. I'm an agent for the government and I need to get back home."

"Shew got sheets? Drink bad water? Okay, we maybe help you? How help?"

"Could you send someone to Beira or maybe to Maputo to the American consulate?"

"Why send person?"

"To get help, or maybe you could get one of your people to guide me there."

"Shew walk? Why walk? Long walk, take long time."

"I need to get home. Do you have a better idea?"

"Shur," said the old man with a grin pulling a plastic rectangle from the lean-to. "Use cell phone. Call shew people. De come get?"

Ames stared incredulously at the phone. "You have a cell phone?"

"Shur," muttered the old guy with indignation. "What shew tink? We savages?"

CHAPTER EIGHTEEN

Using the chief's cell phone Blonde placed a call to the DORK offices in Washington and explained his predicament. He could not pass on the information he had already collected because the chief started complaining about using up his minutes. With reluctance Ames told R where he was, or tried to.

"I'm in a pygmy village somewhere northwest of the Save' river, I'm not exactly sure where. I walked for a couple of days before getting here." At that moment the chief butt in.

"Why shew not gib him de GPS?"

"Say what?" said Ames looking at the head pygmy. "No, not you fuzzy. Hang on a sec."

"I say why shew not gib him de GPS?"

"You've got GPS?" asked the agent in astonishment.

"Shur, gib me da phone." Ames passed the cell to the chief and then was startled some more when the wrinkled fingers began dancing over the small keypad like a kid on an X-box playing Doom III. Within seconds the chief handed the phone back and said, "Der, gib him doz numbers."

Ames looked at the phone. "Ah, R, it looks like I'm at twenty one degrees fourteen minutes twenty seconds south by thirty six degrees forty two minutes twelve seconds east. At least that's what this guy's cell phone says. Hey, don't ask me why a pygmy has a cell phone, ask him. Hang on." He looked down at the pygmy. "He wants to know the number here so he can call me back with the pick-up information."

The chief looked up at Ames. "I not too sure bout dat. I gib him de number, he gib it to somebody else, pret soon I hab probem wid identity teft, my bank count get screwed up, I go broke, my wife leabs me, my dog bites me. No good idea to gib out de number."

"You can trust him," said Ames. "He works for a department of the United States Government, after all."

"Oh, shure," muttered the chief. "Like we all trust the goberment. Tell him shew call back in de morn."

Ames lifted the phone back up. "He said I have to call you back in the morning. No, he won't give out his number. Okay, I'll tell him that. See you later." Ames snapped the phone closed.

"He said to tell you he already has the number. While we were talking he got in touch with the National Security Agency and had them do a wiretap on the line. He has the phone number, your Swiss bank account, your three closest buddies in the Congolese army, the broad you shacked up with in Leopoldville, the names of your three illegitimate kids, how you cheated on the SAT test and he knows about the two missing spoons when you worked in Pretoria."

"Chit," muttered the chief. "I knew I choud no let some merican spy mess wid my phone." He shook his head and muttered under his breath. After a moment he looked back up at Ames. "Okay, but when chou see him chou tell him I want parations for special groups from Department Economic Development. We could use stereo, Play Station and ice cream maker. Oh and maybe DVD player wid copy 'Girls Gone Wild.'"

Ames shook his head. "Don't you need electricity for those things?' he looked around at the primeval gathering of naked people, stone bowls and rough lean-tos.

"No problem," grinned the chief. "Got 10KW backup generator from rooskies last year. Dey use us for spy on crazy white people dig'in holes down by de riber"

Ames' ears perked up. "What holes?"

"De dig big holes den fill wid concrete. Tink nobody see dem. De take in puters, Plasma TV and Lazy boy recliner. Say shoot anyone say anyting."

Ames thought hard. Apparently Silverpinky had her base of operations underground down by the river. That would explain why there did not seem to be anyone around or anywhere for people to stay. She could have a whole complex under there and nobody would know about it, except for the contractors, suppliers, workmen, building inspectors, the local electric company, the PTA, school board, CIA, Mossad, KGB, and the guy with the sandwich truck that came by at lunch every day. Heck of a good way to hide a secret operation. Nobody would suspect a secret base hidden underground in Africa.

At that moment one of the women called to the chief. "Goot time for dinner," said the old man. The chief slid under the lean-to and sat down gesturing for Ames to sit down as well.

Ames ducked down and started to slide under the leafy roof. His head brushed the support pole and, with a loud rustle, the whole thing collapsed burying Ames and the chief under a pile of branches. The chief cried out and a group of natives ran over to dig them out.

The chief surfaced, sputtering profanities in Bantu, then switched to English. "What heck matter wid chou? Chou too stupid to figure out dat chou too big to get in hut?" He brushed leaves out of his hair. "Now got to spend ten minutes and build new hut. Come on, we got ober der and eat. Get in line quick for all goot stuff gone. Be goot dinner, hunters did goot."

Ames sat down with the chief in front of another hut. An older woman with a serious sag to her chest, handed him a stone bowl. Inside was some kind of milky looking fluid with black blobs and brown looking noodles. There was no spoon.

He watched the chief to figure out how to eat it. The chief put two fingers together and made dipping gestures at the bowl, indicating that Ames should use his fingers like a spoon. He held the bowl up to his mouth and grinned at Ames.

With misgivings the agent lifted the bowl and sipped the contents. It tasted like used crap. He glanced out of the corner of his eye. The chief was smiling and moving his hands up and down inviting Ames to continue. With a lot of will-power the agent gulped down the rest of the broth.

He then used his fingers to scoop the long noodle things and the blobs into his mouth. The noodles were crunchy and tasteless, the blobs were gooey crunchy and tasted like chestnuts. After the crappy tasting broth the solids weren't actually that bad except for the small hair like things that kept getting stuck in his teeth.

When he swallowed the last bit he asked, "What was in that?" He poked at his teeth with a dirty fingernail.

"Dat be special food," said the chief. "We don get good stuff like dat ebery day. Dat twigs wid beedles"

"Beedle? What the heck is a beedle?"

"Chou know, black bug, walk on ground."

"You mean beetle?" asked Ames beginning to feel the soup in his throat. "I just ate bug soup?" The agent could feel small creepy things wandering around in his mid-section and trying to climb his throat.

The chief grinned. Suddenly a thought occurred to Ames. The things caught in his teeth were bug legs! Ames jumped up and ran into the woods, holding his hand over his mouth. He stopped and "ralphed" loudly. The soup tasted even worse the second time. Behind him he could hear the pygmy troop laughing.

When he got back to the lean-to the chief patted him on the kneecap. "Okay," he said. "Now dat chou got joke, how you like chou steak, wid or widout onions and mushrooms?"

* * * * * * * * *

General "Tenstars" Manystars stared at the odd looking individual standing in front of his desk. This person was short and thin with unkempt white hair, a stain spattered blue shirt with a once-was-white lab coat and rather thick glasses that made his face, when seen through the glasses edges, seem as though there were huge indentations on each side of his face.

"Who'd you say you were?" asked the General giving the individual another once over with his eyes.

"I'm R from down in ASSHOLS," the person said in a high somewhat squeaky voice. "I've worked here for twenty seven years you moron!"

"Hmmph," muttered N. "I don't get down there much. I understand it's dirty and slightly dangerous. What can I do for you?"

"I got a call from Ames. It seems he's stuck somewhere in Mozambique and needs a ride home."

"Mozambique? Isn't that in Arizona?"

"That's Albuquerque, and it's in New Mexico. Mozambique is in Africa. It's a country on the east coast near Madagascar."

"And?" said the General using his hands in a come-on motion.

"Here, let me make this easier for you," said R pulling a remote control from his pocket. He pressed a button and a panel opened in the wall. The General looked startled. "Whoa! Where'd that come from?"

R glanced at the remote. "From my pocket."

The General scowled. "No, I mean that moving panel!"

R looked at the panel and then at N. "It shows up when I push this button." He held up the remote and indicated a blue button.

The General grabbed the remote and pressed the button. The panel closed. "Hey, that's really neat! How come I wasn't told about this before? I've been here six years and I've never seen this before!" He pressed the button again and the wall slid back open.

R grabbed the remote back. "Because they thought you might break it." He pressed another button and a huge screen lit up showing a map of the world. "I'm only showing it to you now so you can see what's going on." Another button and a number of red and yellow lights lit up on the map.

"The red buttons indicate the agents you have in the field right now. Ignore the yellow lights." R seemed to be pressing buttons trying to get the screen to do something.

"So what are the yellow lights, now that you've brought it up?" asked the General.

R quit pushing buttons and his shoulders drooped. "Those are sightings for Elvis. You weren't supposed to know about that project." There were a lot of yellow lights.

"What the heck are we tracking Elvis sightings for? The man died years ago and I doubt that his corpse is wandering around the country."

"Actually Elvis is alive and well and living with a family in Des Moines. He got fed up with the drugs and long hours that come with being the King. Now he works in a McDonald's on Army Post Road. He's the mayonnaise spreader and does some minor work for us from time to time."

"So what the heck are the sightings about?"

"We track the sightings to make sure no one is getting close. MIB wants to make sure the Cloetheans don't get too close to Arnold Shmetzer."

"Who's Arnold Shmetzer?" asked the General with a puzzled expression.

"That's Elvis' name now."

Tenstars stared at the screen for a moment and then shook his head while looking at R. "So where's Ames?"

R used the remote and the map twisted and revolved until a single red light shown on an enlarged map of the coast of Africa. He pressed another button and map resolved again to a satellite image of jungle trees. Another button and the greenery gave way to a weird image of reds, blues, yellows and greens. The red and yellows moved around.

"This is a thermo graphic image of Mozambique. If you look close you can tell that the red and yellow images are people. The big one is Ames and the small ones appear to be pygmies. What pygmies are doing in Mozambique is beyond me, but Ames seems to have found them."

"What do missing oil tankers have to do with pygmies? I thought we were tracking Silverpinky as the possible thief?"

"Darned if I know," muttered R. "This is Ames we're talking about. He called on a cell phone and asked to get picked up."

"Where'd he get the cell phone in the middle of the jungle?" He waved his hand in the air. "Never mind. Get a chopper out there to get him and get him back here so I can find out what's going on."

R nodded and pushed a remote button. The images disappeared and the wall closed. The General watched as R walked out of the office. He then grabbed the phone and punched some buttons.

"Miss Pinchpenny. I want you to find out all about my office and what gadgets are in here that I don't know about. What do you mean I don't have the need to know? It's my office! Crap!" He slammed the phone down and stood up.

Walking over to the wall he tried prying the panel open with his fingers. When that didn't work he walked along all four walls rapping them with his knuckles. On the wall opposite the map a door suddenly slid open. Startled the General backed up two steps. He craned his neck and peered at the opening.

Moving forward he peeked through the door and around the corner. There was a corridor going left running parallel to the wall. Tentatively N stepped through and slowly advanced along the hall. Behind him the door slid shut. Worried the General backtracked and tried to open the door. It had effectively disappeared.

With a shrug he turned back and followed the hall to the end where it curved left around his office. There was another left and then a right. Stoically he followed the secret passageway.

Down in Dirty Tricks R sat in a chair munching a donut and sipping coffee while he watched in a monitor as the General poked at the walls. The elderly inventory snorted and giggled at the senior officer. When that august officer stumbled into the wall passage, R laughed out loud, spraying coffee onto the table in front of him. Giggling he wiped at his chin.

R moved a mouse in front of the screen and a wall in the hallway closed and another on the other side opened. General Tenstars wandered down the new corridor as R pressed another button and changed the walls again.

He giggled again as he thought of how many hours he could keep the tubby head honcho wandering around. Then he had a thought.

Reaching to his right he picked up a phone and dialed a number. "This is R. Shmetzer is blown. Move him to the secondary location in San Francisco. No, I don't care if he does have a problem with the new personae we're giving him, he'll just have to bend over and take it."

CHAPTER NINETEEN

Ames had a terrible night. It seems the pygmies slept inside the rude lean-tos with brush as blankets. The agent was too tall to fit inside and his attempts to create his own lean-to had met with disaster. Never having been a Boy Scout the concept of knots and crude construction completely eluded him, so he ended up trying to sleep in the open with a pile of leaves and branches over him.

The leaves smelled like used toilet paper and the jungle night was anything but quiet. Apparently everything in the forest slept during the day and came out at night to feed. There were growls and whimpers, flapping wings, rustling branches, and strange and scary cries. There was more noise than a Grateful Dead concert.

Then the cold started setting in. While Mozambique is listed as a tropical to subtropical country where the heat is sufficient to make the sale of saunas difficult, the place does get cold. Well, not like icicles or frozen creeks or anything, but cold. Okay, not cold, but chilly. Okay, not chilly. Well, drat. It was darn hot, there was little in the way of a breeze and the place had a serious odor problems. To make matters worse, every time Ames would start to doze off, something with multiple legs would crawl on some part of his body.

It was a long night.

Somewhere along the line the agent must have fallen into an exhausted sleep. He opened bleary eyes to hazy light filtering through the trees and the smell of wood smoke from a pile of withered branches being tended by the old woman with the saggy chest. He lifted a hand to brush at his face, only to stop and look into the huge multi-faceted eyes of this thing on his hand. Beyond the eyes was a body with a vague likeness to a B-1 bomber and almost as large, colored a muted brown and gray. Huge swept back wings extended behind the eyes and long antennae hung down from a bulbous head. Multi-jointed, fur-covered legs dug into the skin on the back of his hand.

It took a moment for recognition to set in. Then the intrepid agent screamed! Yelling at the top of his lungs he jumped to his feet and started waving his hand in the air, trying to dislodge the B-1 mockup. The insect retaliated by digging its feet in and spreading its wings. The agent's screams became accompanied by a loud whirring noise.

His histrionics woke up the rest of the pygmy tribe who all stared at Ames for a moment trying to figure out what he was doing. The chief settled the matter by having everyone sit down facing the bouncing agent and begin clapping in time to his stomping feet. Soon the clearing was filled with the sound of clap, clap, stomp, ah-ah, whir, clap, clap, stomp, ah-ah, whir. The old lady at the fire began filling bowls with some crunchy substance and passing them out to the clappers, who took a moment from clapping to shovel some of the whatever into their mouths before resuming the cadence.

Everyone was enjoying themselves immensely, except Ames of course, but all things must end. With a final whir the B-1 bug let go and took off into the jungle after a final dive at Ames' head. The agent shrieked once more as the bug sailed by and he fell onto the ground. The crowd let out a tremendous yell and began to clap furiously, some calling for encores. A few stood in tribute to the performance.

The chief stood up and walked over to the cringing agent. Nudging Ames with his toe, the chief said, "Dat pretty goot. Only we uchually do dat sort of ting at night. But bre'fast p'formance okay too."

Ames looked up at the diminutive native. "What the hell was that thing?" He rolled over and stood up, examining his hand as he did so.

"Dat bomber bug," said the chief, peering into the forest. "Chew shood hab kept him. Goot luck for chew. Also make goot breakfast. Better dan grits wid budder."

Ames gagged at the thought of eating the humongous insect.

Other members of the tribe were coming up to Ames and patting him on the back while grinning, when a tremendous roar split the air and the wind started whipping leaves and branches around the clearing. Two smaller pygmies were lifted bodily into the air, spun around twice and disappeared into the jungle.

A heavy yellow object with three arms, looking like a surrealistic daisy, dropped through the trees and landed at the chief's feet with a thump. A silver cable extended upward through the foliage. Ames looked upward at the cable and back down at the daisy.

"Looks like my rides here," he said to the chief. He extended his hand. "Thanks for your help."

The chief shook the agent's hand. "No prob'em. Just don forget foreign aide."

Ames climbed aboard the daisy, straddling one of the petals and hugging the central core. The daisy, with the somewhat erotic name of rescue penetrator, bounced up and down four or five times, skittered across the clearing and chased several pygmies into the surrounding forest, before making one final bounce into the community fire and leaping into the air. Ames waved desperately at his flaming shoe while holding on with one hand as the daisy rose rapidly into the air. The agent was forced to forget the shoe as it became necessary to dodge leaves and branches.

At one point one of the penetrator's arms caught a large branch and the whole affair tipped dangerously, threatening to dump Ames back down into the jungle, now some fifty feet below. With a crack the branch broke free and the daisy, with Ames, bounced upward like an up-side-down bungee jumper, dragging the loose branch with it.

With a final yank the penetrator broke free of the trees and hopped upward into bright sunlight. The entire contraption; penetrator, Ames and the branch bounced up and down like a moron on the end of a bungee cord dropped from the Tacoma Narrows Bridge. Ames could feel his stomach doing flip-flops. The only thing preventing a return of Ralph was that the stomach was empty. He did, however, have the resources for a few briips. The agent was enormously grateful when the undulations slowed.

Looking up Ames could see the belly of a helicopter swinging slightly back and forth. The thing had a fat rounded nose with two large tires hanging from struts on each side of the fuselage. Idly his mind cataloged it as a Sikorsky H-19, the fat old monster made famous by the TV show "Magnum PI" and the not so famous Korean War. This one did not have teeth painted on its nose. This one was lucky it had any paint at all. Streaks of red and brown rust created splotches of color on the supposedly olive drab color scheme. A black circle with a red triangle designated the old chopper as a member of the Mozambique Air Farce.

The cable wound upward dragging the penetrator, Ames and the branch closer to the helicopter. The agent kicked out with his foot trying to dislodge the branch, but all that did was cause the branch to slew around and poke at him with the broken end.

He started to spin, causing the world below to become a blur of greens and browns. He looked up and the world was a blur of blues and whites. He closed his eyes and the world was a blur of blacks and grays. He stifled an upchuck that tasted like green and yellow.

There was a "Thunk" as the branch hit the belly of the helicopter and Ames opened his eyes. A dark skinned crewman in tan shorts, tan shirt and black boondockers was guiding the penetrator cable onto the spool of a powered winch. As the rescue mechanism rose along the side of the chopper the branch scrapped against the aluminum side and forced the device out away from the door. The crewman kicked at the branch and almost fell out, his hands scrabbling at the doorframe and pulling himself back in.

In control again, he stopped the winch and backed it up, causing the penetrator with Ames and branch to lower. Once clear of the fuselage he used his hand and tried to spin the cable so the branch was away from the door. When he started the winch upward again, the cable rotated back and the branch caught again. This went on four or five times until the crewman yelped in disgust.

A second native airman came to the door and looked out. There was an animated discussion for about two minutes while Ames hung from the cable. The second crewman left and the engines of the helicopter whined louder. Ames watched as the terrain began to slip past and he realized that the pilot was heading for wherever home was, with him dangling from the winch.

The crewman disappeared inside somewhere and Ames could feel the wind whipping at him as the chopper increased its speed. The penetrator, Ames and the cable oscillated in the manmade wind, while the branch attempted to poke holes through him. The agent was forced to ignore the ground below as he warded off the malicious wood demon.

The flight lasted around thirty minutes, but felt like a short lifetime. The cable swayed back and forth alternating smacking Ames and the branch into the belly of the chopper and then dangling him out in the wind. At no time did Ames see the crewman look out to check on the agent's well being, but then, he did not see much of anything except branch, metal side and air. Blond just hung on and prayed for a rapid death.

At long last the helicopter slowed and started hovering. Ames looked down at a broad expanse of concrete that he assumed was a runway. Looking up he saw the crewman was again standing in the doorway. The chopper started to descend and the crewman turned the knob on the winch. The cable began to play out. Ames looked down and watched as the ground rushed up at him. As it grew close he flinched, waiting for the inevitable impact. Just as his feet touched ground the chopper came to a stop and the branch fell off the penetrator.

Ames quickly stepped away from the rescue device on rubbery legs, tripped on the branch and fell face down into the branches. Even in death the wood demon demanded a sacrifice. With a wash of air the helicopter rose upward and headed down the runway. Ames stood up and untangled himself from the branch. He kicked at the offending branch. It grabbed him and pulled him down again, bumping his nose on the concrete.

At that moment there was a screech of brakes and the agent rolled over to see a Land Rover, with two men in it, grind to a halt. As the vehicle stopped one of the men stepped out and walked up to Ames and peered down at him.

"I say," said the man in a distinct British accent, "Would you happen to be the American that everyone seems to be worried about?"

"I don't know," responded Ames, pulling himself to his feet. "My name is Blond, Ames Blond." He wiped a hand across his nose and inspected the result. No blood.

"Oh, you're one of ours. Sorry, I'm supposed to meet an American out here." He started to turn away.

"No, I'm an American," said Ames. "You're thinking of that other guy."

"You're not MI-6? Or is it MI-4? Never could keep them straight. One involves intelligence and the other is a Russian helicopter." The Englishman looked a bit puzzled. "So you're an American. I always thought you worked for the crown, Royal Navy or some such thing."

"Nope, I work for DORK out of Washington."

"Oh, so you're a dork? I'd rather think they'd keep you out of the field. Hide you in a back closet or some such. Keep you out of trouble, what?"

Ames' face grew dark. "I'm not a dork, I work for DORK, the Department of Reconnaissance and Knowledge. I'm a field agent and I've just been rescued from a pygmy tribe in the jungles. I don't need bull puppies from some Limey. I need to get to a phone and report a black submarine in the river here."

"Well that rather proves you're a dork, eh what? Mozambique has no pygmies, nor does it have any jungles. And black submarines? Is that rather like those black helicopters you Yanks are always on about?"

It took some restraint but Ames did not hit him.

CHAPTER TWENTY

The Englishman finally identified himself as Colonel Herbert Tarryton Smyth Billingsford the Fourth DCM, MDC, PDQ, etc. of her majesties Special Air Service on loan to Mozambique to assist the besieged government in repelling the Marxist, communists, and politically correct rebels who wanted to take over the government. The primary question that Colonel Billingsford seemed to be concerned with was – why? Why would anyone bother to want to take over Mozambique? It had no resources, few roads, bad ports and no economy. The only thing it did have was way too many monkeys. They just ran around causing hate and discontent, dropping foul smelling feces and destroying non-existent crops.

Sometimes Billingsford wondered why the country didn't export the little buggers. There must be a huge market for monkey meat, monkey furs, monkey paws, money skulls, monkey eyes and monkey brains. They also made nice pets if you didn't mind battered furniture, squashed banana all over the place and mounds of monkey turds decorating your home.

Colonel Billingsford had an office in an old building at the Beira airport. From there he supervised the training of the Mozambique military in counter insurgent operations, which mostly consisted of trying to get more than twenty soldiers together at one time. While Colonel Billingsford had had dealings with soldier problems such as drinking and drug abuse, Mozambique had a rather odd problem.

This problem was that the soldiers were too busy meditating. The government's solution to internal strife was to have the military meditate twice daily. Oddly enough, it worked. Crime and violence decreased drastically and the economy improved. The trick now was to get the monkeys to meditate so they would stop eating crops and throwing monkey crap at people.

For a time Billingsford had considered enlisting monkeys to form the anti-insurgent forces, but the monkeys were pretty much insurgents themselves. And like the natives, they had problems with uniforms and standing in formation. Billingsford spent a lot of time cussing.

Ames climbed into the Land Rover with the Colonel and the Sergeant who was driving. The Sergeant was wearing a tan colored bush jacket with tan shorts. He had one of those funny looking Australian bush hats, with the brim turned up on one side, on his head. The NCO spent a lot of time muttering to himself, with the word "sodding" arising frequently.

The Colonel glanced at the Sergeant as Ames climbed into the vehicle. "Well, Sergeant, let's be off. To quarters please. I imagine Mister Blond would like a shower and a change of clothes. Those things he's wearing look a bit the worse for wear."

Ames nodded at the Brit and looked down at himself. He was still wearing the blue jumpsuit that he had gotten on Silverpinky's sub. The color was slightly faded, there were holes here and there and the thing had a definite aroma to it. His shoes were turning green from fungus and the stitching was coming loose. His crotch was sore from the odd shape of the coveralls and the foot from the pygmy. He needed a shave, a haircut and a bath badly. He examined his hands and decided a manicure would also be in order.

The Sergeant glanced at Ames, wrinkled his nose and started the Rover. They shortly began passing the pride of the Mozambique Air Farce. The predominance were aircraft of Russian manufacture – Mig-21's, Mig-23's, a few Mig-29's and a smattering of American things. A Piper Cherokee and a Cessna 180 sat on the tarmac looking out of place among the war birds. Unfortunately they, like most of the other planes were in need of some serious maintenance.

Flat tires abounded, missing nose cones with dangling wires, even a few missing wings. Cracked windscreens, assorted rust patches, duck taped panel opening and missing engines completed the picture. With some serious cannibalization a couple of the planes might actually be made to fly, if you could find someone insane enough to try.

They drove past a formation of what were probably mechanics and pilots. The whole group was sitting in a row of lines facing a defunct Mig-21, with one leg crossed over the other, hands on knees and backs straight. A soft "ommm" sound came from the group. Billingsford snorted as they passed. "That's why the bloody beggars can't get anything done. They spend four hours twice a day ooming and ahming. I think they only come up for air to eat and relieve their bowels and I'm not too sure about the bowel thing. Sodding retards." The Sergeant nodded his head in agreement, adding a few soddings of his own.

After crossing the runway the Land Rover pulled to a stop in front of a white clapboard building that was in much better repair than the airplanes and definitely better than those around it. A red sign with white lettering sited on poles in front of the building proclaimed that it was the home of the Forward Detachment of Her Majesties

Number 12 Company of the Special Air Service, Colonel H. T. Smyth-Billingsford IV Commanding. Three rubber ducks and a dead goose adorned the four corners of the sign or that's what they looked like to Ames.

The trio marched into the building with Colonel Billingsford in the lead. Inside a young Corporal with those funny looking up-side-down stripes was peering distrustfully at a computer keyboard. He glanced up as the group entered the room, spotted the Colonel and jumped to his feet, slammed his ankles together and saluted by smacking himself in the forehead with the back of his hand. He yelled, "Suh" very loudly.

It would have been perfect except for the combat suspension system, a.k.a. suspenders that he was wearing. The edge of his bayonet (knife, stabbing instrument, whatever) caught the keyboard and flipped it into the air as he stood up. The keyboard came back down and banged into a coffee cup emblazoned with an angry brown boar inside a red circle. The boar appeared to have a fork stuck in its behind, or maybe it was a pitchfork. This seemed to make the boar either very angry or in great pain. Its face was thrust forward with its mouth open with tusks thrust upward. The tongue or its necktie hung out. Above the circle red lettering stated that the cup was the property of Number 12 Company, SAS. Below it listed "Saul's fine coffees and cups."

The cup fell over producing a minor brown deluge that poured over the edge of the desk and onto, and into, a computer tower set on the floor beside the desk. The electronics inside the tower reacted rather badly to the coffee and blue and white sparks began to issue from the cream colored cuboid. Bluish colored smoke started rising into the air.

The monitor on the desk began flashing on and off, altering from a black screen to a white one with random images of the queen and various porno sites. With a loud "Bang", the computer quit and the lights in the building went out.

The Corporal was torn between military discipline and anger at his error. The error won out and he compromised by kicking at the tower while maintaining the salute. The computer issued a final, "Bzzzt" and went still.

In typical English stoicism Colonel Billingsford returned the salute and said, "I say Corporal, your computer seems to have had a bit of a meltdown. Do unplug it and see to the lights won't you. There's a good lad." Leaving the Sergeant with the Corporal, the Colonel led Ames down a hall and into a darkened room.

Back in the orderly room the Corporal started to relax until the Sergeant smacked him in the ear. In the darkened office Billingsford moved unerringly to the chair behind his desk and sat down. Ames unerringly banged his shin, first on a chair and then on the edge of a small table. He groped with his hand, found the Colonel's butt, backed off and knocked the lamp off the desk and slapped Billingsford in the forehead before backing up further and falling into the chair. At that moment the lights came back on.

The Colonel glanced at Ames and down at the broken lamp then back at Ames. He blinked his eyes and said, "Right. It seems you would like a ride home to the states. However there might be some delay. The weekly flight to Pretoria has devolved into a whenever it arrives situation. It could be tomorrow or possibly not until next week. The other alternative is to have one of our chaps fly you down there in one of the country's military aircraft."

He picked up the lamp and returned it to the desk. The shade was bent and mashed in on one side. He tried puffing it back out and the whole assembly fell on the floor again. He used his foot to slide it under the desk.

Looking back at Ames as though the lamp never existed he continued, "That also presents some small problems. We would have to get permission from South Africa to fly into their country with a military airplane. That should not be too much trouble. The second problem might be a little harder, that of getting a pilot to fly the airplane. You would have to drag one of them away from their ooming sessions long enough to do something more useful than shoving curried chicken into their mouths."

"So how long would it take to set up the military thing?" asked Ames. "I really need to get back to Washington and take care of this Silverpinky thing."

"We may be able to get something going by tomorrow or possibly the day after, if the natives cooperate a bit. In the meantime, if I might suggest that you clean up." The SAS commander wiggled his nose in Ames' direction. "You seem to have developed a bit of an aroma."

Ames sniffed at his own armpit and gagged. "Yeah, I could use a shower. I'm also hungry as the dickens. All I've had to eat the past few days are some sticks and bugs before finishing off a nicely done steak and fries. And that was sticks without Grey Poupon."

The Colonel raised his eyebrows. "Without Gray? I say, that was roughing it a bit. Let me get my Sergeant to take you over to the barracks and you take a good wash down. He can scrounge you up some clothing to replace those things you're wearing. Then a bit of food, I think. They make some rather good meals here, if a bit spicy."

"That's okay," said Ames as he stood. "I don't mind a little spice now and then."

The Colonel gave Ames a strange look and called for the Sergeant. "Sergeant Jenkins, would you take Mister Blond over to the barracks and get him a shower and some clean clothing?"

"Suh," cried the Sergeant slamming his feet together and smacking himself in the forehead. "If you'll come with me, suh."

Ames shook the Colonel's hand and followed Jenkins out of the building. Ames looked at the Sergeant. "So you're a Jenkins?" The Sergeant nodded. "Would you happen to have any relatives in the American Marines?"

The Sergeant gave the agent an odd look. "Never mind," said Ames. "Just a thought."

CHAPTER TWENTY ONE

The shower felt great. When he finally felt clean he shut off the water and he dried himself with a thick terry towel. He found an olive drab jumpsuit waiting for him on a bench just outside the shower stall. He held it up and noted that it was one of those worn by the British army, but without the unit patches and rank stripes. He slipped it on and pulled on the green socks and brown brogans that Jenkins had left for him. There was no funny hat.

The jumpsuit fit fine, but the shoes were just a tad too big. Ames slipped them off again and stuffed some toilet paper in the toes to make up the difference. Satisfied with his dress he headed out of the barracks and back across the road to the headquarters building. As he walked he noted that the locals had completed their meditation and were now lined up in front of a building to the left of the HQ area.

As he started into the building a Sergeant he had not met grabbed him by the arm and dragged him outside and back toward the barracks, all the while screaming something about sweeping, mopping and soddings. Thrusting a broom into Ames' hands the Sergeant yelled, "What the sodden rat turd kind of a sodden soldier do you think you are? You'll get your sodden arse to sweeping the sodding mess in here before you go sitting on yer sodding duff over at the sodding headquarters. You get this sodding place tidy or I'll have you up on sodding charges. Do you understand me, you sodden witless excuse for a sodding soldier?"

Totally at sea, Ames grabbed the broom and started pushing it across the floor. He looked back at the Sergeant and said, "Look Sarge, I'm not . . . ."

"Sarge? Do I look like a sodden Sarge you you motherless heathen! Oh my gawd, yer an American! There's only one thing lower than a sodding American and that's the shite on the bottom of my sodding shoe. Get yer sodden arse to sweeping and don't you come out until these sodding floors shine like the bottom of my aunt Sally's sodding fanny! How the sodding devil did a sodding Yank get into her majesties sodden army I'll never know!"

The Sergeant stomped out banging the door shut behind him. Ames stood with the broom in his hands, a stunned expression like a deer in a set of headlights on his face. After a moment he shook his head and went back to pushing the broom slowly to and fro, creating a small pile of dust.

The agent worked steadily for about fifteen minutes when Sergeant Jenkins stuck his head in the door. His eyes went up in surprise at the broom. "Here, Mister Blond, what are you sweeping the floor for? We have privates and the odd native for that sort of thing. That's not to say the natives are odd, just that we have a few hanging about, when they're not oohming and aahming that is."

Ames leaned on the broom. "Well, there was this rather large nasty Sergeant who grabbed me and put me to work in here. I think he thought I was that private you mentioned. "

"Why didn't you tell him who you were?"

"Hey, he called me sodden so many times I was afraid to talk back to him. I think if he had soddened me one more time I would have enlisted just to shut him up."

Jenkins laughed. "That would be Sergeant Perkins. He thinks of himself as a Sergeant Major wan'na be. He tends to terrorize the lower ranks until someone puts him in his place. Here, toss that broom down and let's get you something to eat."

The agent set the broom against the wall and followed Jenkins out of the building. The line in front of the other building had disappeared, but that's the direction the Sergeant led Ames. Pushing open a door, Ames found himself in a rather well appointed dining facility.

There were tables with four chairs each scattered around, each table having a bright red and white checked table cloth. A chrome mess line traversed the center of the room with servers behind glass and chrome windows dipped various foods from chrome pans. Off to one side a bright red and silver counter with red and chrome stools offered a variety of colas, sodas, sundaes and malts. A Coca Cola clock brightened the wall behind the counter. In a corner a Wurlitzer jukebox flashed bright red, blue and gold lights while the soft tones of Mel Torme throbbed through the room.

Jenkins led him through a serving line where the Mozambicans behind the counter filled his plate with food that had a rather wonderful aroma. Jenkins explained the items as they arrived on the tray.

"That's Frango a Cafrial," said the Sergeant. "That's chicken the African way. Oh, and that's corn porridge. They do a lot of that here. It's rather good. Here, take a bowl of this. It's Matata, a kind of clam and peanut stew."

They left the serving line and took seats at a table. A white clad waiter placed a glass in front of each of them and filled them from a carafe. At that moment Sergeant Perkins appeared at Ames' side.

"What the sodden hell are you doing sitting in the sodding Sergeant's mess," yelled the overbearing NCO. "And what the sodden devil are you doing in here when I told you to sweep the sodden billet? Are you sodden deaf or just sodden daft?" The Sergeant grabbed Ames' arm.

Jenkins stood up and pushed at Perkins. "Perkins, leave the man alone. He's not who you think he is."

Ames stood up and pulled Perkins' hand off his arm. "Sergeant I'm not a soldier, I'm Ames Blond."

Perkins stepped back and gave Ames a wilting look. "Right you sodding bugger, and I'm sodding Benny Hill. I suppose you're with sodding MI-6 as well? Should I salute your sodden commander's arse?"

"No, no," explained Blond. "I'm not him. My name is Blond, Ames Blond. I'm an American and I work for DORK out of Washington."

"Well there you've got it sodding right. Most of them sodding Yanks are dorks."

"Hey, wait a minute," replied Ames with some heat. "I didn't say anything bad about you sodding Limeys."

"Sodding Limeys is it," answered Perkins stepping forward and pulling his fist back. "I'll . . ."

At that moment Jenkins pushed in between the two. "Perkins, I'm senior to you and I'm telling you to get back to your duties before I place you on charges."

Perkins glared at Jenkins for a moment, gave Ames a rather nasty smile and stomped off to sodden a couple of Privates cleaning their trays at the scullery. Ames' privates shivered and said a prayer for the Privates. "Don't mind him," said Jenkins. "His mum was frightened by an American army mule in the war and he dropped out two months ahead of time and landed on his head. Finish up and we'll head over to headquarters. I believe Corporal Carp has a flight lined up for you."

Three and a quarter hours later, after Ames had slaughtered three more helpings of Frango a Cafrial, two bowls of matata, six Dixie cups of ice cream and a partridge from a pear tree, the Sergeant and agent arrived back at the headquarters office.

The Corporal looked up as they entered. Ames smile ad and asked, "I understand you have a flight for me out of here?"

The Corporal gave Ames a withered look. "I did have. You were supposed to fly out an hour and a half ago on Linhas Aeroas de Mocambique. You weren't here so I had to start all over again. Unfortunately the LAM flight has already gone and there won't be another for a few days. I'll have to see what else I can arrange."

Ames grimaced. "Well I suppose I should sit here and wait while you make those arrangements." He started to sit down in a wooden chair next to the Corporal's desk.

Jenkins grabbed his arm and stopped him. "It's almost time for diner. Why don't we go back over to the mess and the Corporal can come and get you when he has things arranged?'

"Sounds like a winner," said Ames. Then he had a thought. "Will Perkins be there?"

"Not until later. I sent him over to join the Mozambicans. I'm rather sure he needs to do some oohming and aahming for a bit."

CHAPTER TWENTY TWO

After finishing diner, and about two gallons of water, Jenkins took Blonde back to the headquarters building again. Planting the agent in the wooden chair with a copy of the local shopper magazine the Sergeant went off to talk to the Colonel about the flight to Maputo for the man from DORK.

Ames was trying to decide between a 52 Fiat and a 77 Citroen when Jenkins came back.

"Good news," beamed the Sergeant. "Your embassy has authorized you up to five thousand three hundred and ninety two meticais to get to Maputo." He held an envelope up for Blonde to take.

Ames looked suspiciously at the envelope. "What the heck is a meticais? Sounds like a bad colon problem."

Jenkins chuckled. "The meticais is the local unit of currency. It's worth about twenty-five to a US dollar. So you get about two hundred and twelve dollars. But, hey, you're lucky. They revalued their meticais last year at a thousand to one. You could be wandering around with five million meticais."

Ames took the envelope and peeked inside. There was a small stack of multi-colored currency. The largest was a 500 meticais note that was a solid orange with the black silhouette of a train in one corner and a house in the opposite corner.

Ames stuffed the envelope into his pocket as he stood up. "So where to now?"

"I'm going to give you a ride out to the airport where you can pick up your flight to Maputo. Your ticket has already been paid for by the embassy so you can use that money to buy some clothes. Sorry, but you'll have to give back the jumpsuit. The Queen gets annoyed when people run off with her stuff."

"This is the Queens jumpsuit?" asked Ames while tugging at the sleeve. "I thought she wore ermine and silk and stuff? I don't remember her wearing a green jumpsuit in any of her pictures. I seem to remember she was partial to those flat round hats."

Sergeant Jenkins just stared at Blonde with his mouth slightly open, then shook his head and grabbed the agent by the arm. He dragged Ames out of the building while muttering about wanker yanks.

Jenkins stuffed Ames into the seat of a Range Rover and got behind the wheel. Ten minutes and forty wankers later they arrived at the terminal building for the Beira International Airport. Ames was pleased and relieved to see a number of large airlines with red tails and stylized "LAM" in blue and red on the side.

Pointing at the planes, Ames asked, "What's the LAM mean?"

"That's Mozambique Airlines that the Corporal mentioned. The LAM is Linhas Aeroas de Mocambique."

"Well, it's nice to know that there's a decent airlines here. How often do they fly to Maputo?"

"It's actually kind of hit or miss but the flight only takes about forty five minutes."

"Terrific," said Ames with enthusiasm. "You can just let me out at the terminal."

"Not on your life, Yank," muttered Jenkins. "I'll wait 'til you've got a change of clothes. The queen wants that jumpsuit back."

The concourse shops ran the gamut from coffee to Wranglers. Nothing else. Just coffee and Wranglers. Ames settled on a pair of wranglers, a purple shirt and green tennis shoes. That was all they had in his size that was available for 5,000 meticais. If he had had two thousand more he could have gotten a pair of socks, and a belt, but he did not so he settled for holding his pants up with his hand.

Jenkins stood outside the changing room until Ames handed out the jumpsuit. The agent sat down and tied his shoes, then stood and stepped through the curtain. "Well, now . . ," he started to say. The sergeant was gone.

"Well, bugger all," he muttered and walked out into the terminal concourse. Across the way was a brightly lit counter with the blue and red Linhas Aeroas de Mocambique displayed over it. Confidently he crossed over and joined the small line in front of the neatly dressed ticket agent.

After a few moments wait he arrived at the counter.

"Hi, I'm Ames Blond."

The pretty dark skinned ticket agent looked startled, and then smiled broadly. "Oh, my. I've seen all your movies! I didn't know you were a real person!"

"No, wait," responded Ames. "I'm Blond, Ames Blond. You're thinking of the other guy."

"Oh," she breathed as her face fell. "But you're not blond. You are a brunette. Shouldn't you be Ames Brunette?'

The agents face turned dark and he muttered several obscene words under his breath. "Maam, the name is Blond, Ames Blond, not Brunette." He scowled, "Listen just get my ticket would you please."

The girl turned to the computer and started typing. After a moment she looked back at Ames. "I don't find anything here for a Blond. Could it be in some other name or maybe a different spelling?"

"No," replied Ames in confusion. "The name should be Blond, B-L-O-N-D, like the hair color. The ticket was paid for by the US embassy in Maputo."

She turned back and typed some more. "I'm sorry sir, there is nothing for Blond and no one from the embassy has purchased a ticket in some time. Who told you the ticket was here?"

"Colonel Herbert Tarryton Smyth Billingsford the Fourth of the SAS here in Beira told me that the US embassy had bought me a ticket on Air Mozambique to Maputo."

She smiled. "Oh, I see the problem. I'm sorry sir, but this is Mozambique Airlines. We are the nation's premier international air carrier with service to Tanzania, South Africa and other countries. Air Mozambique is a small local airline with service to small towns here in Mozambique."

The agents face fell. "Where do I find this airline," he asked with some hesitation.

"You go down the concourse," she said while pointing to the left, "Until you get to a green door on the right. You go through there and down the hall to the stairs. Go down the stairs to the brown door…."

"Go through it and down the stairs to Air Mozambique," muttered Ames after interrupting her. "I think I've been here before."

"Oh so you know of them," said the girl.

"No, I don't know them specifically, but I do know there are other airlines with similar accommodations. I suspect the same investors own all of them."

Three minutes later he stepped off the last stair and walked into a dimly lit room with overhead pipes and heating ducts. Why heating ducts in a tropical nation? I have no idea.

On the left side were stacks of boxes, while on the right was a counter made of planks stretched across piled crates. Ames stepped up to the counter and looked for the attendant.

Behind the row of planks an enormous man sat in a broken easy chair watching a television that was perched precariously on his stomach. Ames groaned and shook his head.

The large man looked up at the groan and spotted Ames. He placed the TV on the floor and, with effort, stood up and leaned on the counter. "Hey der, watchoo do?"

With misgivings Ames said, "My name is Blond, Ames Blond and I believe you have a ticket here for me."

The man gave Ames a big grin. "Wow, chew are him? I hab seen all ob chore mobies, man"

"No, no. The name is Blond as in the hair color. That's the other guy you're thinking of."

The man's face fell. "Chew not him?"

"No, sorry."

"Chew not de guy wit de girls and de cars?"

"Nope."

"Well chit man, what choo want?"

"If this is Air Mozambique I think you have a ticket here for me."

"Nope, dis be da jan'tors office. Chew go down de end ob de counter. Dat be Air Mocambique."

Ames trudges to the other end of the plank counter. Chubby trailed along on the other side.

"Okay, I find chew tiket." The clerk started pawing through a stack of sticky notes. "Okay, chew say you name is Blond?"

"Yeah"

"Dis here says you got ticket to Maputo."

"That's right," said Ames.

"Okay, dat be two thousand meticais."

"Whoa," the agent exclaimed putting his hand in the air. "That ticket was paid by the US embassy. I don't owe anything."

"Nope," said the clerk. "Dis here is ticket reserbed by chew embassy. De din't pay not'in."

"What?" exclaimed Blond. "They had to pay for it. I don't have any money I spent it all on these clothes!"

Examining the purple shirt and green tennis shoes the fat agent said, "I like chew choice in clots but no money, no ticky."

"Wait a minute," said Ames in a rush. "Maybe we can work something out. How about a watch" He held out his wrist with the Timex that he had purchased aboard the *Exxon Valdez II*. The band was green with mold and condensation obscured part of the dial.

The big man scowled. "Dat watch not look real goot." He stepped back and looked under the counter. "But I chur like dem green sneakers. I gib you ticket for sneakers and dat watch."

Reluctantly Ames slipped off the shoes and passed them over. The concrete floor felt cold on his bare feet. "So now what am I supposed to do for shoes?"

The clerk shrugged, "Doan know, but if chew look aroun' chew see mos' people not wear choes anyway"

Ames took the ticket and started to turn around, then turned back. "Say, you don't happen to have relatives in Baghdad, do you?"

Fatty rubbed his three chins, "Not dat I know 'bout."

"And where do I get this airplane?" asked Blond.

The ticket agent pointed up and to the right, "Up der at de end ob de concourse at gate den."

"Where?" Ames asked.

"Gate den," said Chubs

"What the heck is a den? You got lions around here?"

"No, not lions. I said Den. Den. Chew know, de number."

"You mean ten? This wouldn't happen to be a bus stop, would it?" asked Ames suspiciously.

"No," replied the agent with a frown. "Why chew tink dat? Chew get de plane not de bus."

"Just checking," muttered Ames as he headed for the stairs.

* * * * * * * * *

General Tenstars Manystars banged open the door to Ms Pinchpenny's office startling the old bag, er, aged secretary into banging her hand against the window frame. As she was in the process of watering the many plants scattered around, this resulted in the water pitcher flying out of her hand and dumping in the middle of her desk creating an instant sea of water logged paper, floating pens and dripping erasers.

Blanching, the General started backing out the door pulling it closed as he went. Turning quick as a snake, Pinchpenny grabbed the door and snarled, "What do you want?"

Attempting to regain his composure, and the offensive, Tenstars asked, "Have you heard from Blond?"

"Yeah," grumbled Pinchpenny as she waded up soggy papers and tossed them into the trash. "Dippy showed up with the Special Air Service in Beira, Mozambique. The embassy in Maputo got him some clothes and reservations on a plane to the capital."

"Why'd he need clothes?" asked Tenstars as she swabbed up the water with a roll of paper towels.

"Because the twit didn't have any. Goofy's apparently running around Africa in the buff," she snapped.

"Wandering around Africa without any clothes on? Why didn't he have any clothes?"

She dropped the soggy paper towel roll into the trash on top of the wet papers and said, "Hey, this is Ames we're talking about here. Does that give you a clue?"

'Hmm," the General muttered. "Say, what were those papers you threw away?" he asked pointing at the trash.

"Those were your expense account," she replied with an evil smirk. "And I'm not doing them again."

CHAPTER TWENTY THREE

Ames groaned as the bugs in his tummy danced a two-step down toward his colon. Somewhere below there was a "pttt" followed by a long drawn out "sqursh". His butt immediately began to burn. He pressed harder on his stomach with his forearms and groaned again.

The Mexican two-step had hit him ten minutes after the plane took off and now he was squatted over an enamel pan behind a ragged beige curtain behind the last row of seats. He assumed the bug and stick soup was starting to affect him. Or it could have been the over-eating of the somewhat spicy chicken. With a final groan, he reached for the roll to complete the paperwork.

A few minutes later he stepped through the curtain to a horde of angry faces. Ames smiled sheepishly and waved his hand in the air in a vain attempt to clear some of the miasma. He failed completely. The stewardess tossed a can of Glade at him, hitting him in the head. After regaining consciousness the agent grabbed the can and sprayed the plane with a steady stream of Lavender scent. The seating area rapidly began to smell like an old lady covering an unwashed body.

The plane was an ancient Lockheed Electra L-10 and looked something like a DC-2. It was probably built sometime around 1940 and was supposed to carry twelve passengers in a once lovely twin tail aluminum airframe powered by two 450 horsepower Pratt and Whitney engines. This model was not museum quality and Ames had no idea how the thing managed to fly, or how it passed any kind of airworthiness inspection.

The thing had twenty people jammed into it, some sitting two to a seat or sitting on the floor. While he felt fortunate that there were no chickens, there were two ducks who felt it was their duty to fly the whole route themselves. This meant cruising back and forth over everyone's head and making shallow diving turns at the end of each circuit. It also meant leaving white spots at various points along the way.

Ames felt slightly miffed that the other passengers were upset with him over the toilet issue and said nothing about the birds. With some ill feelings he made his way back to his seat only to discover that a goat had taken it over and was now sleeping, curled up in it. The agent tried to push the animal onto the floor and earned a bite on the hand for his trouble.

Giving up Blond found a clear space on the floor to sit where he could examine the bite. There were some nasty teeth marks, but the skin wasn't broken. He assumed his rabies shots would work just fine.

The plane trundled along for almost an hour dipping down and then back up as the tired engines worked to keep the old bus in the air. The aircraft was on a circular course from Beira to Tete to Blantyre, Malawi to Cuamba to Mueda to Pemba to Nampula and back to Beira, then to Maxixe and Maputo before heading back to Beira again. It seemed that Ames had boarded the plane at the wrong time and was now flying the outward course to Mueda rather than the inward course to Maputo. Instead of reaching the capital in just over three hours, it would be two days before the plane finally made it, if it made it at all. Until then the agent would have to find a way to catch catnaps with a sleeping goat drooling on his head and a little boy playing with his, Ames', bare toes. The agent was slightly miffed that the kid had shoes and he didn't. There seemed to be a lot of miffing on this flight.

Five hours after climbing aboard the ancient aircraft the pilot landed and the flight attendant gestured for everyone to get off the plane. Ames assumed they had arrived in Maputo, but, what with snoozing off and on, and being without a watch, he couldn't be sure how much time had passed.

At the hatchway he was surprised to find that it was dusk and the sun was setting. He climbed down the loading ladder and followed the rest of the herd to the terminal building, a concrete and tin hut set at the side of the semi-dirt runway.

At the terminal he was startled to find that this was not Maputo, but Mueda a small town at the upper edge of Mozambique. This was a far as the plane would go until tomorrow. Apparently the pilot was afraid of the dark or something.

With some effort and much waving of hands he negotiated a piece of chicken for 30 meticais from a vendor who had a cart near the terminal building. With some trepidation he carefully nibbled a piece of the dead bird. Oddly it wasn't too spicy and had a wonderful flavor. Avidly he wolfed down the breast piece and went back to negotiate a second piece. After eating he found a water cooler inside the building and drank his fill.

Then there was the problem of sleeping. He was wondering if there was a motel or hotel nearby when he spotted some of his fellow travelers bunking down in the dirt next to terminal building. Since most of them wore or carried a sort of blanket, this wasn't a problem, but Ames was required to use his negotiating skills and 100 meticais to obtain a covering for the night.

He wasn't sure why he needed a blanket; the night was nicely warm, when he felt a razor sharp pain in his hand. Looking down he saw a mosquito the size of a bull terrier sucking about two gallons of blood. In horror he waved his hand until the thing flew off. Looking around he realized the things were all over the place, their wings sounding like B-29 bombers on takeoff. Seeing him dancing around one of the Mozambicans came over and explained, in broken English, that the "mozzies" were bad at night and then showed him how to wrap the blanket around his head and arms to keep the "mozzies" from sucking him dry.

Gratefully the agent slid down to lean against the building while wrapping himself in the blanket. Then he had to unwrap and pull his pants down a bit to cover his bare feet before wrapping up again.

* * * * * * * * *

Back at DORK, General Tenstars was fuming. He was also smoking and making odd guttural noises. He paced back and forth from one end of his ornate office to the other, glancing at his watch with each rotation. At the end of each circuit he would kick at the leg of his desk. One in five times he would actually connect.

Sitting in a chair off to the side, N.O. Wrights snoozed with his head leaning back against the wall, drool dripping out of his mouth onto his white shirt. Suddenly Tenstars reached out with his foot and kicked the leg of N.O.'s chair. The seat buckled to the right and N.O. dropped to the left, slamming into the floor on his shoulder. His head conked against the carpet, pulling him from his deep sleep.

Sitting up and shaking his head, N.O. exclaimed, "Hit the beach men! Take no prisoners! All the girls are mine!" He then clapped his hands three times and fell back to the carpet.

Tenstars gaped at the balding security agent, then turned and strode out of the office. As he banged open the door to the outer office Pinchpenny hurriedly clicked the minimize button on her computer display and jumped to her feet.

Thoroughly enraged she yelled, "Try knocking before you enter a ladies room you one starred twit!"

Stepping back a pace, the General stammered, "But, ah, but this is an office and you're my secretary."

"It's still my space, not yours, or do I report you to NOW and AARP?" shrieked the elderly harridan her blue hair shimmering with heat.

"Now, wait a minute," said the General, holding his hands in front of himself. "Let's not do anything hasty. I apologize and how about two extra weeks vacation to make amends?"

"Off the books?" she asked, glaring at him through her bifocals.

"Ah, sure, why not. It's only government money and you weren't doing anything anyway."

She immediately turned and started shutting down her computer and putting her stuff away. As she grabbed her coat the General interrupted, "Excuse me, could you get an update on Ames before you go? I'd really appreciate it."

She glared at him again. "Hey, we're on my time now!"

"Okay, okay. I'll get you some overtime money."

"For the whole day?"

"What! It's four o'clock. The days almost over!"

"I could talk to my union rep and the equal opportunity councilor. I'm sure they'd like to know about your harassment and violation of union stipulated rules."

The General's shoulders dropped. "Okay, the whole day, at double time. Now could you find out about Ames?'

She reached down and picked up a sheet of paper. "As of an hour ago the twit was stuck in Mueda in northern Mozambique," she read, "waiting for the morning flight back to Beira. The retard apparently took the wrong flight. I have sent a nasty gram to the US Embassy in Maputo chastising them for not providing our goose with appropriate transportation. The resident CIA man in Mueda will contact Ames tonight and assist him in reaching Maputo and possibly providing him with a secure communications link so he can let us know what the heck is going on over there. With luck he should be in Maputo by tomorrow afternoon and able to contact you directly. Anything else?'

Stunned the General stammered a thank you. Pinchpenny pulled on her coat and grabbed her car keys. "See you in two weeks, blubber butt."

Grumbling about not having any rights he strode back into his office and started poking his foot at N.O. Wrights.

CHAPTER TWENTY FOUR

Ames grasped the buildings spire and took a swing at the tiny airplanes swirling around his head. At his feet tiny people kept stabbing his toes with itty-bitty spears. Thousands of feet below tiny cars, trucks, buses and ostriches had stopped in their tracks or roads to witness the attacks. The ostriches stuck their heads in holes in apparent indifference.

As he swung at the planes again, his hand missed and, as he leaned outward to try again, he lost his grip on the spire and fell off. Head first he dropped from the building, his eyes watching as the cars and trucks grew bigger and bigger. The ostriches pulled their heads out of the holes to watch him fall. The tiny airplanes followed him down tossing tiny bullets and bombs as he dropped. The tiny people threw their spears with unerring accuracy into his feet.

Downward he plunged, smacking his butt into various building levels as he dropped. First one cheek and then the other slammed into the concrete, the force increasing the further he fell. The ground kept getting closer and closer and his butt was hitting harder and harder. And he could now hear the tiny people yelling his name. "Ames! Ames! Hey, Blond, you twit!"

With a jerk Ames woke up and stared blearily at the man kicking at his butt. Glancing down he shook his foot to dislodge the "mozzies" feasting on his toes.

Rubbing the sleep out of his eyes, the agent looked back up at the man hovering over him. The guy seemed very tall and very black until Ames realized that he was looking up and the guy was actually short and was only black because it was still night and very dark out.

"Who the devil are you," he muttered.

"Give me your hand," said the not-short not-black man.

Ames reached upward and the man grasped his hand. Using his middle finger the man stroked Ames' palm three times, then pumped the hand up and down twice. Turning their hands over, the man swung them back and forth three times and then stroked Ames' palm twice more with his finger before releasing the hand.

"Oh, you're CIA," said Ames. "What do you want?"

"Shhh," whispered the CIA agent. "Do you want to give away my cover? Get up and follow me."

Unwrapping the blanket, Ames struggled to his feet and started following the CIA guy. He was immediately assailed by "mozzies" and had to cover his face and hands with the blanket. He could barely see where he was going through the slit in front of his eyes and stumbled over rocks, stones, ant hills and random unknowns. He did note, however, that the CIA man was wearing nothing but a short sleeve shirt and shorts. Ames wondered why the evil flying insects were not chewing on him.

Ames followed the barely visible stranger down a dirt road to a concrete hut with green shingles, a picket fence, brick-trim and cathedral ceilings. The pump for the backyard pool made a slight gurgling sound. The stranger opened a door and waved the agent into the lighted room.

Blond stepped through the door into a white painted foyer with African and western American art decorating the walls and was led into a large living room with an ornate fire place and three leather couches set into lovely conversation groups with brass lamps and glass topped side tables. Pop culture object de art abounded and a few were even unbounded.

"Si'down," said the stranger.

"One question first," said Ames. "How come the mozzies don't bite you?"

The stranger grinned, "That's easy. Everyone knows the CIA leaves a bad taste in someone's mouth. The same holds true for insects. After a while they learn not to bite. Now sit down and don't dirty up the furniture."

The short stranger was of medium height with an angular face and a somewhat hooked nose. His light brown hair was pulled back into a pony tail and round glasses covered his eyes. Ames recognized him immediately.

"Hey," he cried. "I thought you died in 1980? Does Yoko know you're here?"

"Nah," the stranger shrugged. "I just got tired of the whole peace and music thing. I couldn't take a piss without some twit taking a picture of it. Actually it wasn't that bad until I caught the maid trying to sell my used toilet paper. That's when I decided it was time to bail. The CIA helped me cook up the death thing. Me and the King of Rock have been hanging around here since then making crafts and selling them on eBay, mostly baskets and African clay art. Every once in a while the CIA has us do some little job or other. My name here is Connor."

"So what do you need with me?" asked Ames, sliding down into one of the deep brown couches. At that moment a slightly overweight man with dark hair and long sideburns stepped into the room. Spotting Ames he stopped and looked at Connor.

In a musical southern accent he asked, "Am ah interrupting som'thin' here?'

"No problem, Jimmy," aid Connor. "Just one of the little jobs for Mister Andrews."

"Gotcha!" exclaimed Jimmy who then turned and left the room. He'd lost a bit of weight since the 80's and looked quite good.

Ames sat and stared with his finger pointing at the departed Jimmy. "But he's supposed to be at a car wash in Phoenix!"

"Hey this is the CIA," exclaimed Connor. "We can do almost anything. I'll bet you didn't know that Castro died in 1972 and an impersonator named Bruce Finklestein from Dubuque, Iowa has been subbing for him ever since?"

"Aren't you supposed to keep that secret?" asked Ames with a frown.

Connor shook his head. "Nah. Bruce is terminal and nobody gives a darn about Cuba anyway. Gordon Dingus from Apache, Arizona, AKA Raul, is set to take over sometime in the next couple of years. Anyway, on to business."

"Your boss is worried about you, so he's asked my boss to get your butt to Maputo. In the morning a friend of mine will fly you there. You won't have to wait for Air Mozambique. Their plane doesn't generally take off until after noon when daily meditation is over if it takes off at all. They sometimes run out of duct tape and a wing or engine or something else non-essential falls off. In the mean time, you can crash here and I've got a change of clothes for you."

"That's great," said Ames. "How about communications? Is there any way to get a hold of my boss?"

Connor shook his head. "Sorry, man. Communications up here sucks. We only have email, a satellite link, secure television, and my Blackberry. The telephone system is really bad so it sometimes takes days to get a message out. You'll have to wait until you get to Maputo. We got lucky with notification about you. One of the carrier mozzies made it through in time."

With resignation Blond followed Connor into a well-appointed bedroom with a king sized bed and a private bath. After Connor left, Ames stripped off his clothes and started to climb under the down comforter between the silk sheets. A buzzing sound stopped him.

Looking down he spotted a mozzie unfolding itself from the purple shirt. In a rush he slammed his foot down on the bug only to miss. The thing taxied across the floor and began its takeoff roll. Ames grabbed a hand carved clay statue and chucked it at the insect. The doll missed and shattered on the oak dresser, leaving deep scratches.

As the mosquito took off the agent tossed a first edition Poe, but the bug swerved and the book smacked into side table tearing off the cover. As pages from the book fluttered to the floor he grabbed a poker from the fireplace and started swinging it.

The poker slammed into an antique bronze lamp and shattered the Tiffany glass shade. Swinging back the other way he nicked the mozzie's wing and smashed the cut glass mirror over the dresser. As the bug fluttered to the side, Ames swung again and clipped its other wing, before knocking a Ming vase off its pedestal. As the precious urn crashed into the floor, Ames swung again and pulverized the insect against the sliding glass door, killing the bug and cracking the glass.

Satisfied, the agent dropped the poker, which tore a hole in the Persian rug, climbed into bed, fluffed the pillow and tried to sleep. Realizing he was seriously sweaty from fighting the insect he got up and padded into the bath.

A six foot square spa tub with over twenty jet nozzles dominated the left wall set into a tasteful red and blue ceramic tile platform. Across from it a multi-spray shower with variable lighting and automatic temperature controls gleamed in its satiny stainless housing with etched glass doors. Bright red and white tiles glittered on the floor. An automatic toilet, bidet and multi-sink cabinet with gold taps completed the fixtures. Ames was slightly disappointed at the austerity of it all. A government housing unit should be better appointed than this he thought.

Slipping a bottle of champagne from the built in refrigerator the agent settled into the spa and allowed the gentle fingers of water to ease the tension from his body. Sipping at the Dom Perignon Rose Vintage 98 he considered the problem of Silverpinky. What was the evil harridan up to with the stolen oil tankers? Sheila had said it had to do with crap and old oil wells, but how did that work and where was the profit in it?

That submarine had to cost billions of dollars and where did they build a ship like that? Wouldn't somebody notice this monster sub being built? When he got a hold of Washington or got back there he'd have to check into who had the kind of facilities for that. Maybe the CIA or ICC or maybe the FTC or possibly Interpol or maybe the BSA or GSA or GAO or GED. Somebody would have to know something about it.

He would contact his best snitch, Hairy the Homeless Person, AKA the Beggar, and find out what he knew. It might cost him a new shopping cart but Wal-Mart had lots of those so it wasn't a problem.

Feeling refreshed and relaxed the man from DORK climbed out of the tub and toweled off. Taking a fresh cotton robe from a pile he wrapped up and returned to the bedroom, only to find the masseuse waiting for him, a tall blond with a body that would make a dog hump your leg. He considered the possibilities for a moment then, reluctantly, decided to forgo the amenity in favor of badly needed rest. The girl looked disappointed as she trundled her table out the door, her bottom trundling as well. The blond beauty brightened when Jimmy grabbed her before the door closed completely.

Ames got back into bed, pulled up the duck down coverlet and fell asleep to the soft grunts and groans of Jimmy as the masseuse worked the kinks of his body.

CHAPTER TWENTY FIVE

As the Cessna 310 dropped toward the airfield Ames looked out the window to the left and could see a number of old H-19 helicopters without rotor blades sitting in a field near some partially disassembled Russian Sukhoi-17 fighter bombers. A little farther away he spotted two America AH-1 Cobra attack helicopters and a UH-1 Iroquois, both of which looked to be flyable if a tad rusty in spots.

Ames remembered the H-19 as the big bulbous nosed helicopter with teeth from old Magnum PI reruns, while the Iroquois and Cobras made big news in the late sixties and early seventies dropping troops in jungles and tossing missiles at hidden enemies. A number of ungainly C-130's sat in hardstands away from the main terminal. Some of them seemed to be like the AH-1's and UH-1 and actually flyable. All were standard fair for export to third world countries with low dollar power for military hardware, and that included serious maintenance problems for existing hardware.

The Cessna was Jimmy's personal plane, or so it said on the registration form. The Cessna was a gorgeous pink with a red and white interior. Jimmy said it reminded him of a car he once owned. The tail fin had large bright red lights along the trailing edge.

With a "chirrup" the planes wheels hit the runway and Jimmy's foot touched the brake while pulling back on the throttle. The whine from the twin engines slowed as the airplanes speed dropped.

Jimmy deftly maneuvered the small plane down the taxiway ducking in and out of the line of 727's, DC-8's and Anatov's that sat dejectedly and unused near the terminal building. The only aircraft that was usable was a single DC-6 with the red and white color schemes of Linhas Aeroas de Mocambique. A three hundred pound, minimum, stewardess in red and white livery was pushing a goat through the passenger door. Ames hoped that wasn't his flight out of here.

Jimmy slowed the plane to a walk and Ames hopped out. He waved as Jimmy revved the engine and turned back down the taxiway toward the flight line. The former songster didn't want to hang around and autograph sheep skins and rolls of goat cheese. Blond waved as Jimmy drove up the concrete path, ignoring Ames as the plane wobbled back and forth to the beat of "All Shook Up." Ames tried not to stare too hard as the rear half of the plane shimmied back and forth.

Inside the terminal the agent approached the LAM kiosk. Leaning against the counter he waited for the ticket agent to turn around. When that event occurred Ames said, "Hi. I'm Ames Blond. I'm supposed to pick up a ticket here? I'm not sure where it's to. It could be for Pretoria or Paris or Stanleyville or Baghdad or even Washington."

The girl blinked, then shook her head. "You're the man from those movies and books? I've seen all of the films at least three times. Golly, you're just as good looking in person as you are in the films. I would love to have dinner with you and get to know you better. Do you want the key to my apartment now or should we wait until after we eat. Oh, goodness, I'm not sure if I can stand being near you! My heart may leap from my body!"

Ames just smiled, not understanding a single word of the Portuguese she was speaking and looked slightly bewildered when she handed him a door key.

* * * * * * * * *

General Tenstars moved a black checker from one black space to another and lifted his hand. N.O. Wrights instantly grabbed a red checker and jumped over three of the General's black ones. With a look of triumph Wrights swept the three black disks from the board.

With a disgusted look Tenstars leaned back in his chair. "Sure take advantage of me when I'm worried about one of my agents. Ames has been missing in Africa for almost three days and you're stealing all my checkers." The General looked toward the map on the right hand wall, as you're facing the door, I mean from behind the desk where you would normally sit, not from the side where Wrights was sitting which is the wrong side of the desk, if there is a wrong or right side if you know what I mean, and started pouting.

N.O. giggled. "Ain't got nothing to do with that weird agent of yours. You haven't won a game in years. Didn't you take strategy at West Point?"

"Yeah," sighed the General. "But I kept getting lost and losing my army somewhere in Lower Brooklyn when they were supposed to be in Pakistan."

"Speaking of that agent of yours, just how many agents do you have? Couldn't you send another one and have him help Ames with this assignment?"

"That's part of the problem," muttered Tenstars petulantly. "I had a whole bevy of them but now Ames is the only one left and the White House won't give me any more. As if I were losing them on purpose."

"That's terrible. How many have died and how?"

"Died?" asked the officer looking up. "None of them died. They all just got lost. Like McCarty. He disappeared in Macy's just before Thanksgiving. Hasn't been seen since he went into the toy department just as Santa showed up."

Wrights was sitting looking speechless as Pinchpenny rushed into the room at a slow walk. "Yo, fats," she said in way of greeting. "Your boys been heard from."

"Could you stop doing that," muttered the one star as he stood up.

"Stop what?" the secretary asked coming to a halt halfway across the room.

"Using derogatory names while on duty. It isn't professional."

"You giving me orders chubby?" She asked with slightly hooded eyes. "Do I need to file that complaint with EOE?"

The General's hands came up in a warding motion. "No, no. I wouldn't think of giving you orders. My Gosh woman, we work as a team here. Everybody equal. Well, almost equal, sometimes, maybe. No need for those EOE people to get involved. Here would you like to sit in my chair." He rolled the emu clad resting area out from behind the desk. Then a thought occurred to him. "Say, aren't you supposed to be on vacation?"

"I am," she said with an evil grin. "I'm on vacation and working. You're paying me double time for working during my vacation and giving me regular pay for the vacation time."

"But that means you make almost as much as I do for the next week or so," stammered the head DORK.

"Not even close, fat cheeks. I've made more than you at regular hours for the past three years. I'm not a military officer. I'm a civilian and I have a union, so suck on that." She began using her education, she was a graduate of the Colorado School of Mimes, by pulling an invisible rope connected to a large stash of cash.

As Wrights studiously examined a blank wall the General collapsed into his chair and changed the subject. "What have you heard from Ames?"

Pinchpenny peered at him over the top of her bifocals. "Dippy finally reached Maputo and was last seen at the LAM counter hitting on the ticket agent. The CIA followed him to a coat closet were he assumed the ticket agent would meet him to pass on some information or other. After hanging around for two hours, and missing his flight, the twit went back to counter to find out what happened. His lady friend was gone.

"He talked the guy behind the counter into getting him on the next flight out. That's supposed to put him on LAM flight 203 to Jakarta with a transfer to Royal Dutch Airlines to Sydney and a connecting flight on Delta to San Diego. From there he gets the Greyhound to Chicago and a taxi to Atlanta where he gets the commuter flight to Hoboken and another taxi to Jersey City. He then hops the bus for a quick jaunt to Dulles and the flight to Vandenberg Air Force Base where we'll have a car pick him up and bring him here.

"He should arrive sometime around next Tuesday if he doesn't run into any more ticket girls."

The General scratched his chin. "Why doesn't he take that taxi from Chicago to here? It would be easier."

Pinchpenny frowned. "Because it's cheaper. The taxi guy in Chicago is using the cab to go and visit his sister in Atlanta and is giving Ames a reduced fare. I think it saves like a hundred dollars."

"But he wouldn't have to take all those busses and airplanes and that other taxi if he came straight here. That has to save more than a hundred bucks."

Pinchpenny scowled. "You do realize we're talking government accounting here? Showing an obvious saving is better than getting a real saving. Besides he can put it all on his government credit card and it will give me more travel miles."

Wrights chimed in with, "The travel miles go to you? Why would they go to you?"

"Because I signed for the card, doofuss," stated the blue haired harridan with a smirk. "Read the contract from Visa."

Tenstars shook his head. "Can we get back on track here? What can we do to get him in Washington before next week? He's got the information we need. Maybe get him to use a telephone, email or other modern communications method. Heck, I think a letter would get here before then."

"No can do," Pinchpenny said with a shrug. "He's on that airplane to Jakarta and no way to communicate with him right now."

At that moment the aged snake's cell phone rang producing the ringtone for "I am woman." She flipped it open and listened. With a frown she snapped the lid down and announced. "The question is moot. Dippy has disappeared again."

"What do mean disappeared?" asked the General with alarm.

"It looks like he never got on the plane out of Maputo. The agent who was supposed to meet him in Jakarta said he didn't get off the plane and a search showed he was never on board."

"I thought the CIA saw him get onto the plane?"

"No that's not what happened. According to the Mozambique field office, the other of the two agents there, the agent watching our boy started talking with the ticket agent and then went to a closet to wait for that guy. The agent was still in the closet when the plane took off."

"Why the heck is everybody over there hanging around in closets?" asked the General rhetorically.

Pinchpenny and Wrights looked at each other and shook their heads.

CHAPTER TWENTY SIX

Blond opened his eyes to stare at a pile of empty pizza boxes, squashed and dented beer cans, used tissues, wadded up papers, old magazines and unidentifiable things that did not look all that healthy. The pile was inches from his nose and smelled very rancid. One pizza box had grey fungus dripping over its side to partially cover a slice of half eaten pepperoni.

Pulling his head back and looking around the agent found himself on the floor in a room that was slightly recognizable. He looked back at the pile and muttered, "Federowski." Somehow he was back aboard Silverpinky's mystery sub. And worse, Federowski was back messing the place up or someone had thrown all the junk back into his room.

Mentally checking himself to see that everything was in the right places and probably working, he pushed himself up to a sitting position and looked around. The room was just about the same except for the scattered trash on the floor. There was no evidence that Federowski had returned. At least there was no smell from the latrine to indicate his return.

Climbing further up to his feet he went over and sat down on the bed. His last thought had been leaving the closet in Maputo to go and find out why the girl had not shown up. As he stepped from the closet there had been a blur to his right and then the lights went out. Somebody had koshed him and dragged him back to the sub.

He checked his person and found he was still wearing the brown suit with spangles, an oversized collar and bell bottoms he had picked out of Jimmy's closet. In the pocket he found three dollars, two quarters, a penny, the ticket for the airplane he had missed and the government American Express Jimmy had gotten for him.

Standing up he stuffed everything back into the pocket except for the AmEx card. Getting up he went to the door where he poked the card into the gap between the doo and the jamb. Sliding the card up and down he managed to catch the bolt of the lock and gently eased it back while softly pulling on the door. With a "click" the door came rapidly open banging him in the head and knocking him to ground. There was a squishing sound as he landed in the fuzzy pizza box.

Staring upward from his position in the pile of trash he saw Sheila looking down at him. Her hair was in a cute ponytail and she had ditched the blue coveralls to replace them with pale green halter and red short shorts. Gold colored sandal straps climbed her legs to the knees. Her blue eyes looked down at him with affection.

Quickly she turned her gaze and looked behind herself, stepped into the room and pushed the door closed. Squatting down she looked at Ames and said, "Why are you always on the floor? Is this how it's going to be with you? Hanging around on the floor, sitting in trash and getting smacked with doors? If it is we'll have to have one of those emergency kits with us all the time."

Ames got to his feet and pulled Sheila up to hers. "No, you just have a bad habit of not finding me at my best. Why I went all the way through college and only walked into sixteen doors." His brow wrinkled as he thought. "Of course some of them were like two or three times apiece." He shook his head to clear the worms. "Not to change the subject, but why am I back on this submarine?"

"Clarence spotted you at the airport when he went in for supplies and to pick up Bud when his plane landed. Bud is one of our tanker pilots and captains. He and his crew use the ship and then after completing the job they give an antidote to the real crew and leave them to wake up floating on the ship somewhere off the coast of Africa.

"Bud and the guys get picked up by helicopter and catch a flight back to Maputo. Bud didn't get back the same time as the others because he took a detour to see his mom in Brighton. Anyway Clarence spotted you and conked you when you came out of that closet. Say, why were you hiding in a closet?"

Ames looked at the toe of his pointy-toe Italian shoes, "Long story. What happened after he conked me?"

She looked at him suspiciously for a moment, then continued. "He and Bud rolled you in a rug and carted you out of the airport on one of those luggage thingies. You know with the wheels and handle and all."

"Yeah, it's called a luggage cart."

"Really? You're so smart. You knew what it was without even seeing it! Too bad you fall down a lot. We're gon'na have to fix that."

"So they took me out on the luggage cart. Then what? They loaded me into a car and drove me back here to the sub?"

"Wow, that's really impressive, you knew exactly what they'd do, except they didn't put you in a car, it was a van. And they didn't drive you here, they used an airplane that they put you in after they drove to a small airfield outside Maputo. And they didn't bring you to the ship, they took you to holding cell down in the underground headquarters." She frowned. "I don't think I was supposed to say anything about the underground headquarters."

"Don't worry about that, I won't tell anybody. So how did I end up back in Federowski's room?"

"Silverpinky didn't want you waking up and finding out about the underground headquarters so she had Clarence bring you back up here."

At that moment the door flew open and Clarence stepped in, "Hey, Boobs," he remarked, "Da big broad wants chew up on de bridge ob da ship. " He leered at Sheila.

"I'm gon'na sue that twit for sexual harassment," Sheila hissed under her breath. Getting up she walked toward the oaf, picking up a brass lamp as she passed it.

"Would you like to go on a date with me?" She purred as she came up to him. She grinned happily and wiggled her hips. Clarence's tongue dropped out of his mouth and flapped on the floor. His hands came up to chest height and started making grabbing motions. "Chew betch'a, doll. We could hab a great time togeta." His leer could have scared a New York hooker.

Still smiling she lifted the lamp and slammed him over the head with a resounding, "Clonk." He just stood and stared at her so she hit him again. When the third strike failed to fell him Ames walked over and pushed Clarence with his finger. The ugly crewman hit the floor with a solid, "Thump." His belly bounced back and forth for a few minutes.

"You didn't have to hit him again. He was just too dumb to fall over. What now?"

The girl grabbed Ames' hand and stepped over Clarence. She clonked him again with the lamp as she went by. Ames attempted to step over and put his foot into the wiggling belly. The agent shimmied his way across and alit on the other side.

They both looked at the enlarged wiggling mass for a moment then Sheila grabbed the agent by the arm and dragged him down the hall.

After going for miles through hallways and rooms and traversing up and down six flights of stairs, two elevators, an escalator and a dumb waiter they arrived at the *Exxon Valdez II* which was once again neatly ensconced in the belly of the monster submarine. A string of fifty watt bulbs cast a barely visible glimmer over the side of the ship. The hull fell into a deep inky pit where the light could not go.

"Hurry and hide on that ship," said Sheila pushing Ames toward the tanker. "Be careful. Silverpinky has a crew on board and we'll be releasing the boat in about an hour. Stay hidden until they leave *The Pink Gaspipe*."

The agent stopped short. "What the heck is a pink gaspipe?"

"Not gaspipe. *The Pink Gaspipe*. That's the name of this submarine."

"Well that's kind of a stupid name," he muttered.

He grabbed the girl and gave her a quick kiss then turned and ran across the gangway to the *Valdez*. He slid in a puddle of water and hit the superstructure with a solid, "Bong" and slid to the deck. Sheila shook her head and muttered, "There he goes again," before heading back through the door to the submarines innards.

On board the tanker Ames sat up and felt his nose. Although slightly sore it was not bleeding. He stood up and staggered unsteadily toward the door (hatch) into the massive structure. He undogged the hatch (door) and slide through. Ducking down the stairs he headed for the one place he was sure none of Silverpinky's crew would ever go. At the second landing he hurried down the passageway to the third hatch on the right and stepped into Cratchet's room.

Surprisingly, the odd crewman was asleep in his berth with the cat on his chest looking like a lawn gnome lying on its side with a cat holding it down. All that was missing was the beard since Cratchet was wearing a red bed cap. The position of the cat, however, gave the illusion of an orange beard.

Ames had decided to find a different hiding place when there was "Clank" on the stairway. Looking around in haste, the agent spotted Cratchet's locker. Pulling the door open to hide inside was a huge mistake. Piles of junk, clothing, used sandwich bags, a powdered donut and rubber hemorrhoid cushion oozed out onto the floor. Hearing steps closing the distance to the door Ames hurriedly slipped into the attached bath and pushed the door almost closed. As an added precaution he crouched down in the shower stall and pulled the curtain almost closed.

Sniffing he realized the stall smelled worse than the smell of Federowski's room. Black fungus bloomed along the lower edges of the stall and spongy mounds of melted soap cakes created a Picasso landscape along the floor. Some unidentifiable white stuff tied the soap mounds together like Martian canals.

Outside a shoe scuffed as someone came into Cratchet's room. Ames heard a clatter as the stuff from the locker was disturbed. Peering through a gap between the curtain and the wall he saw a shadow cross in front of the gap in the door. He recognized the ugly profile of Clarence. So the hairy gnome was on this trip too.

After poking through the stuff from the locker Clarence pushed open the door to the bath and started to step in. He stopped halfway and waved his hand in front of his face. With a muttered, "Federowski" he retreated pulling the door closed behind him.

Ames waited a few minutes then moved quietly out of the bath and peeked out Cratchet's door to find the hallway empty. At that moment the ship lurched and the agent could feel the thrum of the ships engine rising in vibration.

Blond hurried down the hall and up two flights of stairs that were now lit only be red emergency lights, to the main deck and looked out one of the portholes. For a few seconds all he could see was black that changed to dark gray and finally the edge of the subs mouth came into view as dark became dark sprinkled with stars. The tanker was being released to do whatever it was that the tanker did when not with Silverpinky's sub.

Leaving the porthole the agent crept up the red lit stairwell to the next deck and the one beyond that until he reached the bridge. Peering through the door he saw three unfamiliar people working in the red glow of the night lights. One was seated at the control console, a second was near the bridge window and the last was walking toward the door Ames was hiding behind.

With a start the man from DORK hurried back down the stairs and slipped into an open room on the second deck down. Above he could hear the bridge door open and close and the tap of feet on the metal rungs of the stairs.

Looking around the dimly lit room he determined that it was storage room for mops, pails and assorted cleaning gear. He slipped behind a dimly revealed shelf group and hunkered down. The footsteps came closer until they were right outside the door of the storage room. They paused for a moment and then, with a "thunk" the door to the room closed.

After waiting a few minutes the intrepid agent tiptoed to the door and slowly turned the latch, then turned it much harder when it didn't open. Finally, in exasperation, he yanked the handle back and forth to no avail. The door was locked and he was trapped.

CHAPTER TWENTY SEVEN

Ames put down the chicken leg he had been gnawing on and wiped his mouth with his sleeve. Through his feet he could feel the thrum of the engines slowing. Standing he wiped his greasy fingers on his soiled trousers and peered out a porthole. He saw nothing except the long bow of the ship, pumps, pipes, and a couple of cranes, cloudy blue sky and the froth of ocean water. Oh, and a mass of land off to the left, barely visible by pressing his face against the glass and peering though one eye.

Getting out of the closet eight days ago had been a bit trying. He had spent two days in the thing before he figured out that the door unlocked from his side. He pushed the button in the doorknob and released it. The button popped out and the door slid open. It took a moment before the agent realized he was loose and then he went a little wild trying to find a bathroom.

After that the last week had been a blur of fear and boredom. Fear that he would get caught aboard the ship and not be able to finish his mission, and boredom from doing just about nothing. He had found an unused cabin on the poop deck where he could sleep, take a shower and spend time when not foraging for food and information. He found the kitchen down the hall on the right and been able to put together simple meals such as bologna and cheese sandwiches, PB and J and a nice filet mignon during one of the off shifts.

The big problem had been clothes. The cabin he was in had no clothing in it and his sneaking in and out of other cabins had found nothing that would fit so he had been wearing the same coverall he had gotten on Silverpinky's ship. After eight days it was a bet that a goat would smell better than he did. It was rather surprising that none of the crew had found him by the smell alone.

When not dying of boredom in the cabin, the agent had surreptitiously wandered around the entire ship from the forepeak tank to the after shaft alley. The tanker was built with 5 main tanks and 5 tanks each on the port and starboard sides. Just forward of the superstructure were the port and starboard slop tanks to take any overspill. Aft and under the superstructure were the engine room, pump room, maintenance deck and the shaft alley for the huge bronze props that pushed the 243 meter long ship through the water. That 243 meters was just over 797 feet, about three quarters the length of a football field.

The deck was split by a group of pipes that ran down the center from bow to stern with an upright crane positioned just about amidships. Smaller pipes ran from the center to each of the separate tanks. Ames had wandered through all of the decks. Eventually he had found the communications shack on the officer's deck.

He had planned on trying to get a message out through the radio but there always seemed to be someone near the darned thing. The people who were crewing the ship spent most of their time in the galley, the bridge or the swimming pool on the poop deck. Since there were a couple of girls included this made for a nice social atmosphere, complete with bikinis and Speedos.

Leaving the porthole he climbed the stairway to the officer's deck and snuck into one of the staterooms. This one was inhabited by a girl from the looks of the clothes strewn about unless someone had a need for a man bra. Making sure the place was empty he peered through the starboard porthole.

The ship was moving slowly toward shore pushed by a pair of tugboats. About half-way there was a short pier with a group of valves sticking up. The ship moved closer until it came to a rest about 5 feet from the pier. Lines were dropped and a couple of guys on the pier tied it off. Ames could feel the low vibration of the bow and stern thrusters keeping the big ship on station.

When the "captain" or whoever was running the ship was satisfied with the positioning a group of crewman connected a large hose to the main valve system on the deck. The hose was picked up by the crane and dangled over the side to be connected to the valve system on the pier. When everything was ready the hum in the ship changed as the big pumps came on line and cargo started flowing through the hose and into the storage tanks. Ames was at a complete loss regarding what the ship could be picking up. This wasn't the Persian Gulf and it looked a lot like somewhere on the east coast of the United States if he had to guess. But it could be Europe or somewhere in Asia.

Inshore were a number of large white tank structures similar to those used for water or petroleum but there was no hint of any kind of refinery or cracking towers. Wanting a closer look the agent descended the stairs to the poop deck and, after peering carefully around, stepped out on deck and dashed to the cover of one of the beach umbrellas by the swimming pool.

Pulling his binoculars out of thin air the agent scanned the shoreline and the towers. At about the time he spotted a logo on the towers a seriously nasty stench hit his nostrils. It smelled as though the ships cat had died about a week ago and the carcass was attached to his shoe.

Sniffing his armpits Blond decided it wasn't him and looked around while waving his hand in front of his nose. That did not help but people have been doing that since the caves so he did it too. Why? No idea.

Taking short breaths he decided that the stench was coming from somewhere near the valve system on the pier. Using the binoculars he scanned the area but saw nothing that could produce such a reek. Breathing in as little as possible he returned to looking at the tank farm. He found the logo again.

In bright red and blue letters five feet high was the proclamation:

Anderson National Farming Cooperative
Piggy Wiggy Pork and Bacon

The lettering was followed by a cartoonish pig with Xes for eyes hanging from a meat hook. The logo pretty much put the ships location in the United States. Well, not in it, but off the coast or pretty near the coast, like 300 feet away close, but what that had to do with the pipe, ship or anything else the agent had no clue. What he did know was he had to find a way to communicate with Washington, either from the ship or by getting to shore somehow.

His eyes followed the pier back to land. There was a single lane road leading inland through the dunes along the shore. As he watched as a pickup truck with a crew cab came down the road and pulled up at the head of the pier. It just sat there. Examining the truck with the binoculars he noted that the door had a logo that looked like the one on the tank, the dead pig hanging from a meat hook.

Up on deck two of the crew went down the boarding ladder, down the pier and got in the truck. One of them looked like Clarence. After a moment the truck turned around and headed back down the road disappearing behind the dunes.

Looking around Ames did not see anyone on deck or, after glancing upward, on the bridge wings. Taking a chance he hurried across the deck and down the boarding stairs. Pausing at the bottom he looked back up at the deck. Still no sign of anyone. Keeping his eyes upward he turned to head down the pier toward the shore, missed and fell into the water.

After attempting to climb back on the pier with no success he gave up and swam toward the shore his boots and clothes trying to drag him down. After ten minutes of huffing and puffing he crawled up onto the sand and flipped onto his back. He huffed and wheezed long enough to get his heart rate back under control. He blamed the problem on lying around on the ship for over a week, messing up his muscle tone. He probably should have taken advantage of the ship's gym and spa. He could have used it when the crew wasn't around and the treadmill and elliptical trainer would have helped him keep in shape. The wide variety of strength machines would have helped too. Too late now though.

Standing up he looked up and down the beach. Not seeing any buildings or other roads he trudged up the macadam squishing shoe and dripping water from his clothes as he went. Looking back toward the ship he noticed the colors on the funnel and superstructure had been changed from the black of the *Exxon Valdez II* to a red and gold stripe scheme. That would do wonders to keep others from spotting the missing ship.

As he topped the first dune he spotted the fence. It was over fifteen feet high and ran parallel to the beach for as far as he could see. Access was controlled by a gate that was firmly closed. A sign stated that trespassers would be prosecuted or possibly shot. A large black dog with pointed ears gave Ames a hungry look.

Resigning himself to a long walk the intrepid agent turned around and slogged back to the beach and headed north along the sand.

CHAPTER TWENTY EIGHT

It was getting dark when Ames found the road. It led off to the left away from the beach and he could see the lights of some houses. Glad that he had finally found some sign of civilization he headed up the road to look for the first pay phone he could find. It would be good to get back to Washington, make his report and get back to the apartment that was not his, to soak in his un-owned bathtub and change into clean clothes that fit him but belonged to the government.

The road went past some small bungalow style homes with only one having any lights on and that one had a dog that would not shut up. "Bark, bark, bark, bark." Ames felt like shooting the damn thing. If he had a gun, some bullets and the energy to put it out of its misery. Or, better yet, shoot the idiot who didn't come out to find out why his stupid dog was barking.

All too soon the row of houses ran out and Blond found himself walking along a lonely road that led into gray darkness. There were not even any street lights to mark the road. Just as it started getting too dark to see the moon peaked over the stunted trees and gave some dimension to the gray ribbon of asphalt.

The waning gibbous moon climbed higher in the sky shedding more light on the road but did nothing to reveal anything manmade except the road. He had been walking about twenty minutes when the road ended and met another. Off to the left he could see a rather dilapidated barn and some old farming equipment. Standing in the middle of the intersection he looked both ways up and down the new road. There were no lights or any indication that people lived in the area. Flipping an invisible coin that he didn't have the agent turned and headed north hoping he had chosen correctly. Who knows, he could be wandering around this rural wilderness for the next twenty years and never see anybody.

After walking for about an hour through a tunnel of dark trees that did their best to block out the light from the moon the trees began to close over head and the road went from asphalt to dirt. Ames stopped and looked around. There was nothing to mark why the road had petered out or where the dirt track headed. He could keep going and find out or turn around and head back the other way and see if that led to something more worthwhile. With a shrug of his shoulders the man from DORK listened to his bullheaded side and started down the dirt track. He walked for another five minutes before he fell into the water again.

Ames broke the surface sputtering and spitting unkind and impolite words about idiots who ended roads in rivers without putting up so much as a sign or barrier. He was treading water when his shoe hit a rock and he found out the water was about two feet deep and he could stand up.

Attempting to shake some of the water off his clothes he spotted the glow of lights on the other side of the river. He figured it was about three hundred feet to the other shore and the light was just beyond that. Looking back at the tunnel of trees that did not give a clue as to where the road was he looked at the other bank. Shrugging his shoulders again he waded out into the water until he was in up to his chest. He struck out in a classic dog paddle his arms and legs splashing like a newbie at a Camp Tiliwikaka canoe class. After about ten minutes he was back to huffing and puffing, snuffling water up his nose and burbleing when his face went under. Falling back on his training the agent headed toward panic with screaming, thrashing and generally requiring the services of a life guard when his feet hit bottom again. He had made it to the other side.

The brave agent sheepishly looked around to make sure no one had witnessed his side step into humanity. Spotting no one except two old guys fishing in a boat, the crew of a dredger and some kids having a late night swim, there was nobody to notice his ignominy.

Feeling better about himself he sloshed through the shallows and up onto the shore. He had to fight his way through some brambles, bristly hedges and a barbed wire fence that fought like crazy but Ames persevered and flipped over the top of it with only minor cuts and bruises and the loss of the left sleeve of his coveralls.

On the other side of the fence a single lane asphalt road turned right toward a flat area with a single streetlight up on a pole. Walking that way a short span the agent determined that he was looking at some kind of firing range. There was a long shed in back and positions where weapons could be placed prior to firing. It looked like a hunt or skeet club of some kind. Happy that he had found something of human construction he went over to the shed and looked around for a telephone. He poked around inside and out but no phone. Disgusted he walked back out to the road and started following it.

As before, he found himself following a single lane road into a tunnel of trees. The moon tried to put light into the tunnel but the overlapping branches made the road an eerie and dark place mottled here and there with dim silver light. The kind of place where you kept your hands in your pockets and you whistled a lot. Ames tried whistling but never having been any good at it only managed a sad sounding "whiffifif" that was more like an angry cat hissing than a whistle. After almost working his way through the tortured strains of "House of the Rising Sun" he fell in the water again.

Spitting and sputtering and slapping the water the soggy agent called the rivers, and water in general, a number of foul names, laid twenty thousand years of bad luck on them and any human dumb enough to live and build roads near the nasty things. He could not for the life of him, as he continued in his tirade, determine why people had to have water.

When his panting and huffing finally forced his angry speech to drop to a low croak he slapped the water one more time and slogged his way across the stream, having to swim only a short stretch in the center. On the other side he found the road continued as though no water had ever split it. Blond muttered something about idiots building roads in water and continued squishing and slopping his way up the road.

Again there was no light except from the moon, but the ground here was flat without any trees and he could see that both sides of the road looked like soggy fens. There was a slight rot smell from the wet plant life.

After a bit the road turned through more trees and Ames was back to eerie, lost and without the ability to whistle. It appeared his search for a pay phone might take a tad longer than he anticipated.

Just as he was starting to feel disheartened and really, really lost he crossed a railroad track and spotted a single light gleaming in the distance. With renewed spirits the agent brightened his flagging steps and briskly and confidently headed into the light.

Getting closer Ames realized the light was a spot flood hanging high in the air on some kind of metal structure. Nearing it and peering upward while shading his eyes from the glare of the spot with his hand Ames recognized the boxy looking tower. It was a DARTS tower, a direct acquisition rail-to-ship spreader bar system. The massive crane was used to transfer cargo containers from railroad trains to trucks for movement to cargo container ships.

The system had been developed by August Design Incorporated for the US government to speed up the transfer of military equipment from shore to ship and back again.

He continued walking along a long line of railroad cars and found a second DARTS system with a spot light high up on it. Next to it was a concrete building of some sort. Ames tried the door but it was locked. After going around the structure he found no telephone, but there was a telephone wire leading to the building. He tried rattling the door again to no avail. Looking around he spotted a large rock and threw that at the door trying to break the lock.

After a half a million throws the door was slightly lumpy but the lock was intact. The rock, however, was at least half its original size.

Giving up in disgust he headed back up the road. If there was a train unloading site then there had to be a town around someplace. Then he got an idea.

Walking around the DARTS tower he spotted a metal ladder heading upward (or downward depending on where you are). Grabbing a rung he started upward. By the time he reached the first level he was huffing and puffing and his arms were getting real tired. He looked back down and then upward. Giving himself a mental kick he continued up.

By the time he reached the upper level his arms were shaking and his hands felt numb. With real effort he pulled himself up onto the catwalk near the operator's cabin. Eighty feet looks rather short horizontally on the ground but is rather high and hard to get to when it's vertical.

Ames lay flat on the metal grid of the catwalk floor, panting and getting his breath back - again. With a groan he realized that he would have to do the climbing thing again to get down. Carefully and slowly he stood up while holding tight to the railing. He wanted to keep his eyes shut but figured he would probably make a misstep and fall off. Keeping a tight grip and his eyes open he looked around.

To the south it was pretty dark with only an occasional dim light peeking through trees. To the east were a group lights but in that direction was the channel where the *Exxon Valdez II* was moored. To the west it was back to the dark with dim lights. To the north things brightened up, literally.

He could see the lights of a town and headlights from cars traveling on a large road. The trouble was the lights looked a long way away and there was a lot of dark in between. He looked up at the stars to see if he could figure out where he was. He spotted what he thought was the Big Dipper but that did no good. He had no idea how to navigate by the stars.

Looking down he could see the rail line led off to the north before the light from the spot petered out and visibility became zero.

With a sigh he shook his arms and started back down the ladder. He was three fourths of the way down, his arms shaking and his breath ragged when a bright light hit him in the face. A voice yelled, "Get off the tower and put your hands up!"

CHAPTER TWENTY-NINE

Ames sat in the back of the car trying to get comfortable while looking out the window. Except for the wash of the headlights and dashboard it was absolute darkness outside. He could be anywhere from Albuquerque, New Mexico to Backwoods, Idaho, with just as few people and sights. He wiggled around trying to adjust the handcuffs on his wrists. At least he thought he was in the United States somewhere.

When he got off the tower he had to shield his eyes from the bright light shining on them. He put his hands in the air with one slightly tilted to try and see who was behind the light. A gruff voice told him to walk forward. After a couple of feet he was rudely slammed against a car and his arms twisted behind him. Handcuffs snapped around his wrists and he was shoved into the backseat. Nobody had said a word and now he couldn't. There was a Plexiglas screen between the back seat and the front of the car. The car looked like an SUV from the inside.

He had tried asking the driver some questions but the man did not answer. Ames relegated himself to sitting in silence until they got where they were going. After about ten minutes he could see some street lights up ahead.

The car pulled into a small parking lot with buildings around it and a few widely spaced street lights. The driver got out and opened the back door of the car. "Come out of there," said the man.

Ames slid out of the car while the man held his head to keep him from bumping it on the door frame. The thought flashed in Ames' mind, "Aha, cop!"

The officer pointed at one of the buildings with a lighted doorway. "Get going and don't try to get cute."

The agent walked up to the door. It had a sign beside it that read:

Federal Security Police
Military Ocean Terminal Sunny Point

Firearms Not Permitted Inside Federal Buildings

As he opened the door Ames thought that was kind of silly. Did the cops leave their guns outside?

Inside there was an officer in a blue uniform seated behind a low counter. He put down the paper he had been reading, "What's up Mike?" he asked.

Ames was shoved into a chair as Mike answered, "Caught dippy here climbing around on the DARTS tower. He must have been all the way up and was coming down when I found him. We'll have to have somebody come out and check it to make sure he didn't do any damage."

Ames piped up, "I didn't do anything up there. I just needed to find out where I was. I've been wandering around in the dark and falling in rivers for a couple of hours now."

"Quiet, we'll get your story in a minute," stated the man behind the counter. "You want to process him or wait until morning and let them do it?"

"Nah," muttered Mike. "I'll get him into the system. It'll give me something to do besides reading another romance novel."

"I don't know how you can stand those things," replied the other officer whose name tag identified him as Slobodnik. "Give me a good ol' comic book any day or maybe one of those reality shows."

"I hear ya. As long as it ain't a cop show. Those things give me the creeps."

"Know what ya mean. All them bald heads, flak jackets and donuts. It's enough to make a man want to quit the force." He watched as Slobodnik reached up and scratched his bald head.

Mike shook his head and grabbed Ames by the arm. "C'mon dippy, let's find out who you are."

"If you must know," answered Ames, "the name is Blond, Ames Blond."

Both officers started laughing their butts off. Slobodnik was laughing so hard he fell out of his chair and started rolling on the floor.

After five minutes the laughter tapered off to grumps and snorts. Slobodnik wiped at the snot trail dripping from his nose. It did not help. Every time he had it clean he would snort again and the slime would ooze out again. "Get him out of here," he giggled at Mike.

Mike giggled as well as he pushed Ames down a hallway and into another room. This one had a short counter with a camera mounted on it. Ames was placed against a wall while Mike typed some information into a computer. The camera flashed once. Then Ames was pushed into a nearby chair where the policeman removed Ames' right hand from the cuffs and hooked the cuff to a metal bar connected to a table. The table was bolted to the floor.

"Okay dippy, for the record, what's your real name?"

"I told you, the name is Blond, Ames Blond."

Mike chuckled. "Yeah, right and I'm Kojak. Let me have your proper name so I can get this thing typed up."

With a sigh of defeat Ames said, "Ames Humphrey Blond. That's Blond without an e."

The officer looked up, his face showing annoyance. "You can screw around all you want, but we're gon'na find out who you are. Now give me your real name."

"I already told you," replied Ames with just a hint of his own anger. "My name's Ames Blond and I'm an agent for DORK out of Washington. I just got off a stolen oil tanker and was trying to find my way to a town or a phone or a road or something so I could get a message to my boss.'

The cops face lit up. "So you admit to being an illegal alien who jumped ship! Well howdy do, let me send an inquiry over to ICE and see how they want to handle this."

"I'm not an illegal alien," grumped Blond. "I'm an agent for the Department of Reconnaissance and Knowledge in Washington, DC. I'm tracking stolen oil tankers and I need to get my information back to General Tenstars. Look, let me make one phone call and we can get this whole thing cleared up."

"Not on your life, Pedro or Abdul, whichever it is. This gets kicked over to ICE and probably Homeland Security. You're sniffing around the major trans-shipment hub for munitions and supplies to our troops overseas and you want me to let you have a phone call? I got 8 years to my pension and there ain't no foreign spook gon'na cost me that four hundred thirty dollars and twenty two cents a month. No siree, Bob. That won't happen. Gimme your hand"

The officer grabbed Ames right hand and stuck the end of his index finger on a small square looking box. The box lit up and the light went up and down like computer scanner. On the monitor in front of Mike an image of Blond's fingerprint showed up. With his other hand the cop pressed a letter on the keyboard and proceeded to place each of Ames' fingers on the box, one at a time, with a stab at the keyboard after each.

After completing the man from DORK's thumb the federal cop dropped Ames' hand and pecked at the keyboard for a few seconds. He then stood up and grabbed the handcuff and unlocked it from the table. With a deft twist he reattached Ames' hands behind his back and pushed the agent out of the room and farther down the hall.

Ames was escorted through one door and then into a small cell and the door clicked shut behind him. Mike told him to stand with his back against the bars. The cop took off the handcuffs.

"Now you settle down and get some sleep. The day shift will be in soon and they can finish processing you." He turned to leave.

"Wait a minute," demanded Blond. "I want my phone call or a lawyer or the ACLU or something. You need to find out who I am so I can get to Washington!"

"I already know who you are. Your information came back while were sitting in front of the computer. Instantaneous communications ya know."

"So how come I'm still here and where's my phone call!"

"You're here because your prints came back blank. Nada, nothing, no dope. In other words, you don't exist. Just what we'd expect for an illegal alien."

"What?" cried Blond. "There must be a mistake! I'm an agent for the US government. I get paid by direct deposit just like you do. I pay Social Security just like you do. I give most of my check to the IRS just like you do. I have to be in the computer!"

"No dope, dude. You don't exist in the United States. We'll have to wait to see if something comes back from

Interpol, Mossad or Fox News. Until then, get some sleep."

The cop went out the door leaving a dejected and slightly soggy agent leaning his head against the bars.

CHAPTER THIRTY

General Manystars Tenstars sipped coffee from a blue mug with the Army eagle on one side and a large silver star on the other. He set down the cup and looked over the report in front of him. The document was titled, "Guidelines to the Federal Paper Reduction Act: Procedures, Actions, Demands and Mandates." The book was ten inches thick. A second book read, "Guidelines to the Federal Paperwork Reduction Act: Appendices, Tabs, Tables and Forms." It was fourteen inches thick and sat on the floor.

With a sigh of dread the General opened the document to the first page. It was blank except for the words, "This page intentionally left blank." The General went through four intentionally blank pages before reaching the documents title page. Tenstars sat back in his chair and grabbed the coffee again. He knew it was going to be a long day.

The General was wishing he had a secretary to go through documents like this for him when his secretary, Pinchpenny, slammed the door open and advanced into the General's office like Sherman going through Atlanta, blue hair bobbing, rhinestoned eyeglasses glaring and laying down a thunder of thighs crashing together.

Her hob-nailed sneakers slammed to a halt in front of the cowering officers desk and a chicken-like voice spat out, "You're boys been heard from again."

The General took his arms down from around his head and stammered, "What?'

"Blond. You know, the boy wonder where the hell he is? The last agent you have who hasn't transferred to the CIA, FBI or Boy Scouts? Ames?"

"Oh, yeah, him." The General sat up straighter in his chair and stopped hiding behind, "Guidelines to the Federal Paper Reduction Act. "So what have you heard?"

"Dippy is in the custody of the Immigration and Customs Enforcement people and is currently being processed for return to Mexico, Bulgaria or Iran, whichever will take him first."

"Why is being processed for deportation by ICE? Don't they know he belongs to us?"

"Apparently not. The Federal Police at the Sunny Point Military Ocean Terminal in North Carolina ran his fingerprints and didn't get a hit. They assumed he was an illegal and turned him over to ICE. ICE didn't get anything from Interpol so they're now checking around to find out who owns him and who wants him. So far they haven't had any luck." Pinchpenny let out a smirkish giggle.

Tenstars sighed deeply and wished he were a drinking man. He then realized he was a drinking man and took a bottle of Jamison's from his desk drawer and took a healthy pull. Being a gentleman he then offered the bottle to Pinchpenny. She wiped the neck on her blouse and chugged off the remaining half of the bottle. With a "Burruppp" she set the empty on the General's desk.

After taking a moment to look from the bottle to secretary and back to the bottle the General asked, "So how did you find out where he was?"

"ICE sent out a blurb to various agencies to see if anyone had any idea who he is. We got copied on the B list. Of course, B-listers only get stuff three days after the event so Ames could be in Belgrade or Tijuana by now."

"Okay, contact ICE and tell them he's ours and find out what it'll take to get him back."

"Already did that before coming in here to explain things to you, and drink up your whiskey."

"Fine," said Tenstars. He then had a thought. "Ames has clothes on and isn't stuck in a beard or anything is he?"

Pinchpenny chuckled at the thought. Ames had a few similar problems on a previous assignment. "Not this time. The only problem seems to be a rancid smell from water-logged clothes, some cuts and bruises from falling off things and a couple of leeches picked up along the way. When I say leeches I don't mean the little black things, I mean the business suited lawyer types."

* * * * * * * * * *

Ames sat on the floor with his back against the wall, his knees drawn up and his arms wrapped around them. The cell was small and crowded with people of every nationality but with a preponderance of short dark haired, ruddy skinned men with multiple tattoos. Through the cell door and across the hall was a similar cell crowded with short dark-haired women with ruddy colored skin and multiple tattoos.

The agent sat in the upright fetal position while keeping a wary eye on a very large man with long greasy black hair, six gold teeth and arms the size of oak trees. The man had been eye-balling Ames for the past half hour.

Just as the agent was preparing to fend off the muscular advances a guard appeared at the cell door and called out, "Ames Blond! Ames Blond get over here."

Immediately all eyes scanned the room looking to see who had been called. Ames hurried to his feet and pushed his way to the door. Along the way he was asked for his autograph twelve times before he could tell people they had the wrong man.

At the door the guard looked him up and down. "Sure don't look like in your movies. Come on out of there. Somebody up front wants to see you."

Ames muttered, "That's not me in the movies," as he preceded the guard down the hall.

Ames had no idea where he was. The morning after his arrest at Sunny Point he had been shackled hand and foot and led out of the building with a bag over his head. He was herded forward until he barked his shins on a metal support of some kind. When he was told to step up he realized he was boarding a bus, probably for transportation to some other facility. When he cracked his head on the top of the door he found out the bus was a van. While stars sizzled behind his eyes he thought, "Aren't the cops supposed to hold your head to keep that from happening?"

He heard some chuckles from outside the bag.

At a guess Ames put the van ride at about an hour. Somewhere after about a half hour they had entered a city. He figured this because the van started doing starts and stops like there were traffic lights. Finally the van thumped over some railroad tracks and came to a stop.

The agent was hustled out of the van and pushed forward until he smacked into a wall, or more to the point, into a door. The door was opened and he was pushed through. Once inside the agent was shoved into a chair and the bag pulled off his head. He blinked his eyes at the sudden infusion of light.

The room was painted an institutional green with the requisite metal desks and uncomfortable chairs. There were about twenty desks and each held a person typing at a computer with a second person shackled to a chair next to the desk. In most cases a third person stood beside the desk and kept up a constant conversation between the chair bound and computer typist.

As Ames was shackled to his own chair two men dashed over toward him. One of them pushed the other who slid into a chair and fell over a desk knocking over a computer and causing the typist to fall on the ground. A coffee cup flipped into the air and a stack of papers flew into the air creating large scale confetti.

The pusher slid to a halt beside Ames and flashed a somewhat ragged business card in the agents face.

Harold B. Shylock Esq.
Attorney at Law - Abogado Mandatario
Deportation Specialist – Especialista Deportacion

(910) 080-1141
Wilmington, NC

Ames wiggled his hands which were shackled behind his back and hooked to a bar on the floor. Harold nodded and put the card back in his pocket. Blond guessed the lawyer had only one card and never gave it to the "client."

The computer operator looked up at the attorney. "Get lost Harold. You can't have this one he belongs to Homeland Security."

Harold's eyebrows shot up and he rapidly headed for another shackled personage.

"Where am I and what's going on?" Ames asked the computer person.

The operator was dressed in a blue shirt and trousers with a circular gold colored patch on the upper sleeve.

The patch had an eagle in the center with the words "Immigration and Customs Enforcement" around the circle. A patch below that proclaimed "ICE – an attitude to live by."

The ICE man looked at Ames for a moment. "Where you're at is deep doo doo. What's going on is we're going to find out where you came from before we turn you over to some people from Serbia for questioning."

"Serbia?" asked Ames with some apprehension.

"Nothing to worry about. We just contract out some of our interrogation services," stated the ICE agent matter-of-factly. "What's your name?"

"Blond. Ames Blond."

The ICE guy leaned back in his chair. "Your report said you had a bad attitude. That won't help you here so let's just play nice and you give me your real name."

With some heat Ames replied, "My name is Ames Blond and I'm an agent for the Department of Reconnaissance and Knowledge out of Washington. I'm on an assignment to find out what's happening to stolen oil tankers and I really need to get to a phone!"

The ICE agent chuckled, "Well, that's about the best one I've gotten in here since the Mexican who swore he was a ambassador from Pancho Villa here to negotiate a treaty with the president. Funny though. He turned out to be the real ambassador who'd had a bit too much of his homegrown cocaine."

"Nice story, but I'm the same thing but without the cocaine," explained Blond.

"Nice try amigo, but that guy is British and comes from London not Washington."

"I'm not that guy! He's not real. I am!"

"Okay Tweety, I'm gon'na put you in the cage until Homeland gets here to collect your butt. I'd suggest you be nice to Sylvester while in the cage."

"Who's Sylvester?" asked Ames with lowered eyebrows.

"Sylvester is a rather large Mexican who thinks he runs things in there and I'm pretty sure he actually does."

The ICE agent waved at another ICE guy who collected the DORK agent and escorted him from the room and down a hallway. Along the way they passed a large room with a bunch of men and some women yelling, screaming, punching each other and swinging briefcases. The melee swirled around the room and was kept from spilling out into the hall by a large metal grill.

"You ain't going to stick me in there!" exclaimed Ames with alarm.

The guard looked in the room. "Nah, that's not where we keep the prisoners."

"Then what's going on?" asked the agent with some relief.

"According to the government every illegal immigrant captured has the right to a deportation hearing before we can the sucker back where he or she belongs. That means every illegal gets a lawyer to defend them in front of the hearing judge. The government is nice enough to provide a lawyer for each of them and pays the lawyers for their services. The work is easy, the hours are short and there are lots of customers with a guaranteed paycheck. So lawyers line up for the privilege of defending the illegals and making a nice living with mostly no work involved."

"So those are lawyers in there fighting over cases?" asked Ames naively.

"No, those are the legal assistants. They get paid by the number of clients they get for their masters, er, attorneys so the competition is fierce and violent. Only the top dogs get the clients and the government bucks. Sort of like an election for president."

Ames was still shaking his head in confusion when the door to the holding cell closed behind him.

CHAPTER THIRTY-ONE

The man from DORK was escorted up the hallway to a small office just outside the big office where all the computers, desks and handcuffees were. As they passed the grated door Ames noted that the fight for clients was still in progress. A new feature was a line of suited individuals outside the door. These gentlemen carried on hushed conversations, clapping each other on the back and shaking hands. Intermittently one of the legal assistants would break free from the clash for clients and pass a piece of paper to one of the suited guys outside the fracas. This individual would then dash through the doors into the big room with the computers. Ames assumed the suits were the actual lawyer.

Inside the smaller room an old friend was seated at an aged metal desk.

"Well if isn't T," said Ames extending has hands toward the man. This entailed turning around and wiggling his hands near his butt, since he still wore handcuffs. The other man signaled to the guard and the handcuffs were removed. The guard was shooed from the room while Ames was offered a chair. T did not shake hands.

T was an attorney from the legal division of DORK who had gray hair, wore gray suits, gray shoes and had the pallor of a dead man. The Legal Division was high sounding name for an office next to Pinchpenny's with a desk, a phone and an overhead fan that didn't work. T only had a chair because he had borrowed one from the General's stash. Ames had met the gray looking man on a previous mission.

Pulling a gray pen from his vest pocket T said, "Sign these release forms and we'll have you out of here."

Ames took the pen and scribbled his name on a half a dozen papers. "How come it took so long for you guys to come and get me?"

"You forget, you're not real. You don't have a Social Security number, your fingerprints are not on file anywhere, and your picture isn't in any databases. No passport, no driver's license, no job, no bank accounts. In other words, you don't exist. So when you disappear off the radar you really disappear."

"So how did you get here?" asked Ames with a shudder at being the invisible man.

"Thank Pinchpenny. She's constantly looking for slightly dumb good looking young men on the Internet. When she came across your description in an Interpol query she got interested. She thought it possible she could get the dumb young man assigned to her and have some fun. While fantasizing she pulled up the suspect photo and realized that the doofuss she was looking at was you. She thought about leaving you here but figured even she could get in trouble. Plus it would make you look even dumber to General Tenstars."

"How do you know all this? Pinchpenny has her pudgy little fingers in everything."

T chuckled. "Even Pinchpenny has her controllers. We've known about her little boy scheme for quite some time. As long as she keeps it legal, not a problem."

Ames grinned. "Well it's nice to know that even Pinchpenny isn't omnipotent!"

T grinned back. "As far as you're concerned she still is. You mention any of this to anyone and you end up raising radishes on a farm in Idaho."

Ames' grin disappeared at the reference to his father who had once been a DORK agent and ended up raising radishes in Idaho.

T pointed to a white valise on the floor. "That suitcase has some clean clothes for you. Go ahead and change."

Blond looked around. "Where do I change at?"

"Right here. Just drop your drawers and put on new ones."

"But there's no privacy?"

"Don't mind me, I have a wife and two kids so I could care less. I'll even turn my back if you'd like" With that T turned his chair to face the opposite wall.

With some apprehension Ames stripped down, taking off the rumpled and still somewhat damp jumpsuit he had been wearing and put on a clean brown suit, starting from the underwear and sox up. The suit did a lot to hide the rumpled creases of his water logged butt and the red rash under his arms and in his crotch.

As he was tightening his tie he glanced at the door. Two female ICE agents were standing in the doorway giggling and whispering. When they spotted him watching them they hurriedly closed the door and disappeared up the hall.

"Terrific," muttered the DORK agent.

With that T turned around, collected the stack of papers and gestured for Ames to follow him. They left the office and went down the hall to the big room where they were met with whistles and catcalls. Ames flashed his middle finger around while T handed the papers to an ICE agent behind a counter. The whistles followed them as they walked out the front door.

Blond found himself outside a non-descript concrete building near a group of railroad tracks. The area looked slightly run down and he heard the toot of a ship in the near distance.

T led him to a mud colored Crown Victoria that had seen better days, about 10 years worth. The car had a cracked windshield, dents along both sides and two Bondo patches, one on the left rear fender, the other on the right front fender. The seats were saggy and the car had a musty smell. The thing reminded the agent of a blue Pinto in much the same shape.

As T got into the driver's side Blond asked, "This thing is a piece of crap. How come a high powered lawyer is driving something like this?'

T Sighed. "Apparently R is on another of his cost saving kicks. I used to have a really nice Escalade, but R traded it for this and used the extra money to pay to get some blue car back from the middle-east. He also mentioned a couple of watches that were missing and had to be replaced."

At the mention of the car and watches Ames looked out the window to keep from showing his grimace to T. Looking at the boarded up warehouse across the street he asked, "So, what now?'

"Now you take the packet in the glove box and follow the instructions there. I'll drop you at the Wilmington airport and drive back to Washington."

"Why don't I just ride back with you?" asked Ames as he opened the glove box and took out a bulky manila envelope.

T didn't answer as Ames opened the envelope and pawed through the stuff inside. There was a new passport with his picture and the name Dilbert Floyd, and airline ticket to Maputo, Mozambique with connecting flights from Washington to Paris and Cairo. He also had a new wallet with a number of credit cards, a couple of photos of people he didn't know, a Wal-Mart receipt and a few hundred dollars in cash.

T glanced over. "Don't use those credit cards," he warned. "R says they are the ones he maxed out buying Christmas presents last year and he hasn't made any payments on them."

"Why doesn't he pay them?" Ames asked looking up.

"Why should he? Those cards are for some guy named Holder. That isn't R and he could care less about somebody else's credit rating. Besides R says he's working on a new invention to make credit scores obsolete. Something to do with trust and logic. Probably won't work."

T put the car in motion and they drove away from the building, out a gate and down a rustic looking residential street.

They rode in silence for about fifteen minutes before T stopped in front of a low brick building with a green roof. The structure looked something like an old train station but with more doors. They had stopped under a long canopy. T motioned for Ames to get out then sped off as the agent closed the door.

Ames watched the car as it went around the airport driveway, followed by a trail of dark smoke, then turned and headed inside through the glass doors. Inside he found a light and airy concourse with the requisite airline counters on one side and the entry doors on the other. Pulling the airline ticket back out he glanced at it. A puzzled expression crossed his face.

Walking over to a sign listing services inside the terminal he ran his finger down the menu. The puzzled expression deepened.

Glancing around he spotted a TSA guard lounging against a wall. When Ames approached him the guard put his hand on his gun and narrowed his eyes. "What do you want," he said with a belligerent tone.

Ames stopped short and glanced down at the ticket. "Can you direct me to Hubey's Worldwide Charters?"

The guards eye narrowing became narrower. "Why?'

"Because I have a flight on it and I'd like to know where their counter is."

The narrow eyes became slits. "Why?'

"Because I want to go somewhere," said Ames with the sneaky suspicion the guard was a moron.

The guard suddenly slapped himself in the face and his eyes opened wide. "Darn I hate it when that happens. Lazy eyes ya know. Now what did ya'll need."

Uh, where can I find Hubey's Worldwide Charters?'

"The eyes narrowed again. "Are ya'll sure ya want them? Delta has some real nice flights out'a here."

With a sinking sensation Ames replied, "Because I have a flight on them."

The guard scratched his head. "Ya'll sure ya don't want USAir maybe? They're pretty good ol boys."

With resignation Ames replied, "No thanks, just point me to Hubey's."

The guard shrugged. "Okay, your choice and your life. Go down to the end of the concourse. Go out the door and head down the road about a half mile. You'll come to a big white building. Ignore that. Go into the small shack to the left of the big building. That's Hubey's. Ya'll sure ya don't want Delta?"

"No, thanks," Ames muttered as he headed for the end of the concourse. He was walking and shaking his head. "Why does R always do this? Find the nastiest, cheapest airline around. The guy must really dislike me."

After a sweaty walk in the hot sun Ames found the decrepit clapboard shed next to the large warehouse building at the side of the runway. A sign painted with faded black lettering indicated that "Hubey's Wurldwyde Chartars" was housed within. The agent openly groaned as he opened the door and stepped inside.

Hubey's reception lounge consisted of an ancient scarred desk with one corner held up with two bricks, a tattered easy chair in an odd floral pattern that looked like it had been owned by a dozen cats, a fan that made sputtering noises, two beat up filing cabinets and a gray haired guy with a handlebar mustache and about seven pounds of meat on his wiry frame.

Mustache looked up when Ames entered and a big grin spread across his face. He stood up and extended his hand. "Mistah Blond! I been waitin' fer ya. Got de bird all set fer ta take ya ta Washington. C'mon in, c'mon in. Have a seat."

Ames eyed the springs peeking out of the chair. "No thanks, I really need to get to Washington as soon as possible."

"Yeah, yeah, sure. Let me grab de keys and we out'ta here." Hubey started lifting papers, moving coffee cups, checking his pockets and poking his feet around under the desk.

Ames pointed at a set of keys hanging from a hook on the wall. "Would those be the keys you're looking for?"

Hubey looked up. "Yeah das dem. Lez go." He led Ames out of the building through a door opposite the one Ames had entered through.

The pilot led the agent out onto the tarmac in front of the office. The only airplane close to the office was ancient looking faded yellow single propeller thing with the wings above the fuselage. With a strained voice Ames asked, "Hubey, that ain't the plane we're using is it?'

"Hubey?" asked the pilot. "I'm not Hubey. Dat was my brudder. He died last year and I got de company. My names Throckmorton and yeah dat's our bird. Sweet little ting. That there's a PA eleven Cub Special built in 1949."

"That thing is going to make it to Washington?" asked Ames with misgivings.

"Nah, it's only got a range of tree fifty miles. We'd be landin' on fumes. Da FAA ain't real happy 'bout sitiations like dat. We stop at Richmond and top off, den head to Washington."

"So how longs it gon'na take to get there. What's that got, a top speed of about fifty miles an hour?"

"Oh she's bedder den dat. I can get her up ta sebenty five wid a tail wind. We get ta Washington 'bout five maybe six hours."

A groan escaped from Ames. "We could get there faster driving! Heck we could get there faster walking!"

"Yeah," said Throckmorton with a smile, "but den ya miss da in-flight movie."

CHAPTER THIRTY-TWO

The trip to Beira was probably one of the worse that Blond had ever taken. The road was horrible for much of the trip; there were few gas stations with bathrooms and virtually no snack shops. The air was dry and hot, the landscape was brown scrub or shanty towns of concrete and tin. For over seventeen hours Sergeant Jenkins guided the Land Rover the twelve hundred kilometers from Maputo to Beira.

Throckmorton had delivered Ames to Washington National Airport after seven hours of being cramped into the back seat of the Cub Special. The agent could have handled that but something in the plane smelled like old sweat socks and the pilot spent the whole flight whistling "Skip to My Lou" with a very nasal shriek. After the fourth hour Ames was wishing for a plane crash to put him out of his misery. The only positive was the just released movie during the flight.

From Washington to Paris to his favorite place in the world, Baghdad, not. Then onto Maputo. Three days of little sleep, over-priced airline food, nasty ill-trained customs inspectors and really horrid third class seats with third rate B-movies had Ames in a foul mood and even fouler clothes when he deplaned in the run-down third-world former Portuguese colonial national capital.

After clearing Mozambique customs, with a hefty five dollar bribe, Ames met Sergeant Jenkins on the concourse. Jenkins met him with a scowl and a, "Cripes mate, don't you ever wash your clothes?"

With a straight face Ames said he was glad to be back, then broke out laughing so hard he fell over. He was really overjoyed when Jenkins told him that flights to Beira were not possible due to some strange regulation passed by the government and overzealous meditation, they would have to get there using the roads. Or what, in some places, passed for roads.

In Beira, in the afternoon of the second day since leaving Maputo, Ames met with Colonel Herbert Tarryton Smyth Billingsford the Fourth in his office at the Beira airport. As he listened to Billingsford sum up the situation, Ames watched as a United flight landed and wondered why the heck he and Jenkins had spent two days on the road for no reason.

"The situation is this," stated the Colonel, "I have no idea what the situation is, haven't seen any of your black submarines and quite frankly, have no idea what you or government are on about. However, her majesty has directed me to support you in your endeavor I shall provide you with what assets I have available. I do understand though, that MI-6 is sending some chap over here to assist you. Has a name that sounds like yours – Bland, Blend, Band or some such."

Ames turned away from the window and looked the Colonel straight in the eye. "What?"

"I say old chap, you didn't hear a word I said did you?"

"Nary a one," replied Blond. "Care to try again?"

"Rather not. Just let me know what you need and I'll see if it's available."

"Well I could use a fully trained and armed recon force, six helicopters, a couple of armored vehicles, some body armor, a skilled tracker and an interrogator."

Billingsford blinked. "I might be able to part with Jenkins and one or two lower ranks with a car or a bus or some such. I could pry a couple of the locals away from their meditations for a few hours, possibly."

"But you had a helicopter!" whined the agent.

"Right. Wasn't ours. Belongs to the Mozambique air force. Doesn't work anymore. I understand some monkeys ran off with the flight controls of something or other."

"But I need to get back to Silverpinky's hideout and find out what she's up to!"

"Rather. You do know where's it's at right?"

"Haven't a clue. Somewhere south of here I think. Or maybe north. Don't think its west, too much land that way and east is out. Too much water."

"The how do you propose finding the place?"

"The helicopter would have been nice."

The Colonel went to the door. "Sergeant Jenkins could you come in here."

Jenkins dashed into the room, slammed to attention and hit himself in the face with that odd British salute. "Suh," he yelled while stomping his foot.

"At ease Sergeant," said the Colonel. "Blond here isn't quite sure how to find that Silver person's hideout. Do any of your local contacts have anything that might help?"

Jenkins relaxed. "Not really, sir. The only thing I have is that thing about a hidden submarine base by the Save near Nova Mambone."

"Hmm," mussed the British officer. "That could be a lead."

Ames thought for a minute. "Wait. I recall Sheila mentioning the Save and some Nova thing or other. That could be a good starting point."

Both Britishers looked at Ames, "Sheila?"

Blond blushed slightly. "Just a girl I met. How long to get to Nova whatever and how do we get there. The route I took through the scrub, jungle and pygmies seems a might out of the way."

The Colonel looked at the Sergeant.

"Easy enough," stated the NCO. "Down route one to route six then cross country a bit. About five hundred kilometers I should think."

"Right," exclaimed Billingsford. "Gather your group, some supplies, a few of the locals and head off. Give Blond here a show of what SAS is all about, what. Get some food, sleep and start out in the morning. Be sure to communicate two or three times a day. Off you go."

Jenkins slammed his feet again, hit himself in the head again and marched out of the room. Ames followed without the foot stomp or head hitting.

The remainder of the day was locating a truck that actually ran, some supplies, a guard who wouldn't steal the supplies and run off, and getting Ames some clothes other than the rumpled business suit he'd arrived in Maputo with.

The change resulted in a green uniform that looked to be daubed with brown paint. Jenkins called it DPM, disruptive pattern material. Ames called it ugly. There was a black beret to go with it but Jenkins took off the metal SAS flash, a pair of wings with a dagger and the logo "Who Dares Wins." Ames was a tad disappointed that he wouldn't get to wear it. A pair of black boots completed the ensemble.

The Sergeant finally stashed a weary Blond at the enlisted barracks and told him to get some sleep, they'd be leaving early the next morning if the supplies were still where they had left them.

Feeling dirty and tired Blond stripped out of the suit, grabbed a towel and headed for the shower. There he luxuriated in a stream of tepid water and some local soap that had a strange smell to it. Feeling refreshed he wrapped in a towel and headed back into the bunk area.

"Just what the sodding devil do ya sodding think yer doin' slacking off ya bleeding sod!" a voice yelled in his left ear.

Ames flinched and looked around. Sergeant Perkins had his face stuck close to Blonds and yelled, "Get yer sodding uniform the sodding devil back on! I'll have yer soddin stripes fer slacking off. What's yer soddin name ya sodding sod?'

Ames gulped and stuttered, "Blond, Ames Blond."

Perkins eyes went up. "Oh, so now yer a sodding secret agent are ya, ya sodder! I'll have ya on sodding bush detail til yer sodding arse falls off. Get yer sodding self to attention ya sod!"

Instead of attention Ames scuttled over to the bunk were his clothes were. To Perkins surprise he dropped the towel and shinned into a pair of under shorts and trousers.

Facing the stunned Sergeant, Ames yelled, "I'm not a sodding secret agent! Well I am a sodding secret agent but not the sodding secret agent you're referring to. I'm a sodding American sodding secret agent! You're a sodding Limey sodding soldier with a sodding evil sodding mouth who has a real sodding problem saying any sodding thing without sodding it up. Get yer sodding arse out of here!"

Ignoring the Sergeant Blond sat down and pulled on a pair of socks and the boots.

Perkins stood with is mouth open and eyes blinking rapidly for about a minute before turning and walking out of the barracks.

"That'll sodding teach the sodding twit that," muttered Ames.

From the other end of the barracks a couple of troopers started clapping. Ames stood up and took a bow before finishing dressing.

Pleased with himself the agent left the barracks and headed for the chow hall. There he had just started on a wonderful Feijoada Mocambicana bean stew with rice when Jenkins came in.

The Sergeant spotted Ames and sat down with a big grin on his face. "I heard about you and Perkins. That's the first time that sodding twit has stopped sodding anyone in the two years I've been here. How's the Feijoada?"

"Pweey gwooh," stated Ames through bean stew, causing rice to dribble down his chin. He wiped at it with his hand.

Jenkins smiled, "That's as good as you'll get at any restaurant around here. However, you'll get better in London. More Mozambicans there than here. Eat up, we leave in the morning. No beef stew on the road, only ORP's, Operational Ration Packs. Rather like your MRE's but stay away from the oatmeal block. You could build a house with the bloody things."

Ames grimaced, recalling a pork patty that could break teeth. He took another spoon of stew to remove the phantom taste.

CHAPTER THIRTY-THREE

Ames and Sergeant Jenkins looked across the flat scrub toward the trees along the shore of the Save River. Barely visible was the green and brown pattern of the camouflage on the huge building hiding Silverpinky's massive submarine, or would be hiding it if the thing was still in there. The two men were almost two miles away and had no idea if the sub was in the building. Only a close recon could tell that information.

The DORK agent took his eyes from the binoculars and looked over at Jenkins. The Sergeant continued to examine the building. Ames whispered a low, "Sarge." Jenkins didn't respond. Ames again said, "Sarge," a little louder. After a third try gave no response Blond smacked the SAS trooper in the head.

Jenkins' head whipped around with the binoculars still glued to his eyes hitting Ames in the nose with the optical devices. As Ames grabbed his nose the Sergeant set down the long-viewers. "What'd you do that for? You getting a bit dodgey?"

Ames checked his hand for blood. Finding none he said, "I was trying to get your attention. Does using your eyes shut off your ears or something?"

Jenkins blinked rapidly for a moment.

"Right. What did you need?'

"I think what we're going to do is I'm going to head over there and take a look. See if the sub is there and what else might be going on. You stay here with the troops and I'll signal you if you should come on in."

"I should go with you," said Jenkins with a frown.

Placing his hand in his hip, a little hard to do since both of them were lying on the ground, Blond asked, "What can you do that I can't?"

"Umm, let's see here," replied Sergeant. "I've spent the last twelve years learning and using recon techniques, have traveled and lived in a long list of environments, am qualified in most firearms and hand to hand combat, can sneak up on the flea on a fly's arse without disturbing the fly, have been through two wars and six conflicts and I've spent the last two years living in this gawd forsaken country."

It was Blond's turn to blink a few times. After completing his obligatory blinks Ames grabbed a pack and headed off across the scrub leaving Jenkins to shaking his head as he watched the agent trip over a bush.

As he neared the building Ames spotted a multi-headed pipe valve thingy attached to a pipe that went toward the camouflaged structure. Her crept closer and put his hand on the metal of the pipe. It was warm and he could sense movement inside. Something was flowing either from the valves to somewhere or from somewhere to the valves. There was a slightly rancid odor in the air.

Crouching down even lower he slunk along the length of the pipe, following it toward the huge building that had, or still did, house the giant submarine.

Getting closer to the building he brushed aside the leaves of a bush and could now see inside the open end of the submarine dock. The pipe he had been following led up to the side of the building and went inside. He couldn't see where. But through the open door he could see the huge black shape of the submarine. Silverpinky was still here, or more likely, had come back from one of her nefarious trips with a stolen oil tanker.

Feeling secure in the green and brown camouflage of the disruptive pattern material clothing he wore, Blond slid to the ground and began to low crawl toward the dock, first bringing one arm and leg forward, then flipping his body to bring the other arm and leg to the front, looking rather like an elongated offset crab with a motor malfunction.

As he reached the side of the dock building and stood up against the metal wall he felt a hand on his shoulder. Looking around, the ugly visage of Clarence came into view followed by the round black hole at the end of a gun barrel. Clarence's head was misshapen by a large white bandage covering one side.

'Chew shoudn'a come back here, dude. Miz Silverpinky really wants ta get her hands on chew." Clarence grinned, making his face even more misshapen. "An I really want'ta get back at chew fer da hittin' me wid da wrench." He used the gun to point for Ames to move forward.

Inside the building Ames was pushed along the dock to the side of the big submarine, up the gangplank and through a hatch to the interior of the sub.

Eventually Ames found himself back in the pink living room. There was little difference from last time except for a cluster of stains from dog accidents. Clarence pushed him into a chair and produced a pair of handcuffs that were used to connect Ames to the chair. The ugly rogue then left through one of the back doors.

Ames examined the room for a moment, then slipped the handcuff off the arm of the chair where Clarence had hooked it. It would have probably worked better being hooked behind the arm support rather than on the open side. The agent went to the TV and turned it on.

The man from DORK had just found the meditation channel when Silverpinky and her entourage came into the room. Clarence looked surprised that Ames was up and walking around. Sheila had a quizzical look, possibly wondering why he was back.

Silverpinky stopped in front of the agent. "Ah, we meet again Mister Blond. Did you enjoy your little walk through the wilds of Mozambique?"

"Ames smiled at her. "Sure did. Met some really nice people, had some good food, enjoyed the local rides and entertainment. Oh, and notified Washington of what you were up to."

Silverpinky frowned. "I'm sorry to hear that, but it will make no difference in the long run. My project here is almost complete and I will no longer need this base for a while. The underground has been emptied and all of our things have been removed leaving no traces or evidence behind. We leave here tomorrow night and anyone coming here to investigate will find nothing."

"Cut it kind of close didn't I?" asked Ames with a smile and a wink at Sheila.

Silverpinky caught the wink. "What was that wink for?" she demanded spinning around to look at Clarence and Sheila. She looked back at Ames. "You got the hots for Clarence? That ain't right! Sheila, take this pervert and lock him up! Clarence you stay away from him!"

Silverpinky stalked off out the door with Clarence following. As he started to close the door Clarence looked back at Ames and winked a very misshapen wink. Ames blanched.

When they were alone Sheila threw herself into Ames' arms only to get clobbered in the head by the handcuffs on Ames wrist. After a long, "ouch!" and a rub at the spot, she settled for kissing him long and hard while Blond attempted to get a breath of air.

Finally she released the lip lock and said, "What are you doing back here? Are you stupid? Will our children be morons too? Why are you here and what have you tripped over recently?"

"I'm here to find out what Silverpinky is up to. Washington needs to know her plans and how to stop her from stealing more ships."

With a puzzled look Sheila said, "But I already told you what she's up to. Are you dense as well as not too bright and uncoordinated?"

At that moment Clarence pushed back through the door.

Sheila pushed Ames away and slapped him hard across the face. "Don't you try to take advantage of me you evil spy!" she yelled. She grabbed him by the shoulder and pushed him through the door as a befuddled Clarence watched.

Unable to see because of the sting to his cheek and eyes, and with Sheila pushing him along Ames blundered into a metal wall and conked himself on the forehead. He fell to the floor with a bright red cheek and a red dent in his head. As Sheila pulled him to his feet he muttered, "Darn glad you love me."

Minutes later he was locked away in Federowski's cabin – again. He didn't actually mind since Sheila locked herself in with him.

CHAPTER THIRTY-FOUR

Ames woke the next morning to find Sheila just kicking the door closed while carrying a large tray. She set the tray on Federowski's desk and handed the agent a cup of coffee. She looked elegant in pink pajamas with Hello Kitties on them and the word "SEXY" in yellow thread across her butt, purple puffy slippers and ruffled hair that would have made Frankenstein scream. Ames was resplendent in blue Batman boxer shorts.

"What time is it," Ames asked as Sheila sat on the bed and spilled his coffee. The brown liquid dribbled down the sheet and onto the floor. He reached for the coffee carafe as she replied, "Tenish. You kind of overslept. I had to get the cooks to make up a special breakfast for the prisoner. Breakfast ended at eight. The best I could get was a half dozen eggs, sausage, bacon, ham, toast and hash browns with coffee and orange juice.. Sorry, but no marmalade or kippers."

His brow knit as he asked, "What the heck are kippers?"

"Small oily herring popular in England for some odd reason," she replied.

"I keep telling you I'm not British. That's that other guy and why the devil would I want oily fish for breakfast? Eeeww! Sounds like a great way to get bad breath. Maybe that's what caused the decline of the empire." He waved his hand, knocking her cup over. "Whatever. What's on the agenda today?"

"First is cleaning up this mess," she stated looking at the puddles of spilled coffee. "Then I gather Silverpinky wants to get the ship ready for departure just after dark. That will give you just a few hours to figure out what you're going to do. Just what are you going to do?"

Blond mulled that over for a moment. "I left Sergeant Jenkins of the SAS with a number of troops sitting in a truck about two miles from here. If I can get to him I can send a report on Silver back to Washington and get an air strike or cruise missile or maybe a couple of darts to stop her."

"Cruise missile? Kind of overkill isn't it? I mean she's just one person with a rather large submarine and she hasn't really done anything except borrow some ships and give them back. Nobodies been hurt or anything."

"Hey if an American president can toss a dozen cruise missiles to cover up a BJ in the oval office I can toss one to stop a ship thief!"

"Still, maybe you should, like, arrest her or something first. Wouldn't that be easier and cheaper?"

"I don't know. I don't have any powers of arrest and even if I did they would be useless here in Mozambique. Besides, we're talking about a bunch of bureaucrats who get a thrill out of wasting money, knocking stuff over and then denying it happened."

"Sounds like a secret agent I know," she muttered under her breath. Then more loudly she stated, "Still seems a bit much."

"I guess I'll have to see what they want to do. You gon'na eat that last fritter?"

Two hours later, fed, showered and dressed in matching blue jumpsuits with yellow belts and orange deck shoes, Sheila led Ames up onto the ship's deck where Silverpinky was waiting with what looked like the entire crew of the submarine.

The overstuffed maven eyed the matching clothes and gave Sheila a stern look that went right over the girls head.

"Mr Blond we will soon part company. I have instructed Clarence to find a nice anthill to stake you to when we leave. I will have him leave you a dull knife since I don't want the ants to eat you, just cause you enough pain and misery so that you will leave me alone."

As she was talking Ames noted a small black shadow near the opening to the building. He squinted but the shadow disappeared. Possibly some animal or other he decided.

"Clarence," she called. "Take Mr Blond to the anthill and prepare him for his ordeal."

Clarence took Ames by the arm and started to guide him down the dock. "And keep your hands to yourself", Silverpinky called after them.

The pair had taken no more than ten steps when a rope dropped in front of Ames. Looking up he saw a brown clad figure sliding down from the ceiling. Looking around he spotted a large number of brown clad figures hanging in the girders or descending ropes. All wore berets and carried some kind of large stick.

As each of the brown figures hit the dock or the deck of the ship it disengaged from the rope and began chasing a crew member from the ship. Soon there was a frantic chase going on with brown and blue clad figures battling over sticks, falling in the water, climbing out of the water and running hither and yon. A few were even running yon and hither.

As Ames ducked a tossed stick he noted that they really were sticks and the brown clad figures were Colonel Billingsford's SAS troopers. Sgt Perkins started to run by chasing Sheila. Ames lifted his arm and caught Perkins in the throat causing the sodding Sergeant's upper body to stop dead in its track while the lower body kept going. Perkins did a beautiful complete flip and landed smack on his face. Sheila looked back and gave Ames a "My hero!" smile, then grabbed Perkins stick and lit out after one of the other battlers, hitting blue and brown alike..

Silverpinky began screaming, "What the devil is going on here? Who are these people? Why are they chasing my people all over the place? Why are they wearing such a nasty brown color for clothing?'

At that moment a small brown figure dashed up to Silver and kicked her in the shin. Looking down she saw this small wizened man with a white beard preparing to kick her again. She attempted to swat at him when a large winged bug swept down and landed in her hair. She started screaming hysterically as the B-1 bug dug in its feet.

In moments additional small brown people entered the fray, tripping blues and getting tripped over by browns.

Sergeant Jenkins ran up to Ames, looked down at the unconscious Perkins, shrugged and produced a handcuff key. "Glad to see you're all right, mate," said the Sergeant in the way of greeting. They both ducked as two pygmies flew over their heads on one of the hanging ropes. They ducked again as the small men flew back the other way. Just as the pygmies started their third swing the two moved out of their way and left them go to it.

"What are you doing here and what's with the sticks?" asked Ames while watching the hordes of blue and brown, with a mingling of short brown people, scatter out the opposite end of the building headed for the bush.

"You don't think anybody's dumb enough to give real weapons to the twits here do you? When you didn't come back yesterday evening I reported to the Colonel and he decided we should do something to assist you. Gave us a lovely way to get in some real training instead of "oohming" and "aahming" all day."

Looking up Ames asked, "What were you doing up there in the girders? Why didn't you just come in through the openings in the buildings?"

"The Colonel thought it would be more dramatic, rather like those stories of your British counterpart. Seemed a bit fun, but it was a bugger of a time getting up there."

At that moment a horde of gray clad figures began sliding down the ropes.

"Who the heck are they?" Ames asked, pointing at the newcomers.

"Those are the lawyers," said Jenkins with a hint of disgust while watching the gray suited men with briefcases chase after the mob. "Both prosecution and defense types. They want to get at their clients and victims as soon as possible so they opted to join the strike force. Rather like an American force going against those terrorists in Iraq and Afghanistan."

At that moment Clarence, in an attempt to escape the melee driving a golf cart, sped past Ames and Jenkins, pushing the small electric vehicle a hard as it would go. The little ugly twit kept looking over his shoulder to see who was chasing him. At the moment that would be nobody. Only Ames and the SAS Sergeant had any idea of Clarence's escape attempt.

Just as Ames started yelling, "Hey, Look out," Clarence slammed nose first into the valve tree on the dock. The cart did a nose down flip tossing Clarence into the air and snapped the valve stem off at ground level.

A loud rumble completely blocked out Clarence's screams as the valve released its contents in a massive stream of brown ooze that shot skyward, slammed into the roof of the building and spread to spray the entire confines of the sub dock.

People, ships and everything were almost immediately deluged with the rankest smelling crud to possibly exist on the face of the planet. All along the dock people started running for the exits, wading through sludge that was rising by inches even as it flowed from the dock into the river.

With an, "Oh my God'" that made Blond wish he had never opened his mouth, the two men joined the rapid exodus from the enclosure and the still spewing mass.

Trudging forward as fast as possible to reach an exit, their footing constantly being threatened by the slimy nature of the former oil wells excretion, they finally managed to get out from under the constant rain of pressurized porcine waste. Without looking back they joined the mass of SAS troops, pygmies, sub crew and lawyers converging on the upstream side of the Save River.

Within minutes the river was crowded with a pile up of humanity scrubbing and squeezing, dripping, dunking and floundering to get the brown ooze of pig crap from the personages. Some were going so far as to remove mired shoes and besotted clothing.

Soon the river and its embankment looked like an illegal Mexican staging area south of Tucson. And even smelled like it.

Finally relieved of muck and stench, people began crawling back up onto the bank of the river, flopping down and trying to get their breath. In some cases the floppers flopped into streams of feces that trailed from people on the way to the river. These personages immediately jumped back into the river for a second go at getting clean.

Ames lay on the ground in his undershorts when a group of SAS led by a wilted Colonel Billingsford and a soggy Jenkins approached. They led a shackled Silverpinky, in a now brown stained coverall without a B—1 bug and carried an unconscious Clarence. Sheila was kicking at one troop who had her in a strange hold that required attachment to a portion of her chest.

Ames stood up and cold-cocked the trooper holding Ms Bitz. The SAS guy did a half-gainer and landed on the ground with a splat. Sheila kicked him in the, ahem, stomach. The girl grabbed Ames bicep and held on. Ames started worrying that his normal male response would become very evident in his somewhat skimpy thongs. He was relieved to find that pig crap trumped female form.

Silverpinky, Jenkins, Clarence who was just waking up, Billingsford and a group of lawyers all looked at the girl, now clad in panties and bra, hanging on Ames.

"Well how the heck did you think he kept getting away," she announced. "You didn't actually think he was doing it on his own?'

The group all did the required blinks and then Silverpinky broke the silence.

"What are you people doing here?" she demanded. "This is a private operation funded by the Mozambique government!"

Billingsford looked at her. "Stealing ships is being backed by the Mozambicans? They're into piracy now?"

"No you twit," exclaimed Silver. "We're not stealing ships, we're saving shit! Well we are borrowing ships but it's for a good cause."

Ames piped up, "Stealing ships and saving crap is for a good cause? Saving crap? Sheila mentioned that. What's saving poop supposed to mean?"

Haughtily Silverpinky raised her chin toward the deluged pier and stated, "We're going to do away with the petroleum market and replace it with a methane market. Natural gas with no carbon signature and an endless supply of fuel!"

"The others looked incredulously at her as she continued. "North Carolina in the United States is awash with pig waste, feces and urine. In some places they are so awash with the stuff caused by over-production of pigs for bacon, hams, pickled pig's feet and other products that entire counties have more or less been evacuated. Well almost or maybe not quite. Anyway, there's so much of the stuff they have no idea what to do with it.

"I use oil tankers to pump up the mess, bring it here and pump it into old oil domes. Toss in some of the right bacteria and the waste gets turned into methane gas. An endless and renewable source of fuel for power," she crowed triumphantly.

At that moment the roof of the building succumbed to the pressure of release pig crap and tore loose from the walls, with a groan the roof capsized into the river dragging the walls with it. A tremendous spout of smelly brown ooze shot high into the air and then subsided to a small waist high trickle streaming off the hidden dock and into the now polluted river.

Ames furrowed his brow at the thought of the size of the environmental encampment and protest this incident would generate and then his eyes lit up as he finally understood the ship berthing in North Carolina and the meaning of the sign on the tank near the pier, "But why steal, okay, okay, borrow the oil tankers? With the money that somebody paid for that huge sub you could have bought a fleet of tankers?"

Silverpinky looked surprised, "What, and have my beautiful boat smell like crap?"

EPILOGUE

Sheila licked the foam from Ames' latte off his upper lip which was rather awkward since she had to lean across the table in the café to do so. This caused her to drag her jacket through corn chowder leaving a white smear on the hem.

Glaring at the smear and trying to wipe it off with a napkin that shredded white lint into the stain Sheila asked, "So what happened with Silverpinky."

Ames blanched. "Well that's kind of a funny story."

Sheila's face lit up and she stopped wiping a hole in the jacket. "Oo, tell me! I love funny stories!" Her chest bounced with her glee.

Ames' brain turned off for a moment as his eyes got stuck to her happiness.

With a click his brain reengaged. "Uh, Pinky, ah Silver, ah, ah, ah." Well, almost engaged.

Sheila stopped bouncing as her face showed a look of concern. "You're not having an Ames moment or something are you?" she asked with a hint of suspicion.

Blond's brain finally fully engaged. "So anyway, Silverpinky was arrested for piracy on the high seas, capital crimes, smelling up the world, assault on federal officers, kidnapping, polluting a polluted river and a host of other charges."

"Well that's good," said the girl. "The nut bag is off the streets then."

"Ah, not quite," replied Ames. "Seems the Department of Energy thought her idea of poopy methane was a great idea and got all the charges dropped. They even went so far as to provide her with one point six billion dollars in loan subsidies to develop the poop to methane project. Sadly, just days after stuffing the loan money into a Cayman Island bank account her project went boobs up. Seems the investors found out that, while she could produce methane from poop, the methane would need a six dollar a gallon subsidy to make it affordable to the average person."

"Ooh, that's not good. Is it?" She started counting on her fingers. Her face became somewhat confused when she got to the tenth finger and had no place else to go.

"Well, it's good for someone. Pinky invested the billion in a Chinese plastic factory that produced cheap rubber ducks for Wally World. Last week the factory had a major meltdown and killed all two thousand seven hundred and eighty two employees. The Chinese were so impressed with her abilities in the population control area that they've hired her to oversee the national child reduction board. She's pretty much set for life."

"What about those pygmies?"

"That's really a sad story as well. The US government okayed their request for foreign aid and reparations. The chief had them build condos on the beach north of Maputo and everybody moved in, away from the jungle. Pretty soon everybody was wearing suits and dresses, carrying briefcases and getting harassed by lawyers and con artists for their share of the reparation money."

"So they sold the condos to rich Americans who thought the area was a wealthy person's get-away spot without checking the mozzie situation first. Then all the pygmies moved to Hollywood where they now star in their own reality TV show, 'The Little's in America.' I guess it's quite popular."

"So how is that sad?"

"Like everybody else touched by the glitz out west they fell into the booze and drug scene, started voting far left, getting divorces and being ripped off by shyster agents. All in all not a pretty ending."

"That's too bad. But wait a minute, what about all that crap that was messing up the land around the sub dock area? That's going to be uninhabitable for a long time."

"Not really. That squirrel R, you remember him from down in Dirty Tricks?"

"Goofy sucker? white hair? Teeth that fall out?" He nodded.

"Seems the old doofuss actually invented something useful. He called it Poo Grass. The stuff eats poop. So they flew in a bunch of Poo Gras and laid sod all over the area down there. It worked so well that it's now a major stop on the Master's tournament. But they're having a small bit of trouble with shoes and golf balls disappearing."

"So you didn't get fired this time either?" she asked, referring to a small problem on a previous mission.

"No, as a matter of fact Pinchpenny found it in her heart to renew the lease on my apartment so I don't have to live on the street. And I only had to give her twenty percent of my salary. And that's the funny one. She doesn't know I don't get paid!"

Sheila smiled, "Well that's good. We'll get to work together maybe."

Ames looked confused. "Work together?"

"Well it's kind of a surprise. Pinchpenny liked me so well she hired me as an agent and at the same salary you get! Isn't that wonderful?'

Ames looked into her eyes. "You do know I just said I don't get paid? If you get the same as I do you don't get paid either."

The confusion returned to her face. "No pay?"

"Nope"

Her face brightened. "But I do get to go to really strange countries with really bad food, meet very odd people, get really dirty and wear bad clothing. That has to count for something. And maybe you can teach me how to fall down a lot!"

Ames sighed and took a sip of his latte.

RECIPES FOR FOODS FOUND IN BROWN GOLD

Spinach soufflé

1-1/2 tablespoons soft butter
4 tablespoons soft butter
3 tablespoons grated Parmesan cheese
1 Lb chopped spinach, steamed
2 tablespoons flour
1/2 tablespoon salt or salt substitute
1 cup whole milk
1/8 teaspoon black pepper
1/8 teaspoon nutmeg
3 egg whites

Spread the 1-1/2 tablespoons of butter around the inside of a soufflé pan or deep casserole dish. Sprinkle the butter with Parmesan cheese.

In a saucepan sauté the spinach until it wilts and there is no more juice. Preheat the oven to 375 degrees. In another saucepan melt the remaining butter and stir in the flour and salt. Cook for 30 seconds while whisking. Add the milk and cook while still whisking for 4 minutes until it thickens. Add pepper and nutmeg.

Whisk 1/2 cup of the spinach into the egg yolk and then add the mixture back into the rest of the spinach stirring to completely mix. Beat the egg whites on high speed until they froth and form peaks. Stir 1/3 into the spinach, then fold the remaining egg white into the spinach. Spoon it into the soufflé or casserole dish and bake for 30 minutes.

Poule en Sauce de Salete (Chicken in Dirt Sauce)

You can't possibly want to make this!

Borscht (Beet Soup)

3 tablespoons olive oil
1 pound beef, cubed
1 white onion, chopped
1 carrot, chopped
1 celery stalk, chopped
2 garlic cloves, crushed
2 cups cabbage, shredded
1 pound beets, chopped
4 cups beef broth
1 tablespoon tomato paste
1/2 cup lemon juice
Parsley
Salt and pepper
Sour cream

Heat oil in large pot on medium heat. Season the beef to taste with salt and pepper then add to the pot and cook until brown, about 5 minutes. Remove beef and set aside.

Add the onion, carrot, celery and garlic to the pot and cook until soft. Add cabbage, beets, broth, tomato and the beef to the pot. Cover, cook until beef is tender, about 39 minutes. Stir in lemon juice.

Ladle into bowls and serve with sour cream and parsley.

Steak Tartar with Cabbage Leaves

Do NOT store more than 2 hours even if chilled.

1 pound sirloin
1 egg yolk
1 teaspoon mustard
1 tablespoon chopped onion
1/2 tablespoon capers
1/2 teaspoon Worcestershire sauce
1 tablespoon olive oil
1 teaspoon parsley minced
1/4 teaspoon Tabasco sauce
Salt and pepper

Trim fat from beef and grind twice. In a bowl add the egge yolk, onions, capers, mustard, Worcestershire, Tabasco and salt and pepper. Mix thoroughly.

Add the meat and parsley. Beat lightly. Serve immediately.

Pomme Frites (French Fries)

6 russet or other large potatoes
1/3 cup olive oil
Salt and pepper

Preheat oven to 450 degrees
Peel potatoes and cut into 1/4 inch slices, then put the slices into 1/4 inch fries. Place the fries into a bowl of cold water to keep them crisp. Before cooking drain water and dry fries with paper towels.

In a bowl add the olive oil to the potatoes mix well and place on a non-stick baking sheet in a single layer. Bake until light brown, about 30 to 40 minutes.

Beouf Ebreche (Chipped Beef)

1/4 cup butter
1/4 cup flour
2 cups milk
3 ounces sliced dried beef
Salt and Pepper

Melt the butter in a saucepan then blend in the flour and milk. Add salt and pepper to taste. Cook on medium heat until the mixture boils, stirring constantly. Reduce the heat and add the beef. Remove from the heat. Serve over toast, potatoes or rice.

Potage d'oignon (Onion Soup)

6 large yellow onions, sliced thin
1/4 teaspoon sugar
2 cloves garlic, minced
8 cups of chicken stock (beef stock may be used)
1 bay leaf
2 tablespoons olive oil
1/4 teaspoon thyme

In a saucepan sauté the onions in the olive oil on medium heat for about 30 minutes until brown. Add the sugar, salt and pepper to taste after about 10 minutes. Add the garlic and sauté for 1 minute, then add the stock, bay leaf and thyme. Cover and simmer for about 30 minutes. Remove the bay leaf.

Serve with toast or cheese or a combination. For cheese, sprinkle on top and put in broiler or microwave until cheese bubbles.

Bacon Rolls

1/2 cup onion, finely chopped
1 tablespoon butter
3 cups cubed dry bread
Celery salt
Garlic powder
Salt
Pepper
1 beaten egg
10 lean bacon strips

In a skillet sauté the onion in the butter until tender. In a bowl mix the bread cubes, celery, salt, pepper, garlic and onion mix. Mix evenly. Add the egg and toss to coat the bread mix. Roll mixture into 10 balls. Wrap a bacon strip around each ball and secure with a toothpick.

In the skillet cook the bacon balls over medium heat until the bacon is crisp. Remove grease with a paper towel.

Peanut Butter Noodles

This recipe contains peanuts that may cause an allergic reaction

4 ounces chicken broth
1-1/2 tablespoons ginger root, minced
3 tablespoons ginger root
2 tablespoons soy sauce
3 tablespoons peanut butter
1 tablespoon honey
2 tablespoons hot chile paste (to taste)
3 cloves garlic, minced
8 ounces noodles (your choice of type)

1/4 cup green onins, chopped
1/4 cup peanuts, chopped
Boil large pot of water and cook noodles until tender.

Combine chicken broth, ginger, soy, peanut butter, honey, chile, and garlic in a pan and heat thoroughly.

Add noodles and toss to coat thoroughly. Serve. Add peanuts and green onions to garnish.

Swedish Dough Balls

1 cup butter
6 tablespoons sugar or sugar substitute
1 egg yolk
1 teaspoon vanilla extract
2 cups sifted flour
1/2 teaspoon baking powder
1/2 cup chopped walnuts or pecans

Preheat oven to 375 degrees. In a bowl cream the butter, sugar, egg and vanilla. Mix with the flour, baking powder and nuts. Roll into balls about 1/2 to 3/4 inches in diameter. Bake on a greased cookie sheet for 5 to 8 minutes until brown. Roll dough balls in sugar and cinnamon to taste.

Pecan Pie

1 cup sugar or sugar substitute
3 tablespoons brown sugar
1 cup corn syrup
1/2 teaspoon salt
1/3 cup butter
3 beaten eggs

3/4 teaspoon vanilla extract
1 cup pecans chopped finely
1 unbaked pie crust

Preheat oven to 350 degrees

Mix the sugar, brown sugar, salt, corn syrup, butter, eggs and vanilla in a bowl. Place the chopped pecan in the bottom of the pie crust. Pour the syrup and sugar mixture over the pecans. Bake about 1 hour until the pie ingredients no longer jiggle. Allow to cool. Serve with whipped cream or other topping.

Kippers

1 Lb smoked herring

Using a tall narrow container, fill with hot water. Pour out the water. Place herring into the container head down and fill the container with boiling water. Seal the container and let stand for 10 minutes. Drain the water and serve with toast and butter.

Twigs with Beatles

You don't think this is a real recipe do you?

Frango a Cafrial (Mozambique Barbecued Chicken)

1 teaspoon cayenne pepper
1 tablespoon salt
1 teaspoon garlic powder
1/2 teaspoon ginger
1 teaspoon paprika
4 tablespoons olive oil

8 pounds of chicken, large pieces

Add all the ingredients together except for the chicken. Mix them well and rub over the chicken. Broil until done. Best served with rice.

Matata (Clam and Peanut Stew)

This recipe contains peanuts that may cause an allergic reaction

1 cup finely chopped onion
1 tablespoon olive oil
4 cups chopped clams
1 cup finely chopped peanuts
2 tomatoes finely cut
1 tablespoon salt
1/2 teaspoon pepper
1 teaspoon red pepper
1-1/2 pounds fresh pumpkin leaves (spinach may be substituted)

Sauté the onions in the olive oil then add in the clams, peanuts, tomatoes, salt, pepper and red pepper and simmer for 30 minutes. Add in the pumpkin leaves and cover tightly until the leaves wilt. Serve over white rice.

Corn Porridge (African Maize Porridge)

4 cups water
2-1/2 cups white cornmeal

Bring 3 cups of water to a boil. Mix 1-1/2 cups of the cornmeal with the final cup of water. Reduce the heat on the water and add the water cornmeal mixture slowly while stirring constantly. Cook on low for about 5 minutes while adding the rest of the cornmeal. Stir constantly. The porridge is done when the mixture thickens and pulls away from the side of the pan. Serve as round balls with stews and other foods.

Feijoada Mocambicana (Mozambican Bean Stew)

10.5 ounces lima or butter beans, dry
8 ounces tripe cut into small squares
1/4 teaspoon baking soda
1 onion finely chopped
5 cloves minced garlic
2 tablespoons olive oil
1 pound spicy sausage (chorizo is normally used)
5 ounces salt pork, cubed
3 very ripe tomatoes without seeds, finely chopped
2 medium carrots finely chopped
1 bunch turnip greens, shredded
2 teaspoons piri-piri sauce (see below)
2 bay leaves
Salt and pepper

In a large bowl soak the beans overnight. The following day wash the tripe and soak in salt water for 2 hours, then drain and cut into squares.
In a large pot of boiling water add the baking soda and tripe. Alllow to boil then reduce to a simmer for 2 hours.
Drain the beans and in a large pan cover with 2 inches of water and cook for about 2 hours until tender.
Heat the oil and cook the onion and garlic over medium heat until soft, then stir in the sausage and salt pork. Fry until meat is brown and tender. Use a little water to prevent burning.

When the beans are done add the tripe, tomatoes, carrots, turnip greens, piri-piri and bay leaves. Simmer for about 30 minutes. Stir in meat and salt and pepper to taste. Cook for an additional 30 minutes. Serve with rice.

Piri-Piri Sauce

This recipe contains peanut by-products that may cause an allergic reaction

This is a very fiery, spicy sauce. Use sparingly.

2 tablespoons red hot chile paste
1/2 cup lemon juice
2 tablespoons finely chopped cilantro
1 tablespoon chopped parsley
5 chopped garlic cloves
1/2 teaspoon salt
1/2 cup olive or peanut oil.

Place all the ingredients except the oil into a food processor and mix on high until smooth then slowly add the oil. Place the mixture in a glass jar, seal and allow to stand at room temperature for one day.

CHARACTERS WHO APPEAR IN BROWN GOLD

Ahmad Jabar	CIA agent in training
Ali Baba	Owner of Muslim Air, former thief
Ames Blond	Agent for DORK
Andrews	CIA chief in Mozambique
Arnold Shmetzer	Elvis Presley
Ben Forte	Former friend of General Tenstars
Bob Cratchet	Cook on the Exxon Valdez II
Britney Spears	Pop singer
Bruce Finklestein	Fidel Castro impersonator in Cuba
Bud	Captain for Silverpinky's team
Captain Blie	Captain of the Exxon Valdez II
Castro	President for life of Cuba
Clarence	Minion of Silverpinky
Colonel Herbert Tarryton Smyth Billingsford IV	Commander of the SAS in Mozambique
Conner	CIA agent in Mozambique formerly known as a pop singer

Corporal Carp	SAS clerk
Da'uud	Former engineman on the Exxon Valdez II
David Copperfield	Stage magician
Elvis Presley	Pop singer, the King of Rock
Federowski	Missing Minion of Silverpinky
Filipe Manuel Ortega Vega de las Montigo con Chile de favor por Mucho Dineros de Rivera	First officer on the Exxon Valdez II
General Tenstars	Head on DORK
Gomer Pyle	TV Marine played by Jim Nabors
Goody DeLay	CNN Reporter
Gordon Dingus	Impersonator of Raul Castro in Cuba
Harold B Shylock	Deportation lawyer
Harry the Homeless Person	Ames' snitch in Washington
Hassim	Ames' CIA contact in Iraq

Hubey	Former owner of Hubey's Worldwide Charters
Jimi Hendrix	Acid Rock, heavy Metal artist of the 70's
Jimmy	CIA agent in Mozambique (Elvis)
Joe Marley	Storekeeper on the Exxon Valdez II
Joe Namath	Football player famous for a pantyhose ad
Kojak	TV Detective of the 70's
Leonardo DaVinci	World's greatest genius
Magnum PI	TV private investigator
McCArty	DORK agent who disappeared in Macy's
Mike	Federal Police officer
Mike Ratlung	Seaman on the Exxon Valdez II
Mister Smith	First Officer on the Exxon Valdez II, also know as Filipe Manuel Ortega yada yada yada
N	Code name for General Tenstars
NO Wrights	Head of POOP

Pancho Villa	Former bandit and president of Mexico
Pinchpenny	Secretary to General Tenstars
Raul	Brother of Fidel Castro in Cuba
Scooby Doo	Cartoon dog, generally smarter than Shaggy
Sergeant Jenkins	NCO with the SAS
Sergeant Perkins	Sodding NCO with the sodding SAS
Sheila Bitz	Former minion of Silverpinky
Silverpinky	Super wealthy evil person
Slobodnik	Federal Police officer
Sylvester	Cartoon cat, also very large Mexican
T	Lawyer for DORK
Thomas Lawrence	Artist, painted "Pinky"
Thomas Smee	Second officer for the Exxon Valdez II
Throckmorton	Current owner of Hubey's Worldwide Charters
Tweety	Yellow cartoon bird

Ugly	Another name for Clarence
Yoko	Wife of John Lennon

ACRONYMS USED IN BROWN GOLD

AARP	American Association of Retired Persons
ACLU	American Civil Liberties Union
AH-1	Attack helicopter named the Cobra
ASSHOLS	Advanced Special Sciences and Hidden Office of Laboratory Studies
B-1	US bomber aircraft used since 1986
B-52	US bomber aircraft used since 1955
BSA	Boy Scouts of America
CIA	Central Intelligence Agency
CLOD	Coalition to Lose Oil Dependency
CNN	Cable News Network
DARTS	Direct Acquisition Rail to Ship bar System
DCM	Distinguished Conduct Medal, English given for extreme bravery
DHS	Department of Homeland Security
DORK	Department of Reconnaissance and Knowledge
DPM	Disruptive Pattern Material, English camouflage clothing

EOE	Equal Opportunity Employer
FAA	Federal aviation Administration
FBI	Federal Bureau of Investigation
FEMA	Federal Emergency Management Administration
FTC	Federal Trade Commission
GAO	Government Accounting Office
GPS	Global Positioning System
GSA	General Services Administration
H-19	Old helicopter design used during the Korean Conflict
ICC	Interstate Commerce Commission
ICE	Immigration Customs Enforcement
IRS	Internal Revenue Service
KGB	Committee for State Security, former Soviet intelligence apparatus
LAM	Linhas Aeros de Mocambique, Mozambique Airlines
MDC	Medal for Distinguished Conduct, not a real medal

MI-4	Russian helicopter designated the Hound
MI-6	British secret intelligence service
MIB	Men in Black
Mig-21	Russian fighter jet used since 1955
Mig-23	Russian interceptor used since 1967
Mig-29	Russian multi-role fighter used since 1977
MRE	Meals Ready to Eat, US combat rations
ORP	Operations Ration Pack, combat rations
PDQ	Post Double Quick, same as ASAP
POOF	Police of Overt Force
POOP	Petroleum, Oil and other Propellants
PTA	Parent Teacher Association
SAS	Special Air Service, British commandos
SCUD	Russian R-11 and R-17 series missiles
TSA	Transportation Security Administration
UH-1	Helicopter named the Iroquois.
URGE	Urban Grandmothers Environmental Society